Amy Cross is the author of more than 100 horror, paranormal, fantasy and thriller novels.

The Curse
of Wetherley
House

AMY CROSS

First published by Dark Season Books,
United Kingdom, 2017

ISBN: 9781520698281

Also available in e-book format.

www.amycross.com

CONTENTS

THE CURSE
OF WETHERLEY
HOUSE

PART ONE
TODAY

ROSIE

"I'M CURSED," I SAY with a sigh, stepping back from my broken-down car as I realize that not one, not two, but three whopping coincidences have conspired to leave me stranded at the side of the road. "I have to be. Nobody can be *this* unlucky."

Cars rush past just a few meters away, heading home in the evening gloom, but at least I've got my hazard lights flashing to minimize the risk that someone'll plow straight into me and just end everything right now. Checking my phone, I see that it's almost 6pm, which means that at this exact moment I'm supposed to be walking through the front door at Lorna's house, ready for her baby shower. Like, at this exact moment. I even have a gift wrapped and ready to go on the back seat, but I'm still a couple of hundred miles from her place and there's no chance I'll make it now.

Not after this litany of disasters.

First, my alarm didn't go off this afternoon. And since I was on a night shift until eight this morning, I slept through until two hours after I was supposed to leave the house.

Second, the friend who was supposed to watch my cat suddenly took off on her own little trip, leaving me frantically scrambling to find someone else to take the job.

And now, not long after setting off, my car has ground to a halt with several flashing warning lights, and I'm starting to seriously think that some kind of hidden force has just decided that today is the day when everything goes to hell.

Maybe I really *am* cursed.

Sighing, I reach into my pocket and take out my phone, so that I can call Lorna and let her know I'm not coming, and then get the number for a garage. After tapping the screen a couple of times, however, I find that nothing happens. It's as if my phone has died, which just seems so completely perfect on an evening like this.

Yep. I'm cursed.

"Ugh!" I mutter, leaning against the side of the car and trying to get my head straight, as cars roar past.

Okay, I can do this.

I can figure something out.

Worst case scenario, I'll walk five or six miles back to the service station I passed a while ago, and I'll ask for help there. I'm sure I'll end up with a massive repair bill, but it's not like I have a choice. This entire evening officially sucks. Already, my mind is racing as I try to work out how I'm going to dig myself out of this unexpected financial hole, but I guess I can pull overtime for a few weeks at the hotel and then maybe by the end of next month I'll break even. I shouldn't complain, really. As my foster parents always used to remind me, worse things happen at sea.

"Rosie?"

Startled, I turn and see that a car has pulled over just ahead of mine, and a figure has stepped out. I can't really see him very well, since he's silhouetted against the lights of passing traffic, but he's coming this way and not only does he apparently know my name, but his voice seemed weirdly familiar.

"It *is* you!" he says, as he finally comes close enough for me to see a handsome, smiling face. "Rosie, right? Is this a hell of a coincidence, or what?"

***

"AFTER SCHOOL I JUST drifted from job to job," Toby says as we sit in the service station's almost-deserted restaurant, overlooking the motorway. "Nothing really stuck, and university wasn't for me, so I just did a little of everything. Cook. Cleaner. Office monkey. Drummer in a band. Charity sign-ups. You name it, I tried it. But what about you? It must be five years since the last time I saw you. What've you been up to?"

"Night shifts on the front desk at a hotel, mainly," I reply, still warming my hands on the sides of a polystyrene coffee cup. "Nothing too glamorous."

"You didn't go to uni or anything like that?"

I shake my head. "Didn't fancy the debt."

"And now here we are!"

"Here we are."

We sit in silence for a moment. This impromptu reunion keeps teetering on the brink, between comfortable and awkward. I knew Toby pretty well at school, but those days are long gone and I'm not sure we have *that* much in common anymore. As I force a smile and then look down at my cup, I can't help thinking that we should get going soon. Besides, there was that one time Toby and I shared a kiss at lunch break, and I'm feeling just slightly embarrassed. After a moment, just for something to do, I reach down and check my phone, which is charging in a socket beneath the table. I now have precisely 4% battery.

"I still can't quite believe it," Toby continues finally. "I was just driving along and I saw someone pulled over at the side of the road, and as I passed I got a glimpse of your face and I just immediately recognized you. Like, snap, there you were in my rear-view mirror. I mean, I often wondered what had happened to you after we all left school, and I looked you up on Facebook a few times, but I just figured you'd dropped off the grid or something."

"No such luck," I mutter.

"And then fate threw us together like this."

"I guess." I can't help smiling. He's right, this *is* one of those once-in-a-lifetime coincidences.

"Well, it's good to see you," he adds. "Really good. I mean, we should never have lost touch after school finished." He hesitates for a moment. "I've got to admit, I didn't really keep up with anyone at the time. I was way too into my own thing and life was pretty chaotic. I definitely went off the rails for a while, but eventually I realized there were a few people I wished I'd still seen now and again. Tom Bradley and Jake Hughes and Martin Wilson, to name a few." Another pause. "And you."

"So where were you off to tonight," I ask, changing the subject, "before you stopped to rescue me?"

"Oh, I think if I tell you, you'll think I'm nuts."

"I already think you're nuts. I remember when you swung from the roof of the science block and landed in a bin."

He bursts out laughing.

He has a nice, infectious laugh.

"So where are you going?" I ask again. "A party? A gig?"

He shakes his head, but he seems a little reluctant to tell me.

"Where are you going?" I ask for the third time.

"I'm going to..." Again, he hesitates, and he really seems a little uncomfortable. Finally, he reaches into his pocket and pulls out an old-fashioned key. "Believe it or not, I'm on my way to check out a haunted house."

I wait for the punchline, but after a moment I

realize that he actually seems serious.

"Yeah," he continues with an embarrassed laugh, "I know, right? I told you you'd think I'm nuts."

I open my mouth to tell him I don't think that, but I can't quite get the words out.

"A little," I say finally.

"And I don't blame you," he continues, "except this house is, like, one of the most notorious places in the country. I mean, it's got a real reputation, it's the kind of place that a lot of people don't even like to talk about. I guess you could call it the Macbeth of the ghost-hunting world. A lot of people lower their voices when they talk about this house. I don't suppose you keep up with ghosts and the paranormal and stuff like that?"

"Not really."

"Not into that kind of stuff at all?"

I shake my head.

"People talk about Wetherley House a lot," he continues. "Like, *a lot*! It's been abandoned for years. Fifteen, twenty, something like that. I'm part of this online group that talks about haunted properties, and sometimes we organize visits to these places."

"You break in?" I ask, raising a skeptical eyebrow.

"No! Definitely not! We always get permission from the owners. That's not always easy, and in the case of Wetherley House it seemed impossible for a while. I mean, we were completely stonewalled. It was kinda rude, really. They could at least have just told us to go screw ourselves, but we never even got a reply from the executors of the estate. Until..."

He sets the key down on the table between us.

"Until this little beauty showed up in the mail."

"The owners finally gave in?"

"Beats me. It just showed up without so much as a note. The only reason we know it's the key to Wetherley House is 'cause of some fine, dedicated research by yours truly. Now, as the more practical member of the online group, I've always been the one who contacts property owners to get permission to go inside, so I guess I finally reached the right person and they mailed the key to me. Either way, I think this counts as permission, so I'm finally heading over there. The house is just half an hour from here. I was on my way when I spotted you."

"Huh." Picking up the key, I find that it's surprisingly heavy, and also a little rusty. "So you're meeting a bunch of ghost-busters, are you?"

"I was, but the others had to drop out. Kieran came down with flu yesterday, Marty had to take some overtime, and Bobby's wife wouldn't let him come."

"So you're going to this haunted house alone?"

"I was all ready and geared up," he continues. "I figure I'll just check it out, and then the others can get their asses along some time next week." He watches for a moment as I continue to examine the key. "Do you believe in the paranormal, Rosie?"

"Me? No. Not really."

"Not even a little bit?"

I open my mouth to tell him that I've never been

into that kind of thing, but suddenly as I stare at the key I get this really strong mental image of an old wooden door swinging open, and for a moment I swear I can see an old, dirty hallway with a set of stairs leading up into darkness. The image goes away as quickly as it came, but for a fraction of a second there it was really strong and really clear.

I quickly set the key down.

"No," I tell him, forcing a smile. "I mean, it's crazy. I like horror movies, but that's as far as it goes. I'm pretty sure that if there was anything to all that stuff, it would've been proven by now. It's not like there haven't been a ton of people trying to find evidence. I remember hearing about some nutters at an old hospital near my place. They spent a few nights there a while back, trying to catch photos of ghosts, stuff like that. Of course, they came away with nothing. I mean, when you really look at it, the whole thing's crazy."

I wait for him to admit that I'm right, but suddenly I realize that I might have been a little insulting.

"Not that I'm saying *you're* crazy," I stammer. "I wasn't -"

Before I can finish, he bursts out laughing.

"You know what I mean," I continue, trying to find a more tactful response. "I just don't think there's anything to it. Real life can be spooky enough, and creepy enough, without having to drag ghosts and all that bull into the mix."

"You don't believe?"

"I don't believe in ghosts."

"Alright, then," he says, picking up the key and holding it between us, letting it glint under the restaurant's low lights. "It seems you've missed your friend's baby shower, and we know each other so it's not like I'm some weird stranger who's trying to lure you into a dark building. So how about it?"

"How about what?" I ask, feeling a faint tingle of nerves as I realize that I might have inadvertently talked myself into something.

"Wetherley House is half an hour away," he explains, still holding the key up as if he's trying to tempt me. "I'll drop you off at your place when we're done, I'll drop you off anywhere you like, but first... Why don't you put your money where your mouth is, and come with me? Let's go explore Wetherley House together. If we're lucky, we might even meet Evil Mary herself."

ROSIE

I DON'T LIKE THIS, but I guess it's way too late to back out now.

As Toby parks the car, I look out the window and see the faint, dark shape of a house just a couple of hundred feet away. There are no lights on at all. Like, zero. I don't know what I expected, but just the appearance of the house is so cold and remote, and I'm already wondering whether I could just sit here and wait in the car while Toby goes inside. At the same time, I don't want to seem like a total wuss, and I guess we'll be in and out pretty fast. Besides, I don't believe in ghosts, so there's no need to be nervous. I just have to keep reminding myself of that fact.

I don't believe in ghosts.

"Ready?"

Turning to Toby, I see that he's smiling at me.

"Sure thing," I reply, forcing a smile.

He reaches over to the back seat and grabs a

thick, padded jacket.

"For your warmth, my lady," he explains.

It's the ugliest jacket I've ever seen in my life, but right now I'm insanely grateful.

"Thank you."

"Bet you didn't think your evening would end up like this, huh?" he continues.

"Never in a million years," I admit, and for a moment I can't help thinking back just a few hours, to when I thought I was on my way to a baby shower. Funny how a few little incidents can change everything.

"You can stay in the car if you want," he tells me. "I can turn the engine back on so you're warm, and you can have the radio on. You don't really have to come inside that cold, haunted place with me."

"Are you kidding?" I reply. "I've come too far to back out now."

Even though I desperately, desperately *want* to back out.

"You must really not believe in ghosts, then," he says, as he takes what looks like an old toolbox from the back seat. "Either that, or you genuinely don't know anything about Evil Mary or Wetherley House."

Sighing, I realize that he's mentioned the name Evil Mary several times now, and he clearly wants me to ask what he means.

"Fine," I say, raising a skeptical eyebrow. "Out with it. Who's Evil Mary?"

***

"HER NAME WAS MARY Carmichael," Toby says as he struggles for a moment with the key, trying to get the door open, "and they say that even now, she haunts this house and waits for her chance to strike again. To see her face is to know pure evil, and to feel her touch on your shoulder is to feel the chill of death itself."

"Oh yeah?" I reply, still shivering slightly despite the thick jacket.

"She'll be waiting for us inside."

"Sure she will."

"If I can get this goddamn door open, anyway."

"Maybe it's not the right key after all," I point out.

"Oh, it's definitely the right key." He wiggles it in the lock for a moment. "Something seems stuck, though." More wiggling. "I guess this door probably hasn't been opened in a long time. You know, it's possible that some kind of residual psychic energy is trying to keep the damn thing locked. Or another explanation might be that the house itself, or something inside the house, would prefer us not to enter. I've read theories suggesting that every negative spirit has an equal or opposite -"

"Oh, for God's sake," I mutter, nudging him out the way and giving the key a good old-fashioned heavy twist, which causes the door to immediately click open. "It just needed a bit of brute force."

"Huh," he replies, as I step back. "Well, that *does* seem to have done the trick."

After taking the key out, he pushes the door all the way open. The wood creaks in the process, and I swear I immediately feel even colder air coming from the hallway. Just as I start peering into the darkness, however, Toby switches on a flashlight and steps inside, and I check that my jacket is zipped all the way before heading in after him. Before I've managed even a couple of steps, however, I feel a board flex under my feet, accompanied by the groan of old, rotten wood.

"Careful," Toby says, as he shines the flashlight's beam around the hallway. "Remember we're intruders here."

"And what exactly is that supposed to mean?" I ask.

He doesn't answer. Instead, he continues to shine the beam all around, and I take a couple more steps inside until I reach the bottom of a set of stairs. Reaching out, I place a hand on the curved section at the bottom of the stair-rail, and I take a moment to look up at the dark landing. The first thing I notice is that the interior of this house is covered in a very detailed, floral-patterned wallpaper, the kind of thing that'd drive me nuts if I had to live with it. Some of the paper is peeling away slightly, and when I touch one of the frayed edges I'm immediately surprised by how cold the wall feels. This house is like an icebox.

"Is it really that chilly tonight?" I ask, immediately seeing my breath's vapor in the air. "It must be, like, minus degrees in here."

When Toby doesn't reply, I turn and see that he's over on the far side of the hallway, seemingly lost in wonder. I guess he's built himself up for this trip, and it's kind of cute to see how seriously he's taking the whole thing. Figuring I shouldn't disturb him too much, I look away, toward the door that leads through to a dusty, abandoned old dining room. I'm about to point out once again that this is a very cold, very pointless waste of time, when I suddenly realize that I've seen this exact hallway before. I look around again, and suddenly it strikes me that this is exactly the place I saw earlier in the restaurant, when I touched the key and got a strong image of a house. I know that's not possible, of course, but it's still a little spooky.

Great. Two minutes across the threshold, and I'm already getting freaked out.

"Did you know there are no photos of this place?" Toby asks suddenly.

I turn to him.

"Not of the inside, anyway," he continues. "I mean, people must have taken photos, but none ever got out. I did a lot of research, but I never came across even one picture that was taken in any of the rooms. I didn't even know the full layout of the place until tonight."

He looks around, clearly awestruck.

"And you're right," he adds, "the temperature *is* very low. There's a noticeable drop once you get through the door. It's an old house, but still, that doesn't entirely explain why we're freezing our asses off in here. There have been studies that show spectral presences have an impact on their immediate area." He takes a device from his pocket and holds it up for a moment. "It was plus five when we were sitting in the car. Then plus two just outside the door. In here, it's minus six."

Stepping over to the doorway, I look into the

next room and see an old dining table with several chairs left neatly in place. It's almost as if, even though Wetherley House has been abandoned for a while now, somebody is still expecting a family to show up for dinner.

"This place is pretty creepy," I continue, "but not in a ghost kinda way. It's just sad."

"She's here, you know."

I turn to him. "Who is?"

"Mary."

Smiling, I realize that he's actually serious.

"Can't you feel the presence?" he continues. "Can't you tell that we're not alone? That there's something in this house with us?"

"Can *you* feel a presence?" I ask, humoring him.

"I've been in troubled houses before," he mutters, heading to the bottom of the stairs and looking up toward the landing, "but I've never felt a presence so fast, or so strong."

I wait for him to continue, but he seems lost in thought.

"So why hasn't she said hello?" I ask finally.

"I guess she's waiting to see why we're here."

He pauses, before turning to me.

"She's being cautious," he continues. "This house has been locked up for more than a decade. In all that time, nobody's been through the door, and she's just been waiting. You can't blame her for being a little suspicious now." He holds up the little device in his hands, and for a moment he seems to be reading something from the screen. "The electron spectrometer

15

is showing elevated readings of five parts per thousand."

"The what?" I ask, raising a skeptical eyebrow.

"It's real science, Rosie."

"I never said it wasn't. I just -"

Before I can finish, a loud bump rings out from one of the nearby rooms, as if wood briefly banged against wood.

I turn and look through a nearby doorway, and Toby quickly hurries past so he can see.

"And that was a ghost, was it?" I ask, trying to ignore the faint flutter of fear in my chest. "I've never understood why ghosts do stuff like that, anyway. Is she auditioning to play percussion in an orchestra?"

I wait for a reply, but he's far too busy with his little machine. In fact, I don't think he heard me at all.

"Or was it a warning?" I continue with a faint smile. "Does she want us to leave?"

Again I wait, but again Toby seems oblivious.

"Or is she trying to sucker us in?" I add, before realizing I'm starting to creep myself out now. "Whatever. It's an old house and you said it yourself, we're the first people in here for years. It's natural that we've disturbed things a little, and that there are some noises. Right? Isn't that totally natural and logical?"

"Mary Carmichael was born here at Wetherley House," he says as he turns away from the open doorway, keeping his eyes fixed on the device. "By all accounts, she was a sweet little kid, but her mother was this monster who tortured and abused her. I mean, you can imagine how all that crazy stuff must've destroyed Mary as she was growing up. Consistent, systematic abuse and violence." He pauses for a moment. "They say that by the time she turned eighteen, Mary was as bad as her mother. Worse, even. Whatever she'd been like before, she'd become this kind of monster zombie cannibal psycho... *thing*!"

"Uh-huh?" I reply, shivering slightly. I swear, the temperature has actually dropped further over the past couple of minutes.

"She killed, you know. Mary, I mean. They say she murdered two members of her own family, and then when the police came she murdered two of their officers as well. She tore their necks out, according to the stories, and sat chewing on their guts until the other officers had no choice but to cut her throat. If you read the whole story, it's just one of the most tragic things you could ever hear. After Mary died, her mother was convicted of murder herself, and ended up hanging for what she'd done. She'd basically taken a happy, carefree child and turned her into a monster."

"Really?"

"Really."

I want to tell him his story sucks, but at the same time it's kind of cute that he seems to believe in all this stuff. To be honest, on the way here I was starting to think I'd been suckered into some lame chat-up routine, but now it's clear that he really, truly *has* brought me on a ghost hunt. Even now, he's staring intently at his little device as he slowly turns away from me.

"And do you know the craziest part of the legend?" he continues.

"I think you're going to tell me anyway."

17

"They say that even today, Mary Carmichael comes and claims any child who's born within the walls of this cursed house."

"Is that right?"

"Why do you think the house is abandoned? No-one dares live here anymore. It's not safe to sell it, it's not safe to knock it down, so it's just left here. I guess they think that if they shut the doors and keep it sealed, no-one'll ever have to deal with the truth."

"And then someone decided to send you the key."

"Yeah, well... Go figure, right?"

He tilts the device in his hands and aims it toward the floor.

"What the hell?" he whispers.

"No kidding," I mutter, looking around and seeing that wallpaper is peeling away in several spots, exposing rotten-looking beams. "I'm no expert, Toby, but it looks to me like this house is ready to be bulldozed. I mean, seriously, what's the point of leaving it standing here like some kind of monument to -"

Suddenly there's a loud bump from beneath our feet. As I look down at the bare boards, I realize I felt a brief but firm vibration.

"I knew it!" Toby says excitedly. "At first I thought the readings were wrong, but they *are* coming from the basement!"

He stares at the device for a moment longer, before heading over to a door in the far corner of the hallway and immediately sliding a rusty bolt to one side. Pulling the door open, he leans through and looks down into the dark space beyond.

"Stairs!" he adds.

"You want to go down into the basement?" I ask, feeling just a little worried. "We're not going to be here all night, are we?"

"It's so cold through here," he replies, holding the device up. "Wow, it's minus nine where I'm standing."

He holds his hand out into the darkness, before taking his phone from his pocket and using the flashlight app to get a better view.

"The steps are still here," he says after a moment. "The air is noticeably colder as soon as you reach through this doorway. Sometimes sudden temperature drops with marked delineations are associated with paranormal manifestations, and it's very clear to me that the cold spot in this house is focused in the basement." He turns to me, and I can see the anticipation in his eyes. "Are you coming?"

"Down there?" I ask dubiously.

"Of course!"

"I think I'd rather not," I tell him, "on account of there maybe being a badger or some other kind of wild animal down there. Or, you know, a mad hobo with a bunch of rusty knives, some guy who doesn't wanna be disturbed while he's cutting up the corpses of his latest victims." Damn it, I know I'm starting to sound cynical, but I can't really disguise the fact that I want to get out of here. "Toby, listen..."

"If I'm not back in ten minutes," he replies, clearly eager to start exploring, "come down and check on me, okay?"

"Down there?"

"Don't worry, I know what I'm doing."

He starts making his way down the rickety steps, and I can already hear wood cracking and swaying in the darkness.

Heading over to the doorway, I'm shocked by the wall of cold air. I look down into the basement, and for a moment I'm just about able to make out the back of Toby's head as he heads further and further down. The wooden steps creak for a few more seconds, and then I hear him reaching what sounds like a concrete floor at the bottom. A moment later, I see the light from his phone's screen.

"I'll be up here!" I tell him.

When he doesn't reply, I roll my eyes and head through to take a look at the rest of the house.

ROSIE

THIS PLACE IS FILTHY.

Running a fingertip across a table in the kitchen, I immediately feel a layer of dust. The more I look around Wetherley House, the more I realize that the place really *does* seem to have been abandoned. Nothing was packed up, there was no orderly process. Instead, whoever was last here seems to have run out and locked the door, and left everything standing. There are several dead plants by the window, and as I get closer to the cupboards I realize I can smell something pretty foul. Pulling one of the doors open, I'm hit by a wall of stench, and I see rotten food.

I don't even dare open the fridge.

When I reach the window, I find that the glass is thick with grime. I guess Wetherley House was probably a pretty cool place in the old days, and it could probably be nice again if someone spent the time and money needed to do it up properly. Looking up at the ceiling, I can just about make out old beams that I guess must be hundreds and hundreds of years old, and I've got to admit that – even if this makes me seem totally old-fashioned and homely – that I could maybe see the appeal of living in a place like this. Somehow it feels like it should be someone's home.

Leaning closer to the window, I peer out through a clear patch and see a large, moonlit lawn with some kind of small forest at the far end. Now that's something I *wouldn't* like to have at the bottom of the garden. For a moment, I allow myself to imagine what I'd do with a house like this, and pretty much the first thing is that I'd...

No.

Wait.

I wouldn't have the forest taken down. What the hell am I thinking? As I continue to stare out the window, I realize that the forest is actually kind of beautiful, although I feel like I can hear a distant sound coming from the dark spaces between the trees. Maybe I'm letting the house influence me, but it's almost as if a voice is crying out, loud but silent at the same time. I guess I'm just letting the spooky atmosphere of this place get to me, but for a few minutes I can't help just staring at the forest and listening to what seems to be a kind of silent calling. After a moment, I realize the glass in the window seems to be vibrating slightly.

Suddenly I look down at my phone, and to my surprise I see that it's already 1am. We got to the house a little after midnight, but I must have zoned out completely. Turning, I look back toward the dark hallway, but there's no sign of Toby. He wanted me to check on him after ten minutes, but he must have been down there for more than half an hour now.

"Hey!" I call out. "Are you still in the basement?"

I wait.

Silence.

Sighing, I make my way back around the table and out into the hallway, where I see that the basement door is still wide open. Heading over, I lean through into the cold passage, but I can't see a goddamn thing. I raise my phone and use the screen to light the rickety, dangerous-looking wooden steps that lead down under the house, but there's still no sight or sound of Toby, and no hint of light down at the bottom. I only have 3% battery left after charging my phone at the service station on the way here, but I guess that'll have to do.

"Hey, Egon Spengler! What's so fascinating down there, anyway?"

Again, I wait.

Again, silence.

"Come on," I continue, "don't make me come down there after you! It's freezing!"

No reply.

With another sigh, I grab a pot from a nearby table and set it on the floor, propping the door open. Then I start making my way down the steps, only for the first wooden board to creak and shift dramatically under my foot. I hesitate, worried that this whole goddamn staircase is going to collapse, but after a moment I tell myself that Toby made it down just fine, so I force myself to keep going even though the entire set of steps is creaking and shifting slightly. By the time I get down to the bottom, I'm glad to set foot on something solid again, even if the basement floor is kind of dusty and cracked.

Holding my phone up, I look around and see that Toby isn't here.

"What the hell?" I mutter, shivering slightly as I look back up the stairs.

I know I zoned out at the window, but that still doesn't explain why Toby would skip out on me. I'm pretty sure he'd have crept up behind me and made me jump. I guess he must have just gone up to the house's top floor, and maybe he was too wrapped up in the spookiness of the place to even notice that I was in the kitchen. Nice. Whatever, I don't fancy spending any more time down here in this cramped, low-ceilinged little room, so I turn to head back up the stairs.

And then I see the words on the far wall.

Squinting, I try to make them out, before ducking under a beam and making my way over. I was half expecting to find that the supposed words weren't words at all, that they were just a bunch of random scratches, but instead I find that the entire wall is actually covered in a series of repeated phrases that have been carved not only into the wooden sections, but even into the stones themselves.

"My name," I whisper, as I run a fingertip across the stones and try to decipher the words, "is Mary."

Kneeling down, I find a section where the carving is a little neater and more ordered, which makes it easier to read.

"My name is Mary," I whisper again.

That's definitely what it says. Hundreds and hundreds of times. Maybe even a couple of thousand. Tilting my phone, I watch as the faint electric glow is cast high across the wall, revealing those same four words scratched and carved into every available surface. Spotting something a little different on the far end of the wall, I get to my feet and take a closer look, and I quickly realize that as the writing spreads across the basement, the letters seem a little less neat and clear, as if the person responsible was starting to get tired.

By the time I get to the far corner, the message has been reduced to just one word, repeated over and over again.

"Mary," I whisper, looking along the wall and seeing that word carved into the stone, as if after a while it was the only important part of the sentence. I can't help feeling a shudder pass through my chest as I try to imagine what kind of person would spend their time down here, carving a name into the wall so often.

I guess the infamous Mary Carmichael must have been here. Even if Toby's ghost story was a load of baloney, it must have been rooted in the life of a real person. Either that, or someone came along later and did all of this, hoping to freak people out.

I guess it kind of worked.

Spotting movement in the corner, I step closer and peer at a rotten timber, and to my horror I see several plump little maggots wriggling in a section of mulchy wood.

"Gross," I mutter. "What -"

Suddenly something bumps against my hand, knocking the phone away and sending it clattering to the floor. Startled, I turn and look, but all I see is darkness. I crouch down and fumble to find my phone, and I can't help panicking slightly for a few seconds until finally my fingers brush against the phone's side. Picking it up, I quickly tap to light the screen and then I turn to cast the light across the basement.

There's no-one.

So what the hell just hit my hand?

Getting to my feet again, I turn and make absolutely certain that Toby isn't hiding down here, and then I look at the far corner, at the spot where the massive scrawl of carved words finally comes to an end. Stepping closer, I see that here the name Mary is barely legible at all, as if the person responsible was losing their strength. By the end, there are just several sets of seemingly random marks, some of which seem to been simple crosses.

It's almost as if this Mary girl eventually forgot how to write her name at all.

***

"TOBY!" I call out as I stand in the hallway, having coming up from the freezing basement and stopped at the foot of the main staircase. "Dude, are we gonna be done here soon? I thought we were just dropping by for a few minutes?"

I wait, but there's no reply.

"This isn't an all-night thing, is it?"

Again, I wait.

"Oh God, it is, isn't it?" I mutter under my breath. "You want to stay until the sun comes up."

He's clearly not anywhere on the ground floor, and I still refuse to believe that he'd just run off and leave me here, so I guess he has to be upstairs somewhere. I really, *really* don't want to go up, especially if he's hiding somewhere and planning to jump out at me. That kind of stuff gets really tiresome really fast, and I'm actually half tempted to just walk out of here right now, and just leave him to get on with all this hocus pocus rubbish.

Not that I'd actually do that, of course.

"Toby?" I call out again, this time unable to keep a hint of a whine out of my voice. "You're right, the house is creepy. Is that what you wanted to hear? I'm cold and I'm freaked out by that spooky basement, and I just want to leave. Why don't we go somewhere else, and you can tell me a load of ghost stories about this Mary Carmichael girl? I promise I'll be scared!"

I wait.

Silence.

"Please? Okay, so if you still wanna look around, can I at least go wait in the car with the engine running so I can warm up a little? You said I could do that earlier."

No reply.

I open my mouth to call out yet again, but the last thing I want is to sound like some kind of asshole.

Finally, realizing that he's not going to reply,

and that I can't just storm off, I start making my way up the stairs. Everything about this entire situation feels wrong, but I don't exactly have a choice. Fortunately, I'm able to remind myself that despite appearances, Wetherley House is just a big, empty old pile on the edge of some dusty little town. I mean, sure, there's a danger that a bunch of crazed hobos might be living here, but I think they'd have made their move by now. As I get to the top of the stairs and look along the landing, I'm resigned to the fact that Toby's just trying to piss me off.

He's starting to do a good job, too.

Listening to the continuing silence, I wait for some hint of Toby's presence. He's blatantly waiting in one of the rooms, probably lurking behind a door, but I don't exactly fancy walking right into some kind of trap. There's no way he can keep quiet for long, but I still need to lure him out a little, so finally I realize that I'm going to have to fight fire with fire. Toby was a bit of a joker sometimes at school, but two can play at that game and I'm going to turn this thing right around on him.

"Alright, then," I mutter with a sigh, making sure to keep my voice up so he'll be able to hear wherever he is, "I guess that asshole left me behind. I'm going home."

With that, I turn and stomp very loudly back down the stairs, before pulling the front door open and then letting it swing shut. Standing in the hallway, I stay completely silent as I wait for Toby to come scampering down after me, but to my surprise the house remains quiet. I turn and look up the stairs, but I guess he's just not convinced yet that I've left. Crossing my arms, I lean back against the wall and decide to wait him out, although I can see my own breath in the cold night air and I'm starting to feel like Toby's a little too obsessed with this place. I mean, it's good to have passions, but I never expected him to cut me loose like this.

As the wait continues, however, I start to wonder whether Toby's a little more stubborn than I'd realized. I was convinced he'd have come down by now.

"Come on," I whisper under my breath, not loud enough for anyone to hear. "This isn't funny. I should be at a baby shower right now, not shivering to death in an abandoned old house."

Turning, I look out the window and see the path that leads toward the gate in the distance. I really want to get the hell out of this house, and I'm starting to think that maybe I don't really owe Toby this much patience. I've tried playing along with his silly game, and I think I've been more than reasonable. Now, as I stand here looking longingly toward the gate and shivering in this cold hallway, I feel like I'm reaching a point where I just have to call it quits. Finally, even though I still feel a little bad for this, I realize I'm done.

"Okay," I call out, as I turn back to look up the stairs, "this time I'm really -"

Gasping, I step back and bump against the door as I see that there's a woman standing at the top of the stairs, staring at me from the landing. The light's too low for me to make out her features properly, but she's definitely a woman and her dress looks kind of old-fashioned. My heart is pounding and all I can do for a moment is watch the woman as I try to work out exactly what I'm seeing. This can't be real. There's no way there can be someone else here.

"Hey," I stammer finally, "so you're, like, a friend of Toby's?"

I try to force a smile, even though I'm feeling really uncomfortable. I keep telling myself that this is a set-up, that Toby's just doing something weird that I don't understand, and I really don't want to give him or his buddy the satisfaction of seeing me panic. Whatever they're up to, they just turned things up a notch and I really don't want to get involved.

"Tell Toby I'm out of here, okay?" I continue, waiting for this woman to actually acknowledge my presence by any other means that this icy stare. "He's got my number, so can you just tell him to call me some time? You know, if he wants. It's not big deal either way. And tell him I really don't appreciate being lied to about what I'm getting into, okay?"

I wait a moment, still trying to act calm, before turning and trying to pull the door open.

Suddenly it's locked.

"Great," I mutter under my breath, trying to figure out what's changed over the past couple of minutes. I try the handle again. My hands are trembling and I'm struggling to keep from rushing, but nothing seems to be working.

It's as if the door just spontaneously locked itself.

Suddenly I hear a creak from the stairs. I freeze as I realize that the woman must be coming down, but I quickly tell myself that I'm only going to play into their hands if I panic.

"Fine," I continue as I turn back to her, "I just -"

She's gone.

I wait, listening to the silence of the house, but now it's as if I'm completely alone.

"Hello?" I call out. "Toby, I want to leave. I'm not into playing games, so do you mind unlocking the door so I can get out of here? I'll walk into town and get a taxi or something."

Nothing.

No reply.

"Is that it?" I call out, feeling a rush of anger in my chest. "Do you think this is funny, Toby? Let me guess, that was supposed to be the terrifying Mary, wasn't it? Yeah, well, it's not scary and it's not funny! I don't appreciate being set up!"

Again I wait, and again I hear only silence.

"Asshole," I mutter under my breath.

Turning and looking around again, I realize that I have to get out of here via the back door. Still checking to make sure that the freaky woman doesn't show up again, I hurry through to the kitchen, bumping into the table as I make my way to the back door. When I try to turn the handle, however, I find that this door is also locked. I try a couple more times, and with each failed turn I feel another flicker of anger. How dare Toby and his asshole friends do this to me? Do they think I'm a complete idiot?

Suddenly I see my reflection in the window's dusty glass panel, and I'm shocked to realize that there's another face right behind me.

Startled, I turn and pull back, but once again there's no sign of anyone.

"This is getting out of hand!" I yell. "Toby, do you realize I could call the cops on you right now? You have to let me out of here right now!"

Unlocking my phone's home-screen, I type 999, but I can't quite bring myself to tap the green symbol and make the call. I don't want to get Toby into trouble, and I also don't want to have to explain the fact that we came here. At the same time, I'm down to just 2% battery, so I don't exactly have all night.

"Toby!" I shout, stepping back over to the door that leads into the hallway. "You're starting to seriously piss me off now!"

I wait, but of course the asshole doesn't respond. I might have been freaked out earlier, but now I'm downright mad.

And cold.

And tired.

And hungry.

With my phone in my right hand, I march past the open basement door and start stomping up the stairs, making sure to make plenty of noise as I reach the landing and head to the nearest door. Whatever game Toby's playing now, I'm sick of being some kind of patsy.

"Where are you then, huh?" I call out, opening the first door and seeing nothing but an empty room with pale, patterned wallpaper. Feeling a tickle in the back of my mouth, I take a moment to clear my throat. "No? Not here?"

I cross the landing and push the second door open, but of course all I find is another empty room.

"Great," I mutter, turning and heading to the third door, "I guess -"

Suddenly I feel something filling my throat, and I reach out to steady myself against the cold wall as I realize that there seems to be some kind of wriggling knot moving up from the back of my tongue. I try to cough it up, and immediately several small, moving chunks splatter into my mouth, along with a foul, bitter taste. Spitting some of them out into the palm of my hand, I'm horrified to see three small maggots, each wriggling in a patch of saliva and twitching their darkened tips.

Before I can react, I feel more maggots in my throat, and I drop to my knees as I start desperately trying to cough them all up. I don't know what's going on or where they came from, but suddenly there's a whole swarm of the damn things not only in my throat but also wriggling all the way down into my chest. Several more are blasted into my mouth when I cough again, but I swear I can feel hundreds of the little bastards falling down the back of my throat and tumbling down my neck.

Doubling over, I reach my hand into my mouth and push my fingers as far back as I can manage, scooping out the knot of maggots and then spitting them onto the bare floorboards. Even as I see a couple of dozen falling out, however, I can already feel more in my throat and suddenly I swallow involuntarily. Gagging and choking, I crawl away from the maggots that have already come out, and then I reach two fingers into my mouth and try to make myself throw up.

"Come on!" I gurgle, with tears in my eyes. "Get out of there!"

Finally I vomit, and scores of wriggling maggots come spewing out my mouth along with the half-digested remains of the burger and fries I had on the way here. As dribbles of vomit trickle from my lips, however, I can already feel more maggots in my throat, along with a sudden tickling sensation deep in my nose, as if some of the maggots have crawled deeper into my face. Hell, I think I can even feel them in my sinuses.

"What the hell are you doing to me?" I gasp, stumbling to my feet as I realize that I just have to get out of this place. I feel dizzy, and the effort of vomiting has made my stomach cramp, but a moment later I throw up for a second time, involuntarily this time.

Doubling over, I take a couple of faltering steps forward before bumping against the next door. As I feel more maggots wriggling through my face, my eyes start watering to the point that I can barely see properly. I turn the door-handle and stumble through, before stopping as I realize that I can just about make out a figure standing in the middle of the room, with its back to me. To my immense relief, I recognize the jacket.

"Toby!" I gasp, trying to get to him but only managing a couple of steps before falling back against the wall. I take a moment to steady myself. "What the hell are you doing? Get me out of here!"

I wait, but he's simply standing calmly, and so far he hasn't even reacted to my arrival. He's just looking toward the far window.

"Toby!" I shout as I clutch my throat. Tears are streaming down my face now, and I swear I can feel maggots behind my eyeballs. "You've gone too far! I need an ambulance!"

Stumbling toward him, I grab his shoulder and try to turn him to face me, but he's standing strangely firmly and all I can manage is to hold on for a moment before limping around him.

"Toby!" I hiss. "You've got to -"

Suddenly I see his face, and I pull back in horror as I see that maggots are crawling through his flesh, wriggling beneath the skin and poking out through gaps around his eyes and cheek. Hundreds and hundreds of tiny holes dot his features, left behind by the maggots as they've chewed through his body, and some of the maggots are even squirming and wriggling in his eyeballs. It's the holes that horrify me the most, though; so many bloodless little holes and tunnels running through his flesh, most abandoned as the maggots move on to the few patches of skin that haven't already been consumed. In some areas, several holes have merged to form gaping chasms in his face.

I don't even know how he's staying on his feet.

A faint, clicking groan slips from his throat and his eyes flick toward me, although some of the maggots catch on his eyelids and he lets out another gurgled cry.

"Please tell me this is a joke," I stammer, taking a step back until I bump against the wall. "Toby..."

My voice trails off as I realize that there's someone standing directly behind him. All I can see right now is the faint outline of a dark dress, but a moment later I see that there are two shadows on the wall: one is Toby, while the other looks to be a woman standing right behind him, barely in my line of view. Before I can ask what's happening, I realize I can see one of her hands, and her flesh looks painfully worn and tight.

"Run," Toby gasps, as more maggots spill from his mouth. "Rosie..."

"This is a joke, right?" I continue, as tears run down my face. "Toby, please -"

"Run!" he groans, his voice suddenly sounding much tighter, as if he's in pain. His whole body is shuddering now, and a moment later I watch as the pale hand reaches up from behind and touches his shoulder.

"Toby," I whisper, "please, tell me this is all a -"

Suddenly the hand pushes down hard on his shoulder and he slumps down, and I'm left staring into the rotten, hate-filled eyes of Evil Mary herself.

PART TWO
1888

MARGUERITE

"THEY'RE WONDERFUL!" I exclaim as Robert takes my hand, helping me up onto the carriage. "I never dreamed they'd look so beautiful."

All around, the port of Dover is bustling on this sunny Monday morning, but I am looking past the throng of workers and visitors, and instead my attention is focused on the vast white cliffs that rise up high and seem to tower not only over the port but over the English Channel itself. I had always hoped that my first view of England would fill me with awe, but I had not reckoned with the majesty of these huge chalky cliffs.

And high up atop those cliffs, bathing in the morning light, there stands the most wonderful castle. From my reading on the subject, I know that the castle is more than seven hundred years old, and I desperately want to go up and explore. At the same time, I feel as if the whole of England is waiting for me, with more to do and more to experience than I can ever manage in a lifetime.

In truth, the sight of the cliffs is a welcome distraction from the din of the port itself.

"Can we stay a night nearby?" I ask, turning back to look down at Robert once I'm on the carriage. "I know it's a lot to ask, but the sea air is bracing and filling. Please, just one night."

"I'm sorry," Robert says, "but -"

"Just one night," I continue, unable to help myself. "Must we really be on our way so soon?"

"Another time," he replies with a smile, as he heads around to the rear of the carriage and supervises the loading of our cases. "We have to get on our way if we're to reach the boarding house by nightfall, and then we must set off early in the morning so that we reach Wetherley House."

"It must be a wonderful house," I tell him, "if it's enough to draw us away from this natural beauty."

"You'll like England," he continues. "Trust me. Soon your old life in France will be almost forgotten."

As he starts speaking to the workers, I remain standing on the carriage, ignoring the strong wind that's blowing in from the sea and watching instead as this busy port town goes about its business. After a moment, as if to join in with the rush of movement and activity, the child in my belly gives out a strong kick, and I reach out to steady myself against the carriage's railing. The child kicks again, and I can only suppose that perhaps he really *is* reacting to the din all around us. I imagine that he, like me, is somewhat overawed by the change in our surroundings.

So far, England is so much busier than our quiet little corner of Provence.

"All's ready," Robert says suddenly, and I turn to see that he's climbing onto the seat at the front of the carriage, where the reins are tied around a loop. Ahead, two fine black horses are being fed by another dock worker.

"Do you mean to drive the carriage yourself?" I ask.

"I do," Robert replies. "If a man can't drive his own wife to their new home, then what good is he?" He smiles as he takes a seat. "I want our arrival at Wetherley House to be memorable, Marguerite. I want to show the others that I mean business. My family can be..."

His voice trails off for a moment. As ever, the merest mention of his family's existence has brought about a change in his demeanor.

"Will your family be waiting for us?" I ask.

"Some of them, if we're unlucky."

"You shouldn't say such things," I point out.

"How's the baby?"

"Kicking."

"That's my boy," he continues as he takes hold of the reins. "Or girl. Now sit down and get comfortable, for we have a long drive ahead of us through Kent. I have told the horses to take extra care, but there could still be a few rocks along the way."

Doing as I'm told, I can't help looking around at the rough, dirty faces of the dock workers. I had heard that England could be a somewhat filthy place, and I can't help noticing that the workers here seem to take less pride in their appearance than the workers back home in Paris or Marseilles. Still, the sheer bright whiteness of the cliffs is more than enough to compensate. As Robert gets us underway and our carriage begins to rattle along the dockside toward the road, I lean back and look toward the horizon.

I'm home. My new home, anyway. With the man I love and, soon, our first child.

***

"IS SOMETHING THE MATTER?" I ask a couple of hours later, as Robert brings the carriage to a halt at the side of a remote road.

"I just need to feed the horses," he replies, already climbing down. "Rest, my dear. This won't take long."

"I think I should like to stretch my legs," I tell him, and he duly helps me from the carriage.

Relieved to be on firmer ground once more, I step around the side of the carriage and look up at a nearby signpost, which informs me that a place called Ashford is just ten miles away. I turn and look around, marveling at the rolling green hills and at the fields that stretch to the horizon. In the distance, sheep are grazing on a patch of land, and the whole scene seems so wonderfully peaceful and divine. Now *this* is the England of Mr. Blake's poetry, the green and pleasant land of which I dreamed as a girl in Marseilles.

All around us, birds are chattering in nearby trees, as if to welcome me with their chorus.

And then I hear a faint gasping sound.

I turn and look at Robert, but he's still busy with the horses. Stepping around to the other side of the carriage, I realize that there's a groan emanating from somewhere in the long grass at the side of the road, and a cloud of flies is buzzing in the air.

Perhaps I should be more wary, but I cannot help wandering toward the source of the sound, worried in case somebody is injured. Sure enough, I quickly spot a human figure slumped nearby, and as I get closer I realize that the figure is an elderly woman, naked and bloodied. She's in a shallow ditch than runs alongside the road, as if she has been tossed aside.

"Are you alright?" I ask cautiously.

She lets out another groan, and I step a little closer until finally I'm able to see her face. I must admit, she's so painfully thin and sick-looking, I instinctively freeze for a moment. Horrified, I watch as the woman tries to raise a hand toward me, but her arms look far too thin to support the weight of her hands. There are even maggots crawling in her flesh. It's quite clear already that this poor woman is starved to the bring of death, and I watch for a moment as she tries but fails to rise from her position slumped in the ditch. At the same time, I suddenly realize I can see the white of her eyes staring at me from behind matted clumps of hair.

I should do something.

I have to help her.

And yet, although I feel the urge to step closer, the sight of this woman is too frightful. It is clear that she must be diseased, although I know my lord and protector would never forgive me if I turned my back. I hesitate for a moment longer, before finally realizing that it's my human duty to help this poor creature.

Despite my swollen belly, I start clambering through the long grass and into the ditch, while waving away the thick flies that are buzzing all around me.

"Marguerite, no!"

Robert grabs my arm, holding my back. When I turn to him, I see an expression of pure horror in his eyes.

"Leave her!" he says firmly.

"But -"

"She's beyond help," he continues, staring past me and clearly disgusted by what he sees. "Look at the poor wretch. There's nothing anyone can do for somebody who's that far gone."

"She's in agony," I point out, with tears in my eyes. "We can't just leave her like this."

"We can and we must."

I look back at the woman. She's still trying to get up, but her painfully thin frame is obviously too weak.

"Besides, she could be carrying any number of sicknesses," Robert explains. "Look further along, my dear. Others have died down there. It happens sometimes. These peasants get thrown out of their towns and villages for one reason or another, usually something criminal that they've done, and they end up wandering the countryside until they can no longer manage for themselves, and then they end up like this." He pauses for a moment, as the dying old woman lets out a faint gurgle. "You cannot tell me, in all honesty, that such things do not also happen in France."

"I'm sure they do," I reply. "It's just that I have never witnessed them."

"There is no need for you to witness this."

"But charity is -"

"The Lord will protect this woman if he sees fit," Robert says firmly. "Although it appears the decision has been made already."

Placing a hand on my shoulder, he guides me away from the roadside and back around to the other side of the carriage. I know he is right, and that as his wife I should accept his decision without argument, but still I bristle at the thought of abandoning another human being.

"I'm sorry you had to see that," he continues. "I just need to adjust a buckle on one of the horses, and then we're ready to get going again."

I nod, although I hesitate as I'm about to get back up onto the carriage.

"Please, put her out of your mind," Robert adds. "Creatures such as that hag are of no concern to the likes of us. Once we're at Wetherley House, you shall never see such horrific things again. That, I promise you. Wetherley is a paradise, a beacon of calm. You will soon forget that there is any meanness or cruelty in the world at all."

He helps me up onto the carriage, where I take a moment to settle my nerves as I wait patiently for my husband to finish with the horses. I cannot help glancing over toward side of the road, but it's impossible to see anything now through the thick branches and the overgrown grass. I can only hope that the woman's suffering is over soon, although I still feel that perhaps Robert could have allowed me to do more. After a few moments of further contemplation, I turn to my husband and see that he's almost done with the horse's buckle. And then, quite suddenly, I realize to my surprise that the birds have stopped chattering in the trees, and the entire world around us seems to have fallen quiet.

I turn to look along the road.

The birds are still in the trees, standing on the branches and silhouetted against the gray sky.

Watching.

Suddenly a figure lunges at me, scrambling over the side of the carriage. Startled, I see that it's the old woman from the ditch, and I'm unable to pull away before she grabs my swollen belly. I cry out, trying to push her back, but she slips one of her bony, dirt-encrusted hands under my dress and I feel her filthy flesh against mine.

"She'll be taken from you!" the woman gasps, leaning closer and bringing with her a foul stench. "You left me to die and now a child will be taken from your family, so that I can live again and -"

Before she's able to finish, the side of her head explodes and her body slumps to the side. As she crashes off the carriage and hits the ground, I'm left shaking and startled on my seat. After a moment, I realize that blood has sprayed not only across my dress but also against the sides of the carriage. There are little white pieces in the blood, too, which I can only suppose are from the woman's brain or skull.

Finally, looking over my shoulder, I see that Robert still has his pistol aimed at the spot where the woman was standing, although he lowers the weapon after a moment.

"Are you okay?" he asks breathlessly. "Did she hurt you?"

I hesitate, before shaking my head.

He steps over to the woman and looks down at her body for a moment, before kicking her head to make sure that she's dead.

"Disgusting filth," he mutters darkly. "We must get going. I'm sorry you were exposed to this, Marguerite, but I assure you that I will never again let anybody frighten you in such a manner."

He kicks her several more times, rolling her body until she tumbles back into the ditch. As he takes a moment to wipe blood from his boots, and then to clean the side of the carriage, I cannot help looking down and seeing the old woman's pale arms still poking out from deep in the long grass.

MARGUERITE

One month later

"ARE YOU READY?" THE photographer asks, once he's finished adjusting his apparatus. "Remember to keep very still."

"What was that?" I mutter, feeling something brush against my shoulder. Turning, I see no sign of anyone behind me.

"You must stay still, my dear," Robert says from my other side. "Have you never had your photograph taken before?"

Turning back to the camera, I cannot help but feel uneasy as I stare into its dark lens. Still, I know Robert is very keen to have a family portrait taken, so I offer my best smile and try to ignore the sensation of a hand touching my belly. I suppose such things are simply by-products of the photography process, which I do not understand at all.

"Okay," the photographer continues. "Here we go!"

I force my smile even wider, although the sensation of a foreign hand persists on my belly.

***

"DO YOU FEEL IT?" I whisper a short time later, once the photographer has left, as Robert's hands rest on my swollen belly. "You must."

"It's like a big swollen bag," Robert replies with a smile.

"But do you feel it kicking?"

"I -"

He hesitates, and as soon as he looks up at me again I can see that something has changed. For the first time, I see him not only as a husband, but also as a father.

"There!" he continues. "Something -"

He looks back down at my bare belly, his eyes filled with shock.

"She's kicking," I explain with a smile. "She's been doing it a lot lately. It seems she's a feisty one."

"Or he," he points out.

I shake my head, while he continues to feel my belly.

"It's a girl," I tell him. "Don't ask how I know. I just do. A mother can sense these things."

"I'm not sure a doctor would agree with you there," he replies, finally getting to his feet and then placing a hand on the side of my face, brushing a finger against my cheek. "We'll know soon enough. Next week, with any luck. And I honestly don't mind if it's a boy or a girl. After all, it might be our first child, but I don't think it'll be our last. I intend for us to have a whole brood to fill this house, and we might not even stop there. The making is, itself, a rather enjoyable endeavor."

"Is Doctor Forbes aware of the date?"

He nods.

"And he'll be ready to come out here to the house?" I continue. "Are you sure we shouldn't go to the hospital instead?"

"The journey would be a risk for you," he explains, heading over to table and picking up his cup of tea. "Besides, Doctor Forbes and Miss Jacobs have delivered many babies in the past, so you'll be in the best possible hands. I've already seen to it that a lad from the town will come out here to Wetherley House and be ready to run back to Doctor Forbes at a moment's notice, to alert him when the time comes. I have spare no expense." He takes another sip, before turning to me. "Everything is taken care of. You have to trust me on that."

"I do trust you," I tell him. "It's just -"

Before I can finish, I hear loud footsteps from the room above the dining room, and those footsteps swiftly head to the stairs. I know I should be more open-minded about Robert's family, but I can't help flinching whenever I know that one of them – especially his sister Eve – will be joining us shortly. When I turn to Robert again, I can already tell that he senses my displeasure.

"She wants to help," he points out, as Eve makes her way down the stairs.

"I know."

"Just give it time," he continues. "She -"

"And how is the mother-to-be?" Eve asks loudly as she enters the room. "My dear Marguerite, I hope you're not overdoing things. In your condition, rest is the only sensible option. Aren't your knees at risk of buckling under such a weight?"

"I'm being very well taken care of," I reply. "Thank you."

"So polite," she says with a laugh, stopping and kneeling in front of me. "Your English is very good, my dear. Much better than my French will ever be, that's for sure. I was never much good at languages. Now let me feel my pending nephew."

Without waiting for me to say anything, she reaches out and places an icy hand against my belly. I flinch and almost pull back, and I see a faint flicker of a smile on her lips as she moves her hand across the dome of tight flesh. A moment later, I feel another kick from the baby, although in truth I would prefer that she keeps still when the hands of others are searching for her.

"He seems strong," she suggests.

"Marguerite thinks it's going to be a girl," Robert tells her.

"Nonsense." She looks up at me. "I know a boy

when I feel one. A mother's judgment is clouded during pregnancy, but as the child's aunt I enjoy a very clear perspective. Trust me, Marguerite. You're carrying a boy. A girl could never kick so hard."

"We shall see," I reply, not wanting to get into another argument.

"There!" she continues. "He kicks again! Why, I shall not take it personally, else I'd be convinced that he doesn't like me. Of course, that'll change one he's out. He'll swiftly come to realize that I'm the best aunt any child could possibly want. Oh, I am going to enjoy teaching him as he gets older. I have so much to offer a child!"

"Well," I reply, "I think -"

"It feels like a big sack of worms!" she adds with evident glee, and while her hand continues to rest on my belly, her eyes are fixed on my face. I fear she's trying to upset me again, and this time I must not fall into the trap. "It feels, dearest sister-in-law, that you are carrying hundreds and hundreds of worms inside you, and they're all jostling for position and trying to gain an advantage over one another. Worms or maggots, anyway." She pauses for a moment. "Obviously I know that's not the case. I'm just telling you how it feels."

"I think I should go and rest," I reply, starting to lower the front of my dress so that she'll hopefully get the message and remove her hand.

She does not, however. In fact, she seems to be challenging me.

"I'm so very tired," I continue, before looking

over at Robert in the hope that he might help. "I shan't sleep. I merely wish to rest on the bed."

"Of course," he replies, "and -"

"Men understand nothing of what you're going through," Eve continues, suddenly taking my hands in hers, as if after all this time she suddenly wishes to be my friend. "Dear Marguerite, my brother can no more guess how you are feeling, than you or I can guess what it is like to be a star in the night sky. And even by the standards of his gender, Robert is especially -"

"How would *you* know anything of womanly matters?" Robert asks, fixing his sister with an angry stare. "How many of those feeble things in *your* belly have resulted in more than a few specks of blood and a fleshy knot to be thrown out with the bath water?"

Eve immediately tenses, and I can see the fury in her eyes. I do hope they're not going to have one of their very loud arguments again.

"Your husband has given up trying to bring an heir from between your legs," he continues, stepping toward me and reaching down, taking my hands and slipping them free of his sister's grip. "Come, Marguerite. If you wish to rest, you should rest. I accept that I know little of what you are going through, but I hardly think my barren sister has any greater insight. She has miscarried five children in five years, and that's just the ones I know of. I'm sure she slipped several others out and threw them away, when nobody was watching."

Getting to my feet, I allow Robert to lead me toward the door, although after a moment I can't help glancing back at Eve. For all his wickedness and jealousy, and despite all her attempts to make me uncomfortable since I arrived in England and married Robert, there are times when I feel desperately sorry for the poor woman. Now, as she remains kneeling on the floor in front of the now-empty chair, with her back to us, I realize that this is one of those times when I feel for her. There was no need for Robert to be quite so harsh, and this is not the first time I have noticed that Eve reacts terribly badly whenever her barrenness is brought up.

"Perhaps you should have been more tactful," I whisper as we reach the hallway and Robert begins to lead me up the stairs. "She *is* your sister, after all."

"She's a wretched creature," he mutters, "with a blackened and twisted excuse for a soul."

"But -"

"I shall send her back to her husband next week," he continues. "The man was foolish enough to marry her. He should be forced to endure her presence at least some of the time."

"I believe they do not speak very often."

"Then they can become reacquainted, can't they?"

"Robert -"

"I don't care what they do," he adds, as we reach the door to the master bedroom and he leads me inside. "You are my family now, and our soon-to-be-born child will make us whole. Then Wetherley House can come alive again, and my sister can take her leave." He helps me onto the bed and then fusses a little, pulling the sheets back so that I can settle. "I won't have Eve interfering. It's bad enough that she has been here for so much of your pregnancy."

"Don't be too harsh on her."

"I must go into town and run some errands," he explains, tucking me carefully into the bed. "Did I tell you that I'm going to invest in old Mr. Trin's new business? He wants to set up a glass factory, and I think he has the necessary experience to pull the venture off. He needs some money, though, to get started, and that is where he has need of a partner. I honestly believe that the business will grow, and that eventually we shall earn great riches. Not just for us, my dear, but for our unborn child. And for all the other children yet to come."

"I am sure you're right," I tell him. "I just -"

Before I can finish, I feel something brushing against my shoulder. I turn, but there is nobody there. Since we arrived at Wetherley House, however, I have noticed this sensation several times.

"Upon my return," Robert says calmly, "I shall see to it that Eve leaves us alone for the evening. She can sit and rot in her room, for all I care. Perhaps that will help her get the message that she's not welcome here."

"But she's your sister and -"

"The matter is settled." Leaning closer, he kisses my forehead, and I instantly feel as if all is well with the world again. "Nothing is going to stand in the way of our happiness, my dear. I promise. And now, if you'll excuse me, I must go and ready the horses for my errands."

Once he's gone, I remain in the bed and listen to the silence that fills the room. Although I confess to feeling sorry for Eve, I shan't be sorry when she is gone, and when our first child arrives. Resting my hands on my belly, I close my eyes and let thoughts of motherhood lull me into a much-needed sleep. I hear a couple of creaks outside the room, as if someone is on the other side of the door, but I suppose that is just the nature of this old and remarkable house.

This is my home now, and for the first time in my life I feel so very safe.

MARGUERITE

THE FOREST IS DARK, and I do not know how I ended up out here.

Stumbling between the trees, I look around for some sign of the house, but I seem to be all alone. Patches of moonlight fall across the uneven ground, bearing the shadows of the high tree canopy, but I cannot make out the lights of the house in the distance at all. I know I must be in the forest at the end of the lawn, I know Wetherley House must be just a few hundred meters away, but the more I look around, the more I fear that I seem to be utterly lost.

"Hello?" I call out. "Can anybody hear me?"

I wait, but the only sound comes from an owl in the distance.

Stopping for a moment, I look around and try to work out exactly which way I have come. I do not remember entering the forest at all, and I do not know this part of Wetherley House's estate at all. I cannot be *too* far from the main building, but I'm so very cold and I want nothing more than to get back to bed and rest. Feeling a faint kick in my belly, I also begin to worry that I might be stressing my child. I am shivering in the cold night air, and -

Suddenly I hear a crunching sound over my shoulder, as if somebody stepped on some dry twigs. I turn and look, but I do not see anyone. I see only the cold, moonlit trees. Then again, out here in the dark, somebody could be just a few feet away and I would not necessary be any the wiser.

"Hello?" I call out again, praying that Robert has come to find me after waking alone in our bed. "Robert, is that you?"

The only reply is the sound of a light breeze blowing between the trees. Even the owl has fallen silent now.

A moment later I hear a loud, deep creaking sound. I look around, but all the trees look so still.

I start walking in the direction of the sound, supposing that perhaps the Lord has seen fit to offer me a path through this wretched forest. I am still getting used to England, but so far I am finding that the place seems to have hidden dangers at every corner. Frankly, I am minded to stay inside the house for the rest of my days, and to never again venture out. And perhaps I shall teach my children to do the same.

Reaching another tree, I stop for a moment to get my breath back, before suddenly hearing another crunch over my shoulder.

I turn and look, but once again I see only

darkness. I know Robert always has a light kept in the house's rear window, so I should be able to see something in the distance. Instead, however, I see nothing at all.

"Hello?" I whisper cautiously, barely even daring to speak. "If somebody is out there, I demand that you make yourself known. Robert, if it's you, can we please just go back inside?"

I wait.

Silence.

"Dear Lord," I continue, hoping that my prayer will be heard, "please guide me to the safety of the house, and ensure that my child shall be returned to warmth."

I hesitate for a moment, still looking over my shoulder, before finally turning so that I can walk away.

Suddenly a figure lunges at me, slamming hard into my belly and sending me crashing to the ground. Landing on top of me, the figure grabs the fabric of my nightdress and tears it apart, exposing my large, swollen belly. Horrified, I look up at the figure's face and see the awful old woman staring back down at me, the same awful old woman from the roadside last month. I want to scream, to push her away, but my body is frozen and my limbs feel too heavy to move as the woman slowly places her crusty, bony hands against my belly and pushes hard.

"You left me to die," she croaks, her voice sounding so utterly dry and ravaged, as if she has a throat full of old twigs. "A little human kindness would not have gone amiss. Now in each generation, the firstborn child of your line, born on this land, shall be taken from you. The way you took life from me!"

I try desperately to cry out, but all that emerges from my lips is a faint gurgle.

"I will reach your children," she continues, as she starts digging the tips of her bony fingers into my belly, "no matter where you hide them! And there is no god in all the world that can stop me!"

Blood starts trickling from the holes she's begun to force, and now I can feel her fingers slipping deeper and deeper into my body. At the same time, my child is kicking furiously, yet I can't cry out or do anything to help. I strain desperately to push the old woman away, but now her knuckles are buried deep in my bloodied belly and I can feel her scratching at my unborn child. She's laughing, too, and finally I manage to tilt my head back until I'm able to see the lights of the house in the distance, and I scream as the old woman's fingers reach into my belly and scratch against my wriggling, unborn child.

**

"ROBERT! SOMEBODY HELP! ROBERT!"

A scream wakes me, and I immediately sit up in bed. My mind is racing, and I can hear footsteps hurrying through the gravel below the bedroom window, followed a moment later by heavy footsteps thumping into the kitchen. A few seconds after that, I hear another sound, and I think perhaps somebody is sobbing in the room below. For a moment, however, all I can think about is that awful dream, and I quickly pull my night-dress up so that I can check my belly is undamaged.

I feel a rush of relief as I run my hands over the smooth flesh. There are no holes, there's no blood, and it's evident that the vile old woman's visit was all just a terrible nightmare.

Downstairs, voices are still calling out in the house.

"Everything's okay," I tell my child, as tears run down my face. "You're safe, I promise. No-one's going to hurt you. No-one's *ever* going to hurt you."

Still, my heart is racing and I'm desperately out of breath, and it takes a moment before I realize that people are still shouting downstairs, as if something is terribly wrong. Looking over at the other side of the bed, I see that my child and I are alone here in the room.

"Robert?" I whisper, my voice filled with uncertainty and fear. "Where are you?"

I wait, but all I hear is more sobs from downstairs, followed after a few seconds by the whinnying of the horses in the stable. I need Robert to calm my nerves, for him to tell me that everything is alright, but evidently he has left the bed.

So I wait.

I sit on the bed and wait for his return, even as I hear more voices outside in the night. I cannot imagine what commotion could have drawn Robert and the others out there, but I know that they shall have no need of me.

And yet, the longer I wait, the more concerned I become.

"Robert?" I whisper.

I must stay here, I know I must, and yet...

Finally realizing that I simply must go and check for myself that everything is okay, I ease myself out of bed and start making my way across the room. I'm so stiff and ungainly, I can barely manage to shuffle out onto the landing, and by the time I get to the top of the stairs I feel as if I might be about to collapse. Now that I'm here, however, I can also hear the sobs more clearly than before, and I can tell with absolute certainty that something seems to be dreadfully wrong with Eve.

"Robert?" I call out again, before starting to make my way carefully down the stairs, wincing slightly as I feel a creaking pain in my knees. "Robert, where are you? Robert, what's wrong?"

Reaching the hallway, I shuffle past the door to the basement and finally I reach the kitchen, where to my shock I see Eve weeping at the table with her face in her hands. Her shoulders are shuddering and her body seems gripped by wave after wave of violent convulsion, and I must confess that I have never in all my life seen her in such a frightful state. In fact, I do not think I have ever seen another soul weep with such fear. All I can see of her really are her rounded shoulders, shaking violently as the most awful sobbing sound comes from her hidden mouth.

"Eve?" I say cautiously. "Eve, whatever is it?"

Heading over to her, I stop next to her chair and look down at the side of her face. Just as I'm once again about to ask what's wrong, however, she suddenly looks up at me with tear-filled eyes, and I immediately understand that something is terribly wrong.

"Where's Robert?" I ask, trying but failing to keep a rush of panic from rising through my chest. "Eve, where is my husband?"

"He's..."

Her voice trails off for a moment as tears stream down her face.

"Robert?" she whispers, almost as if the name is suddenly foreign to her.

"Where is he?" I ask again. "Tell me!"

"He's in the stable," she whimpers finally. "Robert's in the stable."

"And whatever's the matter?"

"He's in the stable," she says again. "Robert's... He's in the stable. He's not coming out."

She opens her mouth and tries to say some more, but instead she simply collapses into the most horrific series of violent sobs, and it's clear I shall get nothing sensible out of her. Telling myself that everything will surely be okay, and that I must not panic lest I disturb the baby, I make my way around the table and over to the back door, and then out into the garden. It's at times like this that I dearly wish Robert had seen fit to employ staff at Wetherley House, instead of insisting that we fend for ourselves, and all sorts of dreadful thoughts are rushing through my head as I shuffle around the side of the house and toward the stable.

Suddenly a horse races toward me, startled and frightened, and it's all I can do to step back out of the way. As it thunders past me, the horse lets out a frightful whinny and then stops, and I see that there appears to be thick red blood glistening on its front left hoof and running up its leg.

"Robert?" I call out, turning and making my way toward the stable, where the door is wide open. The other horse is just inside, though loose, and I cannot begin to imagine whatever is going on there. As I reach the door, however, I spot a figure slumped on the ground at the very far end of the stable, and I immediately recognize the outfit that he's wearing.

I step forward, but already a knot of fear has tightened in my chest.

"Robert?" I stammer. "Robert, what are you doing? Robert, you must get up at once."

When he fails to respond, I shuffle into the stable and start making my way across the dirty, straw-covered floor. I have been avoiding the horses and the stable as much as possible during my pregnancy, fearful that the filth in here might cause some complication, and even now the stench of horse droppings is quite overpowering. As I get closer to Robert's prone form, however, I cannot help but notice that there appears to be a great deal more blood on the floor. Robert is resting on his front, with her head turned away from me, and I'm starting to fear that one of the horses must have taken fright and caught him a blow.

"Robert? Say something, Robert."

I wait, and then I start making my way around him.

"Robert, I -"

Stopping suddenly, I see that the front of his head had been utterly ravaged, with the flesh having been ripped away from the skull and mashed against the wooden boards. A shattered eye socket bears signs of a heavy impact, and fragments of splintered bone rest glistening in the blood. His mouth is wide open, as if frozen in a scream, but his lower jaw has been shattered in the middle and ripped with such violence that one section rests on the ground.

"Robert!" I scream, stumbling back against the wall. "Help! Somebody help!"

This is a dream.

It has to be.

It's another nightmare, and I just have to find a way to wake up. Slumping down, I close my eyes and wait a moment, before opening them in the expectation of finding myself safely back in bed with my husband at my side. Yet when I *do* open them, I am still here in the stable, and a large pool of blood is slowly trickling toward me from Robert's body. I close my eyes again and wait longer, but the result is the same. The third time, I squeeze my eyes tighter still, determined to force myself awake from this nightmare. I just have to find a way.

This cannot be happening.

MARGUERITE

"YES, IT'S TERRIBLY SAD and -"

As soon as I reach the doorway, Eve stops speaking and turns to look at me. For a moment, just a moment, I see a flicker of irritation in her eyes, but her usual calm demeanor quickly prevails. She seems capable of restoring her mood at the drop of a hat.

"And here is Robert's widow now," she continues. "Good afternoon, Marguerite. Are you feeling a little better now? If not, I have chamomile tea."

"Who is..."

My voice trails off as I look at the gentleman sitting on the sofa, facing Eve. Well-dressed and middle-aged, with a rather bushy gray beard and mustache, he's quite the thinnest man I have ever seen in my life, albeit with an extremely large and pointed nose that seems as much like a beak. He stares at me from behind small round spectacles, and then he gets to his feet and steps toward me with an outstretched hand. I want to turn and run, but I force myself to stay.

"Josiah Edge," he says, his voice sounding harsh and rasping.

"*Doctor* Josiah Edge," Eve adds.

The man's hand is still held out toward me.

"My sister-in-law struggles with shock," Eve explains. "Poor Marguerite is so alone now. You must try to understand."

"Oh, I understand all too well," he replies, keeping his eyes fixed on me and his hand outstretched. "The female mind is not good at dealing with horrors. Such things are best left to the male mind, but sometimes these things cannot be helped. Time, however, can be a very good healer."

I wait, but now they're both staring at me, as if they believe me to be a simpleton. Finally I realize that though I feel desperately unwell, I simply must speak.

"Good afternoon, Doctor Edge," I say cautiously, reaching for his hand, only for him to take mine and kiss it gently.

I was not expecting that.

"I am so very sorry for your loss," he tells me. "I cannot claim to have known Robert well, but we met a few times at market and he always struck me as a fine and sturdy man. To lose him now, so close to the birth of your first child, must be an especially cruel blow."

"I was just telling Doctor Edge how badly you've taken everything," Eve says, still sitting in the armchair next to the fireplace. "I said that after the initial hysteria had worn off, you've largely been in bed. Not that there's any shame in that, of course, but... Well, it is what it is."

"I have been resting," I reply, even as a fresh wave of weakness passes through my body.

"And you are due now, are you not?" Doctor Edge asks.

"Where is Doctor Forbes?" I ask.

"Doctor Forbes could barely deliver a letter to his neighbor," Eve replies, rolling her eyes, "let alone a baby. With Robert no longer around to take care of your health, dear Marguerite, I took it upon myself to get in touch with a doctor in whom I have at least a modicum of faith. Doctor Josiah Edge has his own surgery in Bristol, you know. We're very lucky that he could come out here at all. I have used my own purse to acquire his services, but honestly, there is no need to thank me."

"I've become accustomed to Doctor Forbes," I remind her, before turning to this new gentleman. "You'll understand, I'm sure."

"The truth is," Eve continues, "Doctor Forbes and that frightful Jacobs woman are not available. Therefore I have, at great expense, arranged for Doctor Edge and his -"

"I should like to speak to Doctor Forbes," I tell her.

"Well, I believe he has gone to Edinburgh," she replies.

"He mentioned no such thing to me the other day."

"Then his journey must have been a sudden one."

"I assure you, M'am," Doctor Edge says, "that I

shall ensure you receive nothing but the best care. I have been retained by your sister-in-law to offer you around-the-clock, one-on-one attention. She has even very kindly allowed me to stay here in your home, so that I am always available."

"What woman could ask for anything more?" Eve asks.

"Doctor Forbes said he would be back to see me today," I remind her. "He was very keen to follow my progress and he mentioned nothing whatsoever of Edinburgh."

"I cannot answer for Doctor Forbes and his actions," Eve replies, "nor can I answer for his broken promises. All I can do is pay Doctor Josiah Edge handsomely, from my own pocket, so that my dear late brother's child is given the best possible start in life. After all, Marguerite, I'm sure you'll understand when I say that I have a rather vested interest in the life that has been growing in your belly. Robert and I had no siblings. Your belly, therefore, contains our only real chance to continue the line. We owe this to poor Robert."

"I am becoming faint," I whisper, and Doctor Edge immediately helps me over to one of the armchairs. As I take a seat, I feel as if the entire room is spinning around me.

"You have been through a terrible ordeal," Doctor Edge points out, "and it is entirely possible that the experience has left you weakened. I should like to perform a full examination as soon as possible."

I open my mouth to tell him that such a thing will be impossible.

"Of course," Eve says calmly.

I turn to her.

"You need to be checked," she adds. "It's what Robert would have wanted."

"I want Doctor Forbes," I stammer.

"He's in Edinburgh, my dear. You're in no fit state to go to Edinburgh."

"When will he be back?"

"How can I possibly know? The man is free to come and go to Edinburgh as he chooses."

"I really must examine her," Doctor Edge says, turning to Eve. "It's out of the question for me to provide the requisite treatment if I do not know her current state of health."

"Of course you shall give her an examination," she tells him. "It's out of the question to think otherwise."

"No," I reply, struggling to haul myself up from the chair, almost falling in the process. "I think I shall return to bed and -"

Suddenly I slip, almost falling forward before Doctor Edge manages to grab my arms and hold me upright. I try to turn away, but my knees feel terribly weak, as if they cannot support my weight at all.

"Steady," the doctor says, still holing me firmly. "You mustn't push yourself."

"Where do you wish to perform the examination?" Eve asks.

"I want Doctor Forbes," I stammer, as I feel a cold, prickly sweat breaking across my forehead. "I only trust Doctor Forbes."

"Doctor Forbes is in Edinburgh," Eve says yet again, "and -"

"I know he's in Edinburgh!" I gasp, trying to take a step forward but feeling, for a moment, as if I am already leaning at an alarming angle toward the floor. Attempting to steady myself, I turn to Doctor Edge, but somehow I cannot quite focus on his face, and I am starting to feel extremely nauseous. Finally, even though I want to go up to my room, I find myself leaning back and slumping into the armchair. The doctor supports me all the way down, and then he presses two fingers against the side of my neck, checking my pulse.

"Has she been given anything to help her sleep?" he asks.

"Nothing," I try to whisper, but I'm not sure the words come out. "I was worried about the baby."

"Only the supplements you recommended," Eve explains. "I slipped them into her drinks."

"What?" I gasp, as I feel cold sweat starting to run down my face.

"I think I got here not a moment too soon," the doctor mutters. "This woman is almost ready to give birth."

"Can you perform the initial examination there in the chair," Eve asks, as I feel myself slipping into unconsciousness, "or do you need me to help carry her to the bed?"

"Stop!" I gurgle, trying but failing to reach out and steady myself.

"Calm down, you silly thing," Eve says, leaning toward me with a smile. "I know what's best for the child, Marguerite. And for you, too. After all, you're family now, and I always take very good care of my family."

***

"NO, I WANT DOCTOR Forbes!" I gasp, suddenly opening my eyes and trying to sit up, only to find that thick restraints are tying me to the bed.

"Don't strain yourself," Eve says. "You're doing just fine."

Startled, I turn to see that she's sitting next to me, holding a cloth and a metal pan of water. Dipping the cloth into the water for a moment, she wrings it out and then uses it to wipe my forehead. I try to pull away, but I'm powerless to stop her, even as cold drops run down the side of my face.

"You're going into labor," she explains. "Doctor Edge was most insistent that it would be unsafe for you to give birth while still sedated. I'm sorry, but I can't overrule him. He *is* a man of medicine, after all."

"What are you doing to me?" I stammer, looking down and seeing that I have been stripped naked. My enormous belly is still protruding, glistening as if some kind of waxy substance has been rubbed across the tight flesh, and when I try to move my legs I find that my ankles have been securely tied to the bed posts, leaving my legs wide apart with my knees poking up.

"Don't strain," Eve says again. "It might not be good for the baby."

"Why am I tied down?" I shout, trying not to panic.

"So that you don't do anything foolish. Don't be such a silly goose."

"Where's Doctor Forbes?"

"I told you, he -"

"Where's -"

I catch myself just in time, as I realize that there's nobody else to call for. Robert is gone and Doctor Forbes has evidently departed for Edinburgh, which means that I'm all alone here. My parents and siblings are still in France, and I have lived a sheltered life here at Wetherley House ever since I arrived. I have made no friends and precious few acquaintances, and it's extremely clear to me now that I cannot possibly hope for anyone to come and help me. Instead, I try pulling on the restraints, only to find that they're tied uncommonly tight, and that the fibers are already starting to burn my wrists as I struggle to get free.

"It's going to be a boy," Eve continues after a moment. "I can feel it."

"I want to get off this bed!" I say firmly, turning to her.

"A big, strong boy."

"Untie me!"

Staring at my belly, she seems lost in thought for a moment.

"This family needs a boy," she whispers finally. "I know Robert humored you, Marguerite, and said that a girl would be fine, but deep down he wanted a son. Someone who could take over the family business, someone who could keep the family name in a good light. A girl would be acceptable, I suppose, but not as desirable as a boy."

"What are you talking about?" I ask. "I'm not -"

Before I can finish, however, I notice that there is now a second bed in the room, right behind her.

"What's that for?" I stammer.

"What's what for?" she replies innocently.

"There's another bed in here!"

"Oh, that?" She calmly looks at the other bed for a moment, before turning back to me. "Well, that's for me, silly."

"For you?"

"Just have a little patience," she continues, reaching over and wiping my forehead once again, "and everything will become clear in time. Believe me, this has all been thought through very carefully, and no corners have been cut. Doctor Edge is one of the very few men in England who possesses the necessary skills to deliver your child in the required manner, and -"

"Required manner?" I gasp. "What are you talking about?"

"Oh, you're so sweaty," she mutters, wiping my forehead yet again, even though I try to turn away. "It's not very attractive, you know. Not very ladylike. If I were you, I'd try very hard to keep from screaming during the birth. You don't want the little boy's first moments in this world to be so utterly terrifying, do you? I always feel that a woman has a duty to usher her child into life with as much decorum as possible. These things can really affect the -"

"Help!" I scream suddenly, turning to the window as I realize that Eve must have lost her mind. "Somebody help me!"

"Whoever do you think can hear you?" she asks.

"Help!" I scream again, pulling on the restraints and causing the bed's frame to rattle against the wall, making a little extra noise. With tears streaming down my face, I know full well that there's likely no-one around for miles, but I have to get out of here. "For the love of God, somebody help me!"

I continue to cry out for several minutes, trying to make as much noise as possible. My throat is already beginning to hurt, but I know I cannot stop yet, I know I must hope that by some miracle I shall be heard. Finally, however, I slump back down against the bed, breathless and exhausted, trying to think of some other way out of here.

"There, now," Eve says, "does it feel good to get all of that out of your system?"

"Dear Lord," I whisper, "I pray that you will -"

Before I can get another word out, Eve starts laughing.

"I pray," I continue, "that you will deliver me from this nightmare and help me ensure that my child is born safely and properly. I am your humble servant, your child in this life, and I want nothing more than to safeguard my child. If I have to give up my own life, then so be it, but -"

"God's not going to pay any attention to *you*," Eve says firmly, setting the bowl of water aside and getting to her feet. "You're French!"

"Why are you doing this?" I gasp, turning to her and watching as she calmly walks toward the door.

"Robert and I made a pact when we were children," she replies, stopping and turning to me with a curious smile on her lips. "Did he ever tell you about our childhood days here at the house? He and I used to play together in the forest, away from the prying eyes of our dear, late parents. We used to play with each other in the most delightful ways, and we used to talk about continuing the family in the most intimate manner possible. But then shortly after he turned eighteen, Robert suddenly decided that what we'd been doing was wrong, and he shunned me. He said our pact had been a childhood folly, but he was wrong. The pact was for life, and it's going to come true, one way or another."

"What are you talking about?" I stammer.

"Such a shame about his accident," she continues, "but then, he should have been more careful around the horses. It's astonishing how much damage a hoof can cause, isn't it? The brutish thing must have stamped on his head repeatedly, which seems almost impossible to believe. It's almost as if something else caused the injury. The blade of a shovel, perhaps."

"No," I whisper, as her smile grows. "You couldn't have..."

"I must prepare," she adds, turning and heading out to the landing. "This is going to be a very trying ordeal, I'm afraid. For both of us." She hesitates, before glancing back at me. "By the way, did Robert ever tell you what happened to our parents? They were both poisoned by mushrooms from the forest. Such rotten luck."

With that, she swings the door shut.

"No!" I scream, pulling harder than ever on the restraints, even as they begin to wear through my wrists and as blood trickles down my flesh. "Help me! Somebody get me out of here! Help!"

MARGUERITE

"OKAY, YOUNG LADY," DOCTOR Edge says calmly, has I continue to pull desperately on the restraints, "this might hurt a little, but you must keep a stiff upper lip. That's how we do things in England, you see. Remember to remain ladylike and calm throughout the birthing process, and all will be well."

MARGUERITE

A SECOND PAIR OF hands pushes the flap of skin aside and reaches deep into my belly, sending a searing, agonizing burst of pain through my gut. I can feel every single one of those fingers – twenty, five from each hand – arranging and rearranging my bloodied innards as they try to dislodge the child, and a moment later I feel the blade of scalpel cutting through some other part of me that's getting in their way.

The blade hits bone, scraping my pelvis.

I try to look down at my body, to see the horror, but the hand on my forehead pushes my head firmly back against the pillow. Crying out as sweat and tears run down my face, I feel several convulsing waves of pain starting to pulse up through my chest, causing me to clench my jaw so tight that I fear my teeth must surely shatter. When this does nothing whatsoever to alleviate the pain, I try turning my head to one side. The hand on my forehead slips slightly, thanks to the sweat, and I look over at the next bed as a groan of agony slips from my mouth. I just hope and pray that the pain is all mine, and that my child is okay.

Eve is watching me from the other bed, with those calm, expectant eyes of hers.

"Put a sheet up," she says as soon as we make eye contact, quickly turning to one of the nurses. "Now!"

"Why are you doing this to me?" I try to gasp, although all that emerges from my lips is a series of throttled, spitty gasps. I can taste blood in the back of my throat, and I'm not even able to focus my eyes properly. I can see two of Eve, almost three, and everything seems to be spinning around me.

A moment later, two nurses hold up a clean white linen sheet, keeping me from seeing Eve at all.

"What are you doing to me?" I try to scream, before the hand on my forehead is joined by another on my cheek, and my head is forced around until I'm once more looking at the ceiling. How many nurses are there? Two? Four? Looking up, I see several blurred faces, but they might all be one person.

And still those fingers are wriggling like fat maggots, intruding in the depths of my belly as they cut and scrape and tear. When they manage to shift the child, I feel a torrent of blood bursting from some part of me, spattering down into some other part at the bottom of the cavity these monsters are trying to make. Then I hear a faint, muffled discussion of some obstruction, before several fingers take hold of a lower section of my rib-cage. I try to flinch, but not quite in time, as one of the ribs is cracked and pulled away. Another jolt of pain shudders through my body, and I open my mouth to scream once more, but then another sound fills the room and stills my agony.

A child is crying.

"Hurry!" Doctor Edge hisses somewhere nearby. "No, leave that! Don't cut it yet!"

"What are you doing to her?" I groan, with blood on my lips. I instinctively try to move my hands down to my ripped-open belly, but the restraints are too tight. Still, I try again and again, as if my hands refuse to accept that they cannot touch the child.

"Let me hold her," I whimper. "Please..."

As I continue to struggle, I can hear the child's cries as she's lifted slowly from my belly and then moved away. A moment later, I feel something warm and wet bumping against one edge of my vast, torn wound, and I realize the umbilical cord hasn't been cut yet.

"Okay, now!" Doctor Edge shouts suddenly.

"Do it!" Eve screams, her voice filled with urgent frustration. "Hurry! Do it!"

"Give her to me!" I sob, turning my head first one way and then the other, trying to slip free of the greasy hands that are trying to hold my face in place. "Give me my child! Give -"

Before I can finish, another scream rings out, a

woman's voice. I turn and look to my left, but the white sheet is still being held in place, although it's shaking violently and when I look up at one of the nurses, I see that her hands are trembling as she looks down at whatever is happening on the other bed.

"Please," I whimper, hoping against hope that they might suddenly take pity on me, "let me hold my child."

The baby's cries are still filling the room, accompanied by a scream that I now realize is coming from Eve herself. I can see the faintest hints of shadows on the white sheet, but I can't even begin to imagine what is happening on the other side. I can hear people shuffling around, and muffled voices too, and something very urgent seems to be taking place. Already my thoughts are becoming thinner somehow, as if I'm being dragged down into unconsciousness, but I know I have to stay awake for my child. Even now, as she cries just a few feet away, I feel certain that she's a girl, and that she's healthy and that I just need to hold her and make sure that everything is alright. She cannot spend her first minutes in this world, her first minutes of life, in the hands of these barbarians. She needs her mother.

"Give her to me!" I sneer, as a rising sense of anger begins to fill my ravaged body. "I swear, you will give her to me right now."

"Careful!" Doctor Edge calls out from the other side of the sheet. "Gently. That's right. Gently."

"What are you doing to her?" I scream, pulling harder than ever on the leather restraints that bind my wrists to this cursed bed. "Leave her alone! Let me have her!"

"Careful, now," he continues. "Careful. That's perfect."

Pulling on the restraints, I start rattling the bed furiously, and now the hands on my head are finding it harder to hold me in place. I can feel blood cascading down the sides of my ruptured belly, but sheer panic and anger are driving me to keep pulling and pulling, trying to find some way off this bed. My child is still screaming, just a couple of feet away on the other side of the white sheet that's now spattered with blood. I have to get to her, I have to rescue her. I'm her mother. I cannot let her experience the cruelties of the world so soon.

"Robert!" I scream. "Give me strength! For our —"

Suddenly the restraint around my right wrist breaks. Startled, I immediately sit up and reach over, grabbing the white sheet and ripping it from the hands of the nurses. As the sheet falls away, I'm horrified to see Eve naked on the other bed with blood running down the sides of her belly, and it appears that she has been cut open. Several nurses are assisting Doctor Edge, and for a moment I cannot comprehend – nor really make out – what I am seeing. There is blood on their hands, and Doctor Edge is attending to the hole in Eve's belly. The twisted, knotted umbilical cord is held tight, running from my carved-open belly and directly into the mess of Eve's belly, and with a sudden jolt of horror I realize that while my child is still attached to me, she has been taken from my body and directly placed inside Eve's.

"Stop!" I scream, lunging toward them and almost tipping the bed straight over. Several pairs of hands grab me and try to hold me back, but I manage to reach over and take hold of Eve's arm. "She's mine! She's -"

Before I can finish, I see that there's another figure in the room. The naked old woman is at the head of the second bed, leaning down and watching me with a smile as she whispers directly into Eve's ear.

"No!" I shout, reaching toward them. "Leave us alone! Get away from here!"

"Restrain that hysterical woman!" Doctor Edge shouts. "Get on with it! Earn your money!"

My hand is pulled away from Eve's arm and I'm forced back onto my bed. Horrified, I watch as Eve smiles through her tears, resting her hands on the side of her belly as my child is slowly raised screaming from her blood. And then, as I cry out again, the bloodied white sheet is raised once more and a pair of scissors flashes past my face, and the umbilical cord is cut. I cry out again and again, but several pairs of hands are now holding me firmly, and I can feel somebody once again rearranging the mess in my belly. A moment later, a thick metal needle slides into the side of my neck and I feel a stinging liquid being injected into my body. Even before the needle is pulled out, I can feel my thoughts slipping away, but I have to stay awake for my child.

She's screaming.

I have to go to her.

I can't let them take her away.

A moment later, I hear the sound of metal against metal. I turn and watch as another nurse carries what looks like a saw around behind the sheet, toward the other other bed. A moment later I hear the most horrific sound I have ever heard in my life. Somebody is sawing through bone.

***

"MARGUERITE. MARGUERITE, WAKE UP. I'm sorry, but you have to be awake for this part."

I hear the voice, but at first I don't know what it means. And then something presses against my closed eyes, and the lids are forced open by pairs of tongs, and light flood my vision. My mouth opens slightly, even though my lips were slightly dried together, and I try to blink even though I find I cannot. Finally, slowly, as the rush of light begins to subside, I see a blurry figure standing over me.

"Sit her up," Doctor Edge says calmly. "Come on. Hurry."

Hands grab my arms from either side and haul me into a sitting position on the bed, leaning my back against the wall. I'm powerless to resist, and I immediately start to close my eyes again as soon as the tongs let go of the lids.

"No!"

Suddenly I'm slapped hard on the side of the face, and my eyes briefly flicker open for a few seconds before closing again.

"Give her the injection," Doctor Edge continues. "And don't make me keep hurrying you every step of the way."

I let out a faint murmur, but a moment later I feel another needle sliding into my body, this time in my right arm. Whereas the previous injection stung, this is merely cold, and after just a few seconds I open my eyes properly and look up at the doctor, finding that my vision is no longer blurred. Outside the window, birds are singing in the morning light.

"The child needs milk," the doctor explains, "and unfortunately Mrs. Carmichael..."

His voice trails off for a moment.

"Well," he continues, "let's just say that I was correct to have a back-up plan. Mrs. Carmichael has produced only a feeble dribble, whereas your body still produces a great deal." He turns and heads over to a nearby table, before returning with a set of metal clasps and tubes, which he immediately sets on my sore belly. "This is a device of my own invention," he adds, "and it has been thoroughly tested. You want the child to grow up strong and healthy, don't you? Then you must sit still and not make a fuss. You can still help the child by providing milk."

"Where is she?" I whisper, trying to get up from the bed but finding that I'm far too weak.

Ignoring me, Doctor Edge pulls my gown open and attaches one of the tubes to my right breast. I feel an immediate tightness, and a moment later he attaches the other tube to my left breast, taking a moment to check that the cup sections are sealed before arranging the tubes that run across my belly and down off the side of the bed.

"What is this?" I ask. "Where's my baby?"

"You don't have a baby, Marguerite. Stop with that nonsense."

"Where's my baby?"

"You don't have a baby."

"Bring her to me," I stammer. "For the love of God, she needs me! She needs her mother!"

"She's with her mother now," he replies, as he attaches a metal section to one of the tubes and starts screwing it into place. "She has everything she could possibly need, with the sole exception of milk. Now pay attention. Milk is the only thing you can do for her now, and I'm sure you'll want to help, won't you? There's a good girl, Marguerite. Now, I must inform you that there will be some discomfort."

"What are you doing to her?" I ask, reaching out to him, only for him to effortlessly push my weak arm away. I try again, but already I have lost the needed strength.

"It's all for the best," he continues. "Mrs. Carmichael will be able to give the child the life she deserves. I'll admit that the manner of the birth was somewhat unconventional. Pioneering even, one might say. There aren't many doctors in this land who would be able to perform such a feat, nor are there many who would be willing. I would dearly love to write a paper explaining my achievements here at Wetherley House, but of course there are undoubtedly those who would be aghast. It is despicable how crude morality so often gets in the way of medical and scientific achievement. To take a child from one mother and implant it in another, and then to birth it in the usual manner, is no mean feat. I warned Mrs. Carmichael about the dangers, but evidently this method was very important to her."

He takes a moment to adjust the device that is attached to my chest, and as he does so I notice old scars around both his wrists.

"One day," he says, turning to me, "this kind of work shall be commonplace. Of that, I have no doubt, and when it happens I am sure that my name will be celebrated around the world. You should see the joy on dear Mrs. Carmichael's face, now that she has given birth to a child of her own, and -"

"She's mine!" I gasp. "What have you done with my daughter?"

"She's not your daughter."

"Give her to me!"

He shakes his head. "You don't understand."

"You tore her from my body!" I hiss, reaching for him again, only for him to once more swat my hand away. "I carried her for nine months! She's my girl!"

"So you're another one, are you?" he mutters, eyeing me with displeasure. "I had hoped that, since you had such a good view of my work, you'd understand." He sighs. "God will see to it that I am amply rewarded in time. I suppose you to be simply a hysterical and emotional creature, incapable of looking at these things in the proper manner. That is a pity, but not entirely unexpected given your sex. Fortunately, you do not need to appreciate the role you have played in this great work, in order for that role to have value. I have learned so much from these past few days. So very much."

"What are -"

"And for now," he adds, as he starts pumping the lever on one side of the device he's holding, "you can still help the child. Doesn't that thought fill you with some sense of purpose, at least?"

I open my mouth to ask again what he has done with my child, but suddenly I feel an immense pressure in my right breast, accompanied by a growing, cracking pain. I let out a gasp as the pressure builds, and then I hear the sound of liquid dribbling into a metal pan. Looking down, I see that the nipple has cracked open, and that milk is running out through the gaps.

"That's good," Doctor Edge says, leaning over the side of the bed and peering at something on the floor. "Strong, healthy milk. Just what the child requires."

"What are you doing?" I groan, as I feel myself sinking deeper and deeper back into a daze, kept awake only by fear and pain.

"This will take a while," Doctor Edge continues, still working the pump by hand. "While I am here, perhaps you would like to hear how I made these several discoveries, and how a humble, hard-working boy from Kent became one of the country's most preeminent and pioneering medical figures. I suppose I was gifted with a good mind from an early age, but a gift is not always enough. One must work hard and show rigor, and good old-fashioned discipline played no small part in my astounding achievements. Why, by the age of fifteen, I had already invented my first medical device, to the astonishment of my parents. I think that was when they realized that they had on their hands a truly remarkable and intelligent child. And it is when I realized, in turn, that I am a genius."

As he continues to tell me his life story, I turn and look over to the window, and I see that snow is falling outside. And as the pain builds and this cursed man continues to drone on and on, all I can do is tilt my head back and scream.

MARGUERITE

"THIS WILL BE OUR home," Robert says with a smile as he helps me down from the carriage. "Wetherley House. It has been in my family for generations, and here we shall live good, happy lives. I know you have come a long way to be with me, Marguerite. I promise that, in return, I shall provide you with every comfort."

I remember this moment.

I remember it so well.

Even as I step away from the carriage and look toward the beautiful house, at the end of our long journey from the port at Dover, I know that this is a memory. A dream, perhaps. Yet though I am certain I should find some way to force myself awake, I cannot help but let myself enjoy the memory for a moment longer. After all, Robert is holding my hand, and he feels as real as he felt on the day I arrived here at the house.

Perhaps I am weak, but I want this dream to last forever, so that I do not have to wake and return to the nightmare.

"Are you alright?" he asks after a moment.

I turn to him. "Why do you ask?"

"You are crying, my dear."

He takes a handkerchief from his pocket and uses it to dab tears from my face.

"These are tears of joy, I hope," he continues, sounding a little uncertain. "Tears of anticipation and happiness."

"Our child," I whisper, feeling a slow, burning pain in my belly. "I must go to our child."

"We shall have many children," he says with a smile.

"I must go to her."

"She's not born yet."

"But she is," I reply, as a sense of panic starts rippling through my chest. "I must find her."

"Now that we are married," he continues, "we should indeed begin to prepare for the future. There is an excellent doctor in town, and I feel sure -"

"There!" I gasp, looking toward the house again as I realize I can hear a child crying in the distance. "She needs me. She is calling out for me."

"My darling?"

Stepping away from Robert, I start making my way across the lawn, finally breaking into a run until I reach the front door. Finding that the house is locked, I hurry to the nearest window and peer inside, but all I see is an empty room. Hurrying to the next window and then the next, I am still unable to see anybody inside the house, but the child's cries are getting louder and louder, and more pained too.

"Marguerite?" Robert says as he wanders toward me across the yard. "Whatever is the matter?"

"Don't you hear her?"

"Hear who?"

Turning to him, I realize that this is not part of the memory. This is something new, something that is entering my thoughts from the outside world as if the dream and the nightmare are knotting together. As Robert stares at me, in fact, it takes a few seconds before I realize with a growing sense of horror that something appears to be wrong with his face. The flesh has been torn away, exposing a shattered section of bone as if he has been struck by some terrible impact, and the front of his shirt – though white and clean a moment ago – is now bloodied and ripped.

"Marguerite?" he continues, with a faint, nervous smile. "Whatever is the matter with you?"

"I must..."

Behind him, the horses wait with the carriage.

Too horrified by Robert's appearance to utter another word, I turn and run to the next window, but still I can see nobody in the house. Making my way around to the rear, I find the back door but quickly discover that this, too, has been locked. I pull and pull on the handle, and then I try pushing, but it is as if the house has been sealed completely. Still, my child is crying inside and I know I must find some way to get to her. After all, she needs her mother. Finally, overcome by a sense of profound panic, I start banging my fists against the door's glass panel, hoping against hope that somebody will finally let me into this infernal house so that I can nurse my daughter.

"Marguerite?" Robert says as he steps up behind me. "This is no way for a lady to behave."

I can see his damaged face reflected in the glass, but this does not stop me. Slamming my fists harder and harder, I feel the entire door shudder, and a moment later the glass shatters. My hands crash through and thick shards of glass dig deep into my wrists, deep enough that I feel them scraping against bone. Blood begins to pour down my arms, yet somehow the blood feels so very cold, as if I am being chilled. I struggle to free my wrists from their impalement, but now I find that I cannot move my hands properly at all, as if my fingers have stiffened.

"Let me inside," I stammer, shivering now as I feel my entire body starting to freeze. Tears are streaming down my face and I try to grab the door's handle, but I cannot curl my fingers at all. "What is happening to me?" I gasp. "Dear God, help me! I have to get inside! I have to get to her! I have to get inside and -"

***

SUDDENLY THE BARROW JOLTS over a bump and I am shaken from the dream.

"I have to get inside!" I gasp, opening my eyes and immediately looking toward the house. Heavy snow is falling and has already carpeted the lawn. I can hear my daughter crying inside the house, yet after a moment I realize that I am naked in this wheelbarrow, and I am being taken down toward the forest.

Finding the strength from somewhere, I manage to roll out and crash down against the snow. I hear voices behind me, telling me to get back in, but I quickly stumble to my feet and start running toward the house. My feet are already freezing to the point of becoming numb, but nothing can hold me back as I get closer to the house and hear my child's cries coming from within. Still the voices call out for me, telling me to get away, but when I reach the house's back door I turn the handle and find that it is unlocked. Finally I stumble into the kitchen, and now I can tell that the child is crying in the drawing room.

"I'm coming!" I gasp, limping past the burning fireplace and into the hallway, then making my way past the door that leads into the basement and past the foot of the stairs. "I'm coming for you!"

I can see the door to the drawing room up ahead, and I can hear voices talking happily. My legs are starting to seize and I have to steady myself against the wall for a moment, but finally I reach the door and look through to see that several women are sitting on the chairs. They turn to me as I enter the room, and their faces are filled with horror, but I have already spotted Eve at the far end of the room, cradling the crying child in her arms as she sits closest to the roaring hearth.

"Give her to me!" I scream, holding my arms out as I limp toward Eve.

"Whoever is this creature?" one of the women stammers.

"Gordon!" Eve shouts, clearly startled by my sudden arrival. Her face is very pale, as if she has lost a lot of blood, and she looks rather sickly. Dark, heavy rings have developed under her eyes. "Gordon, get in here at once!"

"Give her to me!" I shout, lunging at her. Grabbing the child, I try to pull her away from Eve, but she is held tight and a moment later a man rushes into the room and pulls me back.

"What is she doing here?" Eve sneers. "She's upsetting Mary!"

"Mary?" I gasp. "What -"

Suddenly I'm struck on the side of the face, with enough force to leave me momentarily stunned. The baby is crying out now, and I try to turn and comfort her, only to feel arms grabbing me from behind.

"I am terribly sorry," a man says as I'm dragged back across the room, past the horrified ladies. "I shall see to it myself that your orders are carried out, my dear."

"Whatever is going on?" one of the ladies asks.

"It's nothing," Eve says, clearly struggling to stay calm. "I'm sure all families have their little secrets, do they not? Robert's wife lost her mind upon his death and has to be taken away to an asylum. I do hope that news of this unfortunate event will not become grist for the gossip mill. We've been trying to keep the situation within the family, for her sake and for the child's as well."

"Give her to me," I groan, hearing my daughter still screaming as I'm dragged along the hallway. A moment later I'm pulled outside again and dumped back in the waiting barrow, which is then turned and pushed away from the house at speed.

"I'm sorry," a man says, "but she suddenly woke up and jumped out. We couldn't do anything to stop her."

"We'll talk about it later," another man replies, clearly annoyed. "I should have known it would be too much for you cretins to actually do a job without fouling the whole thing up."

"I understand, but we -"

"You've thoroughly embarrassed Mrs. Carmichael," the second man continues. "We'll have words about this later. Watch out, she's stirring again."

I try once again to rise up from the barrow, but a hand pushes me back down and I see that we are now past the edge of the lawn and into the forest. The trees rise high above me as snow falls on my shivering body, and I can hear my child crying far off in the house. I try to open my mouth and call out to her, but I can't get any sound from my throat at all, and after a moment the barrow comes to a sudden halt. Before I even have time to react, I'm tipped over one side and sent tumbling into a dark pit, finally crashing down hard against frozen tree roots that crack the bones in my right arm.

Shuddering with cold and pain, I manage after a few seconds to roll onto my back, and now I see that I am at the bottom of a deep pit, at least six feet beneath the edge. A man is standing high above, staring down at me as snow continues to fall, and a moment later another man comes into view carrying dirt piled high on a shovel. He turns the shovel and tosses the dirt down, and clumps of frozen soil batter my body like hundreds of tiny rocks.

"Wait!" one of the men says suddenly, just as another man is about to throw more soil down. "Let us show a little respect."

Gasping, I watch his silhouette as he slips something from his pocket, and a moment later I realize he has opened a small book.

"Dear Lord," he continues, "may you look upon this wretched creature and, in your boundless wisdom, see to it that her soul is taken into your care."

As he continues to recite a prayer, I struggle desperately to my feet, straining to reach up and grab one of the many frozen tree roots that are poking out from the walls of this grave. My hands are trembling and I can feel the threads in my belly starting to come loose, and I let out a pained wail as I try to haul myself to safety. A moment later, once the prayer is over, more frozen soil comes crashing down on top of me, and I cry out as I drop back down onto my knees and rolls onto my side. This time, when I try to get up again, I find that my arms are frozen stiff, and I can hear an animal whimpering nearby.

No, not an animal.

I think that wretched sound is coming from my own mouth.

Turning to look back up at the grave's opening, I try again to call out to my child as she screams in the distance, but more soil comes tumbling down and several chunks fall into my mouth. I cannot force them out, and instead I can only shiver as I am buried alive. I reach out again and curl my frozen fingers around a tree root, and as I feel the heavy thuds of more soil landing above me, I try one final time to scream.

And then everything is dark. All I can hear is a series of distant thuds, getting further and further away, as the men continue to fill my grave with frozen soil. Finally, even that sound ends.

Now all is silent, and all is still.

PART THREE
1900

MARY

ALL IS SILENT AND all is still. The forest is so quiet.

Even the afternoon light does not make a sound as it streams down between the branches and leaves.

There is no noise from the forest, or from the house, or from the nearby road.

I am even holding my breath.

Everything is silent, and yet...

I can hear a deafening scream.

Loud enough to shake me, to rattle my bones.

Loud enough to make me want to put my hands over my ears.

Loud enough to cause the muddy ground to tremble beneath my bare feet.

Somebody is in agony, crying out for help, screaming louder than I ever thought a person *could* scream.

Yet still the forest is silent.

***

"HERE SHE COMES NOW," Father says as we stand behind our chairs at the dinner table, waiting for Mother to join us. "Be patient."

I want to tell him that I'm always patient, but I know I should hold my tongue. Instead, I simply stand with my head slightly bowed, staring down at my plate as I listen to the series of creaks and bumps that are oh-so-slowly making their way down the stairs. I can hear a few gasps, too, and it's evident that Mother is having a particularly bad day with her aches and pains. Finally, hearing another bump at the door, I dare turn my head slightly and look past the table, and I see Mother's shadow shuffling into view as she leans heavily on her two walking sticks. Her shadow is like that of a huge, upright spider.

And then Mother herself appears.

"We waited for you," Father tells her.

"Thank you, Gordon," she rasps, as he hurries over and pulls her chair back so that she might sit.

I watch as Mother rests her walking sticks against the table and begins to ease herself onto the chair. I have never seen her without that huge black dress, nor have I ever been told much about her injuries, but I *have* overheard her talking to Father from time to time. So I know that Mother suffered some horrendous damage when I was born. A few times, after drinking wine at dinner, she has even gone to great lengths to remind me that I am the cause of her disability, that it is my fault that her body was so badly damaged in the process. I feel bad for that, honestly I do, and many times I have prayed to God that he might forgive my sin and set Mother's body right. But now, as Mother lets out a groan of pain as she finally settles on her chair, I cannot help but wonder what she looks like under all those clothes, and how badly twisted her hips and legs have really become.

It is wicked of me to think such things, I know, but I am curious.

"Be seated, Mary," Father says finally, stepping back over to his own chair and sitting.

I do as I am told, and a moment later Mr. Carsdale brings the first dinner pot through from the kitchen. I know Mr. Carsdale always waits outside the dining room until he knows that Mother is ready. This is one of the many unmentioned signals to which we are all accustomed here at Wetherley House. I suppose all families are similar to some degree, although lately I have begun to think that Mother's deformities are far more considerable than those of almost anyone else alive. Her upper body seems completely fine, but evidently from the bottom of her ribs down to her legs she is utterly ravaged. Who in their right mind would not be curious about such a thing?

"Ah, pork," Father says with a forced smile as Mr. Carsdale lifts the lid from the dish and leaves the room. "My favorite!"

"You say everything is your favorite," Mother mutters darkly.

"I have a lot of favorites," he replies, glancing at me. "You like pork, Mary, do you not?"

"I do," I lie, smiling at him and then at Mother.

Mother, of course, glares back as if she hates the sight of me.

I look down at the table.

"Shall I lead the prayer today?" Father asks.

When nobody replies, he puts his hands together.

I do the same, and I bow my head too.

"Bless us, O Lord," Father continues, "and these, thy gifts, which -"

He stops suddenly as a spoon bangs against the dish, and even without looking up I am quite certain that Mother has begun to serve herself.

"And these, thy gifts," Father says again, "which we are about to receive from thy bounty."

"That'll do!" Mother barks.

"And which -"

"That will do, Gordon!"

And then silence for a moment, while Father gives in.

Finally I allow myself to open my eyes, and after a moment I dare look up. Father's eyes are open too, and he has separated his hands, as if he has once again abandoned his attempt to say grace. Mother, meanwhile, has almost finished helping herself, and she winces slightly as she leans over and sets the spoon back in the dish. I feel as if I should help her, but I already know from bitter experience that she sometimes reacts very badly to such things. It is better, I have come to realize, if one remains as still and quiet as possible. Sometimes, I believe that the less attention one attracts from Mother, the better.

"I saw there were some slippages in the forest," Father says as he begins to put food on his plate. He's trying to make conversation, as usual. He'll fail, as usual. "Some mud slides, even. I think you should both refrain from going out there until I've made sure it's safe. We wouldn't want any accidents."

"When do I ever go out into that damnable forest?" Mother gasps.

"Mary, you must be careful too," Father continues. "I saw you out there earlier. What were you doing?"

"Just exploring," I tell him.

"Exploring what?" Mother spits.

"I don't know," I continue, forcing myself to turn and look at her scowling features. "I suppose I just wanted to see how the terrible rains had affected the land. I noticed last time that the trees tend to -"

"I don't want you going out there ever again," she says suddenly, interrupting me. "I've told you before, girl. The forest is off-limits."

"I thought -"

"Don't argue with me, girl."

"Of course not, Mother. I'm sorry, Mother."

"I'm sure it'll be safe soon enough," Father says

diplomatically. "Mary, you may serve yourself now."

"I don't want her going into that forest," Mother replies, as I start putting food on my plate. "There's no reason for anyone to ever go out there. I'd sell this house in a heartbeat if I could, but nobody would ever give us the proper price. Those jackals think they can undercut us, but I'll show them. Eventually a real offer will come in and we can get out of here. Wetherley House is a monstrosity."

"I thought it was important to our family," I say, daring to ask a question.

"Who gave you permission to speak?" Mother snaps back at me.

"Sorry, Mother."

Setting the spoon back on the dish, I look down at my plate.

"Why must I be troubled all the time by foolish questions?" Mother continues, sounding a little breathless now. "When I say that something must be a certain way, it must simply *be* that way. Why do you, Gordon, or you, Mary, feel the need to disagree all the time?"

"It's alright, Eve," Father says calmly. "You mustn't let yourself get upset."

"Then tell that stupid girl to keep her mouth shut!"

"Your mother likes to eat dinner in peace," Father continues, and I look up to see that he's watching me now. "Perhaps we should save the conversation for some other time. For now, Mary, simply keep it in mind that you are to refrain from going out to the forest. There's nothing there of interest. If you get bored in the house, you have plenty of studies to be getting on with."

"Yes, Father," I reply, although I can't help glancing at the window and staring for a moment at the dark forest beyond the lawn. Even from here at the dining table, I swear I can hear the silent scream rising up from the mud between the trees.

Why do Mother and Father not hear the scream?

MARY

"I SHAN'T BE LONG," Father says as he leaves the master bedroom. "Are you sure you don't want me to stay and help you with your -"

"Leave me alone!" Mother snaps. "Go and attend to your beloved horses, Gordon, if they matter to you so much!"

Standing just inside my bedroom door, I listen to the sound of Father making his way down the stairs, and then I hear him leaving the house. He always spends at least half an hour out there in the stable each evening after dinner, tending to the horses, and I know that Mr. Carsdale is still busy with his duties in the kitchen. I wait a moment longer, therefore, before stepping out onto the landing and taking great care to avoid the boards that might creak and give away my presence. Fortunately, I know which boards creak; I know all the boards intimately, the way I know the keys on a piano.

Ahead, Father has left the door to the master

bedroom partially open, and I can hear a faint rustling sound as Mother gets ready for bed.

It is wicked of me to even *think* that I might spy on her, yet curiosity has been gnawing at me of late and I feel certain that if I can understand the nature of Mother's injuries a little better, I might be able to get a better realization of why she is the way she is. Even now, as I creep along the landing and listen to the continued shuffling sounds coming from the room ahead, I keep trying to remind myself that what I'm doing is perhaps justifiable if one looks at things from a scientific standpoint. Despite everything we have been told at church, I feel more and more certain that sometimes there is no right and no wrong, and that God must surely understand why from time to time we must make compromises in our own souls.

Besides, though I am but a girl, I want to be a doctor when I grow up.

Reaching the door, I peer through the crack between the hinges, and I immediately see that Mother is over by the dresser in the far corner. She has already slipped out of her black dress, and now she is removing her undergarments. If she spots me here watching her, she'll surely fly into the most intense fury imaginable, so I tense myself in case I have cause to pull back at any moment. I continue to watch, however, as Mother begins to pull her petticoat away, then the last of her underthings, and finally my eyes open with shock as I see that it is not her legs that are damaged at all, but rather her hips.

A huge, thick scar runs down through her rear,

and a moment later she turns slightly and I see that the scar continues around to the front, splitting in two and forming a kind of Y-shape that covers most of her belly. The flesh is mottled and discolored, and there are several smaller scars running like tributaries from the main section of twisted and knotted flesh. It is as if her hips were at some point carved open and separated slightly, and only partially put back together, and as such her legs appear to have gouged up into her waist a little, which I suppose explains the fact that they have become bowed over the years, barely able to support her weight at all. In fact, the arrangement of her hips looks so unreal and so unnatural, I cannot help staring in open-mouthed horror at the ghastly sight.

Letting out a gasp of pain, she steps over toward the far end of the dresser, and I can hear her legs clicking as her knees point out at opposing angles. She really *does* have a rather spider-like gait, and it's clear that she's in a great deal of agony. She has told me so many times that it was my birth that caused this damage, but I do not understand how one small baby could tear a woman's body open in such a manner. I have seen other mothers in town, and I am quite sure that they have all been able to walk around perfectly normally. Some of them have even given birth to several children, and it seems that only *my* mother was almost crippled by the arrival of just one. Was I really so monstrous from inception, so vile and dangerous, that I virtually carved her body open in the simple act of entering this world?

Whatever could have been wrong with me?

Suddenly Mother turns and I instinctively pull

back, holding my breath. A moment later I hear a series of clicks and soft bumps, and I realize that she is coming over to the door. Avoiding the loose boards once more, I pick my way carefully but quickly back to my room and then I gently push the door shut. Fortunately, Mother is unable to move at any real speed, so at least I know that she had no chance of spotting me. Still, I wait with a growing sense of fear as I realize that I can hear Mother coming out of her room.

A moment later, one of the boards creaks on the other side of my door, and I realize she has come to check that I am asleep.

Stepping back from the door, I wait for her to knock, or for her to simply come inside. I have no hope of fooling her into thinking that I have already gone to bed, so I shall most likely be in the most awful trouble if she decides to enter. After a few seconds, however, I hear the same board creak again, and I realize to my utter relief that she has turned to go back to her own room. Sitting on the edge of my bed, I tell myself that I just took an awful and unrepeatable risk, but at the same time I know that the risk was worthwhile. I have now seen Mother's true form, and a shudder passes through my body as I realize that perhaps she was right all along when she said that her disability is my fault.

Finally, getting down onto my knees, I begin to offer a prayer before bedtime, imploring God to forgive me for doing such awful things to my own mother, and asking that she might be spared any further pain.

***

IT'S THE WRIGGLING SENSATION that disturbs me at first. I drift in and out of sleep, occasionally waking for a few seconds at a time, for just long enough to brush a hand across my face and then nod off again. Between these moments, I dream of horrible creatures crawling all over my body, and finally I wake yet again and roll onto my back, opening my eyes and staring up at the dark ceiling.

And then I feel it.

Something is on my face.

Reaching up, I run a hand across my left cheek, and sure enough I find that some kind of small worm is making its way past my nostril. Plucking it from my flesh, I turn and place the offending creature on my nightstand, and then I watch with a sense of both fascination and disgust as a single maggot wriggles in the moonlight. For all of a few minutes, I cannot help but watch the maggot's progress, and I must say that I feel a very faint sense of admiration for the fact that it seems so determined to continue on its way. I have no idea where a maggot needs to be in the middle of the night, but the little chap is evidently in a great hurry. So long as he is not on me, I suppose that his business is really none of mine.

Peering closer, I squint and look closer at its darkened little tip.

Turning to roll back over in bed, I suddenly realize that I can see a figure outside, far beyond the lawn. I pull myself further up the bed and peer out the window, just in time to see that there is indeed someone walking between the trees in the forest. From the fact that the figure is walking normally, I can immediately tell that it is not Mother, and after a moment I realize that the figure appears to be a man. It's not Father, though, and I know that there is nobody else who has any right to be out there on our private property. Bathed in moonlight, the man regularly slips out of view behind some of the trees, only to swiftly appear again a little further along, and I am struck after a moment by the realization that although I cannot make out his features at all, he seems to be looking directly this way.

Directly at me, even.

I pull back from the window, lest I should be seen, but I cannot contain my curiosity for long and I quickly look out again.

He is still there.

Still walking calmly through the forest, just as the maggot still crawls calmly across my nightstand.

"*Your* activities might be none of my business," I whisper, looking down at the maggot, "but that man..."

My voice trails off for a moment, before finally I climb out of bed and take my gown from the hook on the door. Once I am decent, I pull the door open, and then I take the maggot in the palm of my hand and step out onto the landing, although I immediately step on a loose board and flinch as a creak rings out. Staying completely still, I wait as silence returns, desperately hoping that I have not woken Mother and Father. After all, they would undoubtedly send me straight back to bed, and I fail to see why I should not go out and see for myself what the man wants. I am twelve years old now, almost thirteen, and I refuse to be easily scared.

Of course, I would be far less nervous if the figure were a woman, but I am sure I can fend for myself. Besides, one scream and the whole house will hear.

"Anyone would think I'm foolish for doing this," I whisper to the maggot as I tip it from one palm to the other, "but that would simply be because they did not know me very well. I'm tougher than I look."

I wait a moment, but of course the maggot simply continues to crawl across my hand. He would probably be much happier outside.

Creeping past the door to Mother and Father's room, taking care to avoid the rest of the loose boards, I finally begin to make my way down the stairs and through to the back door, where I stop for a moment so that I can peer out across the lawn. At first I see no sign of the man, but after a moment I spot a faint figure moving through the moonlight, and I realize that he cannot have been some wild hallucination that I dragged into the waking world from my dreams. He's real, that's for sure, and without hesitation I reach down and turn the key, unlocking the door and then pulling it open.

And all the while, I am constantly keeping track of the maggot, and transferring him from one palm to the other whenever necessary.

The night air is cool, but I step out and make my way to the edge of the lawn. The man is still in the forest, and now more than ever I'm certain that he's looking at me. I know I should go and wake Father, but at the same time I want to know who the man is and what he wants, and I feel certain that Father and Mother would both make me go to my room while they dealt with him, and that I would never be told the truth. Besides, something about the man seems strangely familiar and calming, and after a moment I realize that while the silent scream is still filling the forest, it seems now to be calling me onward. Perhaps it is the scream that is giving me uncommon bravery tonight.

As I start making my way across the lawn, the man stops walking and seems almost to be waiting for me, just beyond the treeline.

Glancing over my shoulder, I see that the house is still completely dark. I am still, however, well within screaming and running distance. When I turn back to look at the man, I see now that he is well-dressed and fairly respectable-looking, which emboldens me somewhat. Had he turned out to be some kind of hobo, I would surely have hurried back toward the house by now, although I still slow my pace as I get to the end of the lawn, and I am ready to scream and fight back if necessary.

I take a couple more steps toward him, still looking after the maggot in my hands, and then I realize I am now probably close enough for the man to hear my voice.

"Who are you?" I ask, making sure to stand up straight so that I look as tough as possible.

"Who am *I*?" he replies, with a strong accent. Maybe French. He hesitates, before stepping forward across the grass and then stopping again. He seems to be eyeing me very carefully. "I was going to ask you the same question," he continues, "but now I see there is no need. It's uncommonly brave of a young lady to come out alone from a house to greet a complete stranger." He pauses. "You're tough. Unafraid. You look so much like her."

"I look very little like my mother," I tell him.

"Says who?"

"Says me."

"Do you mean that you have seen -"

He pauses again, and then he nods as if he understands something.

"You mean the woman in the house," he continues. "Mrs. Eve Carmichael?"

"She is my mother, yes. And my father is home too, so you needn't be thinking of making a scene. What are you doing out here, anyway?"

"What am I doing?" He seems to find this funny, and he lets out a faint belly laugh. "I suppose you could say that I am checking the area out, in advance of perhaps making some inquiries and -"

He frowns as he looks at my hands.

"What in the name of all that's holy," he continues, "are you doing?"

"That's none of your concern."

"None of my -"

He hesitates again, before shaking his head as if he has given up trying to understand.

"My name is Henri Alesi," he explains. "Does that name mean anything to you?"

"Should it?"

"Not the Henri part, perhaps, but the Alesi part should definitely mean something. If it does not, then this is a terrible shame and it must be rectified as quickly as possible."

"Who are you," I ask again, "and why are you out here in our garden in the middle of the night?"

"*Your* garden, Mademoiselle."

"What?"

"You said *our* garden, as if you meant all of you who live in that house. But in truth, the garden and all of this rightly belongs to you. After all, you are your father's sole heir. Your mother's, too."

"I..."

My voice trails off for a moment as I try to work out what he means.

"What is your name?" he continues.

"I'm not sure I want to tell you."

"Humor me."

"My..." I take a deep breath. "My name is Mary, if you must know."

"Mary? Well, Mary, you look very much like your mother indeed. Here, let me show you." Reaching into his pocket, he takes out a faded old photograph and holds it out for me to see. "Take it. It's yours."

"That's not my mother," I point out, able to see the cracked image of a woman from here. "That's just..."

Again, my voice trails off as I realize that the woman looks strangely familiar. Or not familiar, exactly, but as if I have seen her face somewhere before, or a similar face. For a moment, I cannot fathom where, before finally I realize that I have on several occasions seen that face staring back at me from the mirror. She looks very, *very* much like me.

"Her name was Marguerite Henriette Alesi," the man explains. "Surely you know that name?"

Shaking my head, I keep my eyes fixed on the photograph.

"No?" he continues. "They kept even that from you? Well, I can't say that I blame them. She was my sister, and I have come a very long way to ascertain the circumstances of her death. I have come from France, because to date the answers we have been given have been entirely unsatisfactory. Letter after letter, filled with evasive claims and signed by Mrs. Carmichael and a Doctor Edge, whoever he might be. I promised our father on his deathbed just a few months ago that I would get to the truth, and now here I am. Letters be damned."

"Well," I reply, "I don't know any Marguerite Henriette Alesi, and I think you should go away now."

"We know her death was painful," he replies. "In Paris, we engaged the services of a person who can speak to the dead. After much effort, she was able to draw the spirit of dear Marguerite to our company. She spoke of pain. Indescribable pain as her child was ripped from her. She was weeping, even in death, and she kept talking about the cold ground. It seems she was not buried on church land, but somewhere common and indecent. She spoke of endless ice and darkness. She implored us to put right what had gone wrong, and to save her child." He pauses again, and now there seem to be tears in her eyes. "That child is you, my dear."

I shake my head.

"Oh, it is. This is not the first night I have been out here in the forest, watching the house."

"Well, you shouldn't have been."

"My sister is buried somewhere here," he continues.

"You're not -"

"I hear her scream even now."

I open my mouth to tell him that he's out of his mind, but those last words catch my attention.

"A silent scream," he adds, "but somehow louder than any I have ever heard before. It's here in this forest, I can feel it. Can you not feel it too?"

"I don't know what you're talking about," I tell him.

"Really? That is a surprise."

"I think you should leave," I continue, taking a step back. "If I see you on this property again, I'll make sure Father calls the police. You told me your name, so I shouldn't cause any bother if I were you." Turning, I start walking back toward the house, but suddenly he grabs my arm from behind and I spin back around and look up at him.

"You belong with your real family," he tells me, "not with these impostors. Your aunt is just -"

"I don't have an aunt," I reply, "and you must let go of me right now or I shall scream."

"Eve Carmichael is not your mother," he continues. "Not by birth. My sister Marguerite was your mother, which makes me your uncle, and I am starting to see that something very sinister must be going on here.

Wetherley House and all the rest of your father's estate should rightfully be yours."

"My father is very much alive and well," I tell him.

"Your father died before you were born. You must come with me immediately, and then -'""

"No!"

Pulling my arm free, I stumble back and fall, landing hard on the ground. The man reaches for me again, but I pull away and struggle to my feet before quickly racing back toward the house. I don't dare look over my shoulder, and finally I clatter up the steps to the back door and reach the kitchen, at which point I turn and slam the door shut with such force that it rattles loudly. To my relief, I see that the man is already trampling back into the forest, having evidently decided not to follow me, but my heart is pounding and I can't get his awful words out of my head. His claims were utterly ridiculous, and yet -

Suddenly a naked woman lunges at the door from the other side, screeching and smashing her hands through the glass. Startled, I step back and bump against the table, but already the woman is gone and the glass is undamaged, even though I still hear her cry echoing in my thoughts.

A moment later, I look at my hands and realize that I dropped my maggot friend somewhere outside. Still, I'm sure he'll be okay. As I stare at the door, I realize I can see another face staring at me. For a few seconds, I think it might be the woman from the

photograph, but then I realize I'm wrong.
It's just my reflection.

MARY

I SO RARELY GET a chance to leave the house and come into town. Mother has taken to her bed this morning, however, and Father is away on business, so I have been able to slip away. Now, as I reach the edge of town and see the busy market square up ahead, I feel as if I have come to a completely different world.

"Careful, now!" a woman calls out, and I turn to see that she's pushing a large pram across the street while trying to avoid a ball that some boys are throwing. "Mind out for others!"

As she gets closer, I see that the pram contains not one, not two, but three newborn babies, each wearing a pink bonnet. The children stare straight at me and I smile, but a moment later I look up at the woman's face and see that she's watching me with a faint scowl.

"Good morning," I say, hoping she might let me meet her babies properly.

"Morning," she mutters, but she noticeably

changes course as if she wishes to avoid me, and I turn and watch as she pushes the pram into the yard of the Trin glass factory. A moment later, the wooden gate is pushed shut, as if to let me know in on uncertain terms that I must not follow.

"Nice weather," I mumble, although I suppose she can't hear me now.

Heading further along the street, I see that several stalls have been set up in the square, with local farmers selling their wares. I've heard about the market, but Mother has never let me come to visit before, so I cannot help but feel somewhat awed by the sight of so much wonderful produce. There are dead chickens and ducks hanging from hooks, and one stall even has pig heads all laid out on display. I can't even imagine what one would do with a pig's head, but I suppose it could be used to make some kind of meal and I wouldn't mind trying some day. Stepping closer, I see that the pigs' eyes are open, and I can't help wondering what it was like for them when they died. I know they were probably just dumb, brutish animals, but -

"That's her!"

"What's she doing here?"

Hearing a series of astonished whispers nearby, I turn away from the pigs and see that several women are watching me from next to one of the other stalls. From the expressions on their faces, it's clear that they're shocked and appalled by something, and after a moment I glance over my shoulder, in case I'm mistaken and they're actually looking at someone else. Seeing nobody, however, I turn back to the women and see that they're still staring in my direction. A ripple of discomfort runs through my chest, and I instinctively step out of sight.

I can still hear them, though.

They're whispering about me.

Ducking down, I make my way around a couple of the stalls, edging closer to the women until finally I dare to pop up on their other side. They have their backs to me now, and a couple of them are craning their necks as if they're trying to work out where I've gone. Evidently they have no idea that I'm behind them now.

"Can you imagine?" one of them asks. "I never thought I'd see the day when that little beast would come swanning into town. Doesn't she have enough space up there at that wretched house?"

"Madness is hereditary, you know," one of the others replies. She's wearing a black hat with a large orange feather. "Her mother went insane, and the girl will go the same way."

"What did they do with the mother, anyway?"

"Bedlam, I suppose. Or one of the other asylums."

"Do you think she... Well, I mean, would she even be alive anymore?"

"If she went to Bedlam? I doubt it. Besides, you're forgetting one thing. I was there on that awful day when the naked woman came rushing into the house. I don't mean to cast aspersions, but let me tell you that I saw her being taken away, and I saw her being carried in a wheelbarrow toward the forest."

"The forest? Why would they take her there?"

"Well, that's my point exactly. If you ask me, the

wretch might never have made it to Bedlam at all. Then again, it's often better that way. There's no point keeping the mad alive. They just -"

Suddenly she begins to turn, as if she's heard me.

I duck down, hoping against hope that I wasn't spotted.

"The mad are best killed," she continues after a moment. "I mean, what do they have to offer? Nothing. And if you ask me, that little brat should go the same way, sooner rather than later. Marguerite Alesi was mad, and her offspring will be the same."

Marguerite Alesi.

There's that name again.

"You don't really think Wetherley House is cursed, do you?" one of the other women says, and I duck down further as I realize they're coming this way. "It used to be so lovely up there in the summer."

"I shouldn't like to find out," the first woman replies. She sounds so full of herself, so certain that she's right. "It'd be best all round if the place were to be knocked down, but I doubt that'll happen any time soon. Money's money, and from what I hear, the Carmichael family flatters to deceive in that department. Ever since Robert Carmichael sank all his inheritance into that silly glass factory, they haven't had two shillings to rub together and -"

"Oi! You! Outta there!"

Suddenly the head of a broom slams against my shoulder, and I turn to find a large, dirty man towering over me. Before I can tell him that I'm not a thief, he hits me again, and I'm barely able to crawl out from behind the stall before the broom cracks against my shoulder. Bumping against another stall, I stumble to my feet and run a couple of paces, before tripping and slamming down into the mud.

"It's her!" a woman calls out from nearby. "It's that little brute from the house!"

Turning, I see that the gossiping women are watching me with a mixture of fascination and horror, while the man with the broom is coming for me again.

"We don't want your kind here!" he yells, swinging at me but missing this time as I duck and scurry away through the dirty. "Clear off! If I see you loitering near my stall again, I'll have your hide for leather, do you hear?"

"I was just -"

He swings at me again, this time hitting my waist, and I cry out in pain as I run away. I can hear the women muttering excitedly about me, as if they see me as some kind of oddity that'd be better off in a freak-show, but I don't stick around to hear any more of their gossip. Instead I run along the first street I find, even though I don't exactly know where I'm going. Stumbling several times, I start sobbing as I reach the next corner, and then I hurry down an alley before dropping onto the ground and finally letting myself sob. I feel so stupid and so weak for crumbling so easily, and after a moment I let out a gasp of frustration.

I should have torn their bally hats off and stomped on them.

Slamming my fists against the dirty cobbles, I

feel a rush of rage running through my chest, but hurting my hands only makes everything worse. Finally I wipe tears from my cheeks and lean back against the wall.

And then I realize I can hear footsteps nearby.

Turning, I see that a kitchen hand has just come out from the rear of the inn, carrying a bucket of soapy water.

"You alright there, love?" she asks. "You'd best not stick around here. This water's dirty and it's about to spill all over."

"Sorry," I stammer, struggling to my feet. "I just..."

"Has a boy been mean to you?" she continues with a faint smile. "Don't let it get you down, my little petal. Boys are only ever after one thing, and at your age you're too young, despite what people in some places might say. You're right to run away."

"I'm not running from boys," I tell her, still a little breathless. "I'm running from..."

My voice trails off for a moment. I don't want this woman to be disgusted by me, but at the same time I also want to ask her what she knows.

"I'm from Wetherley House," I continue finally. "Do you know it?"

She hesitates. "Aye," she says finally, a little cautiously, "I know it."

"And *what* do you know, exactly?"

She glances over her shoulder, as if she's worried about us being overheard.

"Do you know something bad?" I ask, taking a step toward her. "Do you -"

"Ah, now stay back, young madam," she says, suddenly raising a hand as if to warn me away. "Don't take this the wrong way, but I'd rather not meddle in anything that's beyond me, if you know what I mean."

"No," I reply, "I don't know what you mean."

"How old are you?"

"Thirteen," I tell her, which is only a lie by a few months. "Old enough to hear the truth, I reckon."

"Is that right?"

I nod.

"And have you asked your... Well, have you asked the people you live with?"

"I don't think they'd want to tell me."

She laughs a throaty, genuine laugh.

"Well, no," she manages to say finally, "I don't suppose they would. There are plenty of people around this town who have bad feelings regarding Wetherley House. They're worried that some of what's in that place might leak out and change things down here."

"What do you mean?"

"You really don't know, do you?"

"I don't know anything," I reply. "I didn't realize until today, I didn't think there was anything much to know. Now I realize that there's a lot I don't know, and I should very much like to know it. If you catch my drift."

"Aye, but you're maybe a little young still."

"Who was Marguerite Alesi?"

She pauses again, before shaking her head.

"Why was she taken to an asylum?" I continue. "Or is that not what happened? I heard some women talking in the square, but I didn't really understand what they were talking *about*. It's all so confusing, but I feel like there's something I should be told."

"It's not my place to meddle," she replies, "but I'll let you in on one thing, little lady." Again, she looks around for a moment as if she's worried about being overheard, and then she turns back to me. "Run away," she adds finally. "Don't go back, not even today. The world is a dangerous place for a pretty young thing such as yourself, and there are no guarantees that you'll last long. You'll most likely be preyed upon by men, and you'll need your wits if you want to survive. You'll need to do things, too. But it's your only chance. Run away from that house, because whatever's in there, it's worse than anything you'll find anywhere else."

"But what -"

"Charlotte!" a voice yells from inside the inn. "You're taking your sweet time, aren't you?"

"Go!" the woman hisses.

"But -"

"Go! Run and don't look back! Not ever!"

With that, she empties the bucket, sending soapy water rushing across the cobbles. I step back, making sure to keep my shoes from getting wet, and then when I look at the woman I see that she's already hurrying inside. I open my mouth to ask her if she can tell me more, but she swings the door shut and I'm left standing all alone in the alley, and to be honest I don't feel much like I've learned a great deal.

Trudging through the streets, I go over and over everything the woman said to me. I'm lost, and for a while I feel as if my tired legs will never carry me home, but all of a sudden I find myself at a junction that I recognize. Sure enough, after walking just a few meters along another street, I spot the road that leads home, and I can just about make out the sight of Wetherley House in the distance.

For a moment, I consider following the woman's advice and running away, but I know I wouldn't last long. Besides, whatever's at the house, I've survived it this long and I want to know its true nature. Feeling determined to show a brave face, then, I set off for home.

MARY

"WHO IS MARGUERITE ALESI?"

As soon as I ask that question, Mr. Carsdale turns to me. I've been helping him groom the horses since I got back from town, and it has taken several hours before I feel ready to ask this most important of questions. I want him to tell me that the name means nothing to him, but already I can see from the look in his eyes that I'm onto something. It is as if I have uttered the name of a ghost.

"Who?" he replies unconvincingly.

"You've worked here for several years now," I continue, "since not long after I was born. Have you ever heard of a woman named Marguerite Alesi?"

"Why? Who mentioned that name to you?"

"Nobody. I'm just curious."

He hesitates, and it's abundantly clear that I've set him on the wrong foot.

"I don't know anybody named Alesi," he tells

me, before grabbing an empty pail and handing it to me. "Now go and fill this up, and mind when you get back that you don't ask any more unfortunate questions. And especially mind that your parents don't hear you utter that name, not ever, because there'll be hell to pay if they do. Especially from your... Well, from the lady of the house."

"Why?"

"Just go and fetch some water."

"But if the name means nothing, why would Father and Mother -"

"Go!" Grabbing my arm, he shoves me toward the stable door. "Be told, child!"

Needing no further bidding, I make my way out into the morning sunshine, although I can't say that I'm satisfied by Mr. Carsdale's response. He's very loyal to my parents, I know that much, and I have no doubt that he would be willing to keep any secrets of theirs that he might learn. At the same time, I also know that he's a fundamentally decent man, and I do not believe that he would willingly be privy to anything truly awful. As I head past the house and toward the well by the old oak tree, I become momentarily lost in thought, until suddenly I realize that I can hear voices talking inside the house.

Slowing for a moment, I find that Mother and Father seem to be speaking to someone, and a few seconds later I freeze as I hear a familiar French voice.

It's the man from last night!

He's in the house!

Unable to help myself, I set the pail down and

hurry to the back door, before slipping through the kitchen and into the hallway. Sure enough, the voices are still speaking in the drawing room, and I make sure to stay very quiet as I edge closer. I don't know the floorboards down here quite so well, and I'm worried one of them might creak beneath my steps and betray me.

"And this payment," I hear Father saying, "is to be the end of it, do you understand? We will not tolerate any return visits or attempts to extract another shilling."

"You have been most generous, Mr. Carmichael," the French man replies. "I must say, I did not expect you to be so understanding of my needs. Why, my family had even assumed that lawyers would need to get involved, which would have been very costly for both sides. But as I said, you have surprised me. I assure you, I shall be departing from Dover tomorrow morning, and after that you shall hear no more from the Alesi family."

"We should have heard nothing in the first place," Mother sneers, with more venom in her voice than I have ever heard before. "Then again, I suppose I should have expected such treachery and deception from the French."

"Mademoiselle," the Frenchman continues, "please, I came only to make sure that my family gets what is coming to them."

"By taking our daughter away?"

"That was one possibility, but now that you have made this most generous payment, I believe I speak for my entire family when I say that the matter is closed."

Suddenly I hear footsteps heading toward the door, and I duck out of sight behind the grandfather clock just as Father and the Frenchman emerge from the room and head toward the front door. Mother, evidently, has chosen not to exert herself.

"The girl looks like her mother," the Frenchman says.

"Nonsense," Father snaps back at him.

"It's true. I saw her last night. I even spoke to her."

Flinching, I realize that I shall surely be punished for this.

"Get him out of here!" Mother sneers. "He's full of nonsense!"

"Tell the girl that the Alesi family wishes her well," the Frenchman says as he heads outside.

"We shall tell her no such thing," Father says firmly, "and if we so much as see another of your wretched lot in this county again, we shall ensure that you are chased out like vermin."

The Frenchman begins to reply, but Father slams the front door and hesitates for a moment before turning and making his way back into the drawing room.

"How dare he come here like that?" Mother asks, her voice shaking with rage. "How *dare* her?"

Suddenly a glass smashes, and I realize that in her fury Mother is becoming violent.

"We should have known that one of them would pop up eventually," Father says calmly. "Still, it's good that he was an agreeable type. I'm actually rather surprised that he was bought off so easily. Some of these fellows can get a right bee in their bonnets, but all things considered he was simple enough to get rid of."

"You shouldn't have paid him anything!" Mother hisses. "You're weak, Gordon!"

"And you'd have preferred him to stick around and ask more awkward questions? Perhaps you'd have liked him to have spoken to the girl again?"

"Don't be ridiculous!" She sighs. "How much do you think she knows now, Gordon? He said he met her last night, and she has said nothing to either of us about the encounter. If she suspects the truth, she will ask more questions. You know what she's like!"

"She does not suspect."

"How can we be sure?"

"She's just a child, Eve. A precocious child, yes, and very intelligent for her age, but still a child. I'm sure that as far as she's concerned, that wretched French idiot was just a fool who stumbled into the garden. You must calm yourself and keep from worrying too much, my dear. This is all over now."

"Why didn't Mary tell us about the man this morning?"

"She was probably scared."

"Of him, or of us?"

"My dear, just -"

"Don't tell me to calm down!" she hisses, and I flinch again as I realize that she is once again becoming very angry.

Telling myself that I cannot possibly risk getting caught eavesdropping, and that I need time to come up with an explanation for my actions, I begin to sneak back through to the kitchen.

"Was he telling the truth, Gordon?" I hear her asking after a moment.

"About what, my dear?"

"About Mary looking like Marguerite."

I freeze, as I realize that at least part of the Frenchman's story must have been true.

"No," Father stammers, "of course not, she -"

"I see it in your eyes!" she shouts, accompanied by the sound of more breaking glass. "You think she does! You think she looks like that awful woman!"

As more glass smashes, I hurry out the back door and grab the pail, and then I make my way to the well. Mother is in one of her moods, she's angrier than I've ever heard her before, and now I have no idea what to think. Who was Marguerite Alesi really, and why do I look like her? And why is Mother so furious? A moment later, I see Father heading out of the house and going to the stables, which is what he always does whenever he wants to get away for a while.

When I walk past the window, carrying water, I hear Mother sobbing in the drawing room.

***

"YOUR MOTHER MERELY WISHES to speak with you," Father says a short while later, standing with me outside the master bedroom. "There's no reason to be afraid, Mary."

"Can you come in with me?" I ask, looking up at him.

139

"She wishes to speak with you alone."

"But -"

"And you know that it is best not to go against her wishes, do you not? That is something we all have to learn in this house."

"But Father -"

Before I can finish, he knocks on the door, and I know with a sickening sense of dread that I cannot possibly talk my way out of this. I do not believe that Mother knows I have been eavesdropping, but she must certainly suspect me of some other infraction.

"Come!" she calls out, and Father opens the door.

"Be honest with her," he whispers to me, before pushing my back gently and forcing me to step forward into the room. "Always be honest. If honesty ever harms you, then the mistake was made in the act, not the telling."

Mother is sitting on the chair next to the window, working on some embroidery. She's wearing one of her usual large dresses with a frilly skirt, which I know is supposed to disguise her deformities. She peers at the embroidery for a moment, as if she's not aware of my presence, and then a shudder passes through my chest as I hear the door bump shut behind me, followed by the sound of Father's footsteps heading away.

"Well, come and sit down, girl," Mother says calmly, still not looking at me. "The way you're standing there like that, anyone would think you were afraid of me."

Finally, she glances this way.

"You're not afraid of me, are you?"

I shake my head.

"Then come and sit." She gestures toward the chair opposite her, in the bay window. "You're almost thirteen years old now. That's an age at which you can be trusted to speak on a slightly more adult basis. I am relieved about that fact, Mary. I am so very glad that I no longer have to talk to you as if you're a child." A faint smile crosses her lips. "Please, sit. It's very important."

Making my way across the room, I cannot help but feel that the air in here is rather thin. Taking a seat, I hear the chair squeak gently under my weight, but I myself do not dare make a sound lest I might disturb or somehow upset Mother. She seems so calm and peaceful, and I know that at times like this she is often at her most testing. At least when she's crying and screaming, the source of her anger is always very obvious. When she is quiet like this, however, one must be on one's toes.

"Do you ever look at yourself in the mirror," she says after a moment, as she continues to work on the embroidery, "and ask yourself where your face came from?"

"I beg your pardon?"

"Why do you look the way you do?"

"I don't know."

"Do you think you look much like your father?"

"No. Not especially."

"And what about me? Do you think, Mary, that you look very much like me?"

I swallow hard, but my throat is horribly dry.

Suddenly Mother glances at me again.

"Well, Mary?"

"I don't know."

"You don't know?"

"I mean, it's hard to say. I mean -"

And now my throat seems to seize up entirely. I hate when Mother questions me like this; I always become so easily flustered.

"This is not a trick question, Mary. There's no right or wrong answer. I simply wish to know whether you ever wonder where your face comes from." She pauses. "Let me try to phrase this some other way. Have you ever seen a picture of anyone else and noted any kind of resemblance to your own features?"

I immediately think of the woman in the photograph.

"No," I lie.

She watches me carefully.

"No," I say again.

Even as that word leaves my lips, however, I can tell that Mother knows I am telling an untruth.

"A man came to the house earlier," she continues. "A Frenchman, of all things. Can you even imagine the audacity of a Frenchman coming to England, to an English home, and trying to tell good, honest English people how they should go about their business? The matter is absurd in its entirety. But tell me, Mary... Have you ever spoken to a Frenchman?"

"No," I reply, before realizing that I have been caught in a lie. "Actually, yes."

"When?"

"Last night."

"Last night? Were you not in bed all of last night?"

"I got up. And I saw a man outside the house."

"Indeed. Then what?"

"I went to ask what he wanted."

"You went outside alone in the middle of the night, to approach a strange man who was loitering in our garden?"

"Yes."

She eyes me cautiously for a moment.

"Why," she continues finally, "that is quite one of the stupidest decisions one can imagine. You are extremely lucky, my dear, that he did not haul you away and do terrible things to you. You do realize, I hope, that you were exceedingly lucky not to get your throat cut?"

"Yes," I reply. "I mean, I realize. I'm sorry, Mother."

"You're sorry?"

I nod.

"Good," she continues. "I'm glad you're sorry. But what concerns me now, is the question of what this Frenchman might have said to you."

"Nothing."

"Nothing?"

"Not a word. I mean, he just greeted me, and I told him to be on his way."

"I see."

She looks back down at her embroidery, and I can tell that she most definitely does not believe me. Ordinarily, she would respond to my lies by banishing me to my room and handing down some form of punishment, but this time she seems inordinately calm and I find myself worrying even more about what she intends to do next. Finally she looks at me again, and I'm certain that she seems to be studying my face most intently.

"Turn a little to your left," she says eventually.

"I beg your pardon?"

"Your left. Turn."

I do not know why she wants me to do such a thing, but I do it regardless.

"He was right," she continues, with a slightly wistful tone in her voice. "You *do* look like her. More and more with each passing year."

I open my mouth to ask who I look like, but I'm not sure I want to provoke her any further.

"Well?" she adds. "Are you not going to ask to whom I refer?"

"I'm sure you would tell me if it were important."

At this, she lets out a brief, seemingly very genuine laugh.

"Oh, I've taught you well," she continues, "but if you look like her, then perhaps there is more of her in your heart than I had dared imagine. And perhaps that aspect will continue to grow and grow as you age. Why, by the time you're eighteen, you might be a veritable facsimile of the woman."

I wait for her to finish, but now she is simply watching me once more. Her eyes are twitching slightly, and after a moment she tilts her head. The more I stare at her, the more I feel as if she seems to be listening to someone else. In fact, as my eyes are drawn to look at her right ear, I feel certain that I can hear a whispered voice.

"Might I leave now?" I ask suddenly, as a rush of panic thumps through my chest.

"No."

I take a deep breath.

"And still," she adds, "you do not ask who I am talking about. I can only conclude that either you are a very incurious girl, or you already know and are therefore too frightened to pose the question. Oh, my dear Mary, you have never struck me as incurious before."

"I don't know what you mean," I reply, but now the fear is so very obvious in my voice.

"You must think no more of her," she continues. "Is that clear? Think no more, and certainly speak no more. Not to me, not to your father, not to anyone. And from now on, child, you are never to look at your own reflection ,is that understood? The mirror in your bedroom is to be removed, and you are to avoid all other mirrors in this house, and you are to never permit anybody to take your photograph." She pauses, eyeing me with a hint of disdain. "And never learn French. Ever. Tell me that you understand."

"I understand."

"And be -"

She stops and tilts her head again, and the whispering voice becomes just a little louder.

"Yes," Mother says softly, as if to answer, while

keeping her eyes fixed on me. "She is. Yes. I know."

I wait, as the whisper continues.

"Now get out of my sight," Mother says finally, gesturing for me to go to the door. "The sight of you makes me feel uneasy. Have a glass of wine brought up to me, and tell your father that I am not to be disturbed for the rest of the day. Tell him I am having one of my bad spells and I must be alone so that I can recuperate. And make sure he understands that it's all your fault."

"Yes, Mother."

Feeling immensely relieved to be let out of her company, I get to my feet and hurry toward the door.

"Oh, and Mary?"

Opening the door, I turn back to her.

"Never disobey me again," she continues, "and never neglect to tell me anything of importance. If you ever lie to me again, my dear, I shall see fit to punish you. As your mother, it is my unfortunate duty to do whatever is necessary in order to beat you straight. And finally, you are never to go to that forest again, is that understood? Not in the day and not at night. Never. Ever."

I hesitate, before nodding.

"Now go," she continues. "I am quite sick of the sight of you for today."

Stepping out of the room, I pull the door shut and then take a step back. Looking down at my hands, I see that they are trembling. In fact, I am trembling all over. And then a moment later I realize I can still hear a whispering voice on the other side of the door, and I can hear Mother mumbling to herself. Stepping back toward the door, I set my ear against the wood, hoping to hear a little better, but in the process I accidentally step on a loose board.

"Go!" Mother screams, and I immediately turn and run away.

MARY

AS THE NIGHTTIME RAIN continues to come crashing down, I stand in the open kitchen door and stare out at the dark lawn. I have been standing here for fully ten minutes now, long after everybody else went to bed, and I know that I am directly breaking Mother's rules. At the same time, I have spent the evening thinking about her warnings, and I have come to the conclusion that I cannot simply shrink back and accept her word on every matter. Perhaps this is a flaw in my character, but I feel compelled to do what she tells me I must not, no matter the punishment I shall receive if I am found out.

Besides, I can hear the silent scream once more.

Stepping outside, I am already drenched by the time I have pulled the door shut. The weather of late has been atrocious, with more rain having fallen in the past few weeks than we have seen for many years. Fortunately, I know that Mother has taken something to help her sleep, and I also know that the sound of the rain will surely make it far less likely that Father will hear me coming outside. It is under this cover, therefore, that I turn and step out across the lawn, squelching through the puddles of mud and heading toward the treeline. Rain is pouring down all around me, hissing as it batters every surface, making this night louder than any place I have ever been before. Even the town, with its vehicles and shouting men, is quieter than this violent night.

The horses sound restless in the stable, but they are securely tied.

By the time I get to the edge of the lawn and find myself staring into the dark forest, I have begun to feel my soaking wet clothes clinging to my cold flesh. I am shivering slightly, but I know deep down that I should not allow myself to show any weakness, in case I am being watched. And as I pick my way between the trees and set out through the forest, I feel as if I *am* being watched. Of course, in this maelstrom I would hardly have much chance of hearing anyone, even if they were standing right behind me and shouting my name.

Although I suppose I would hear if they whispered directly into my ear.

Suddenly my right foot squelches and sinks into the mud, stopping only once my entire ankle has been submerged. I let out a faint gasp, and for a moment I struggle to pull my foot clear, but I set off again soon enough, wading more than walking as I use the trees to support myself. The sound of rain is now a din, as if the natural world has conspired to replicate the immense scream that I have been hearing for days in silence. And now I think I can hear the scream more clearly, ringing out above the sound of the storm, as if someone is screaming in an attempt to attract my attention.

It is coming from ahead.

Straight ahead.

I do not know how I know this, but I know it.

Stumbling slightly, I nevertheless manage to steady myself against a tree. After a few more steps, however, I see to my shock that a mud-bank has given way, with rivers of mud having sloughed down into one of the ditches, leaving several of the trees standing rather precariously with their roots exposed. The sight is quite shocking, as if the forest itself has opened its mouth, and I suppose that this is what Father meant when he warned that the terrain out here might not be entirely safe. I suppose it would be sensible to turn back this instant, but I cannot bear to be such a coward, so I wade forward until my footing becomes precarious and I have no choice but to lean against another tree.

Even now, fresh mud is cascading down the slope as the storm continues to reshape the land. Fresh muddy rivers are finding paths, sometimes joining and sometimes separating.

And then I see the face staring at me.

Washed partially clean by the rain, a human skull is poking out from the mud. I can see eye sockets and a cheekbone, and part of a jaw too. Dribbles of mud are flowing over its surface, and rain water appears to have pooled in the sockets and is now overflowing. I want to believe that this is an illusion, that there cannot possibly be human remains out here in the forest, yet I see the skull as clearly as I have ever seen anything my whole life. And without even stopping to worry about whether I am being sensible, I set out to traverse the river of mud, hanging onto exposed tree roots as I struggle to reach the skull.

In the distance, one of the horses whinnies.

As soon as I am close enough, I reach out and take hold of the skull, lifting it gently from the mud. The jawbone comes loose and is washed away, but I raise the skull and take a closer look. Whoever this poor soul was when they were alive, they seem to have been buried out here in the middle of our forest, and I cannot fathom how such a thing could have come to be. Looking back down at the mud, I spot a couple more bones poking out into the rain, but I suppose there is no need to reach for those. They must, I assume, be the rest of this unfortunate person's body. Balancing carefully, I use the exposed roots to haul myself back up to safety, and then I stumble a little further from the mud until I'm on slightly more stable ground.

Now that I can see the skull properly, I realize that it's quite beautiful. Perhaps it's wrong of me to think such things, but I can't help noticing as I turn the skull in my hands that it has a certain grace and nobility. I run a finger against one side of its face, trying to imagine what it looked like with flesh, but I have no idea. I do not even know whether it belonged to a man or a woman, but the empty eye sockets seem to be staring straight back at me and after a moment I spot something dark stuck to the edge of the socket on the left. Using my finger to dislodge the patch, I realize after a few seconds that it appears to be a small scrap of flesh left clinging to the bone.

"Who were you?" I whisper against the sound of crashing rain, as I stare at the skull. "How did you end up here in our garden?"

I hesitate for a moment, as another question comes to my mind.

"Were you screaming so that I might find you?"

***

AS I MAKE MY way back across my bedroom, still drying my hair after my trip out into the rain, I stop for a moment and look at the skull on my writing desk. I know I must find a safe place to hide it, so that Mother and Father never know that it's here, but for now – in the dead of night – I cannot help but marvel at its features as candlelight flickers against its bony face.

I have so many questions, and I wish I were older so that I could begin to answer some of them.

"Marguerite?" I whisper.

I wait, almost expecting an answer.

"Is that your name?" I continue.

Silence.

"Are you Marguerite Alesi?" I ask. "Is that who you were?"

Again, I hesitate for a moment, but the skull simply stares back at me. I no longer hear a scream. It is as if the skull was calling to me, and I have now done what it wanted.

"My name is Mary," I reply, even though I feel rather foolish. "I am twelve years old. Almost thirteen. I live here at Wetherley House with my -"

The words catch in my throat. Suddenly the word *parents* feels wrong, and I take a step closer to the skull.

"I live here with Eve and Gordon Carmichael," I continue. "Did you know them? Do those names mean anything to you?"

I hesitate, before reaching out and placing a hand on the side of the skull.

"My name," I add, "is Mary, and -"

Suddenly hearing a creak out on the landing, I feel a rush of panic at the thought that Father or especially Mother might discover me. Quickly setting the skull out of sight behind my desk, I blow out the candle and hurry to my bed, scrambling under the covers and pulling them over me. I turn and face away from the door, and a few seconds later I hear the tell-tale sound of the handle turning. As the door creaks open a little, I don't dare turn to look, although after a moment I hear a very faint clicking sound, as if Mother is standing outside and watching me.

She must know that I have been awake.

She must have seen the candlelight flickering beneath my door.

Still, that doesn't mean she knows I was outside, and she surely knows nothing of the discovery I made in the forest.

Sure enough, after a few more seconds, the door gently bumps shut again and I allow myself to breathe a sigh of relief. Turning over in the bed, I push the covers aside and sit up.

And then I see her.

Letting out a gasp, I realize that Mother in fact entered the room and is now standing next to my bed, staring down at me with the door shut behind her.

"Mother?" I stammer, pulling back as panic grips my chest. "What are you doing?"

I wait, but she does not respond. Instead she simply watches me. I'm sure she was a tall woman once, before her injuries, but her badly bowed legs bring her down by at least a foot, perhaps more, and I can hear her low breaths.

"I got up to go to the bathroom," I explain, my mind racing as I try to think of an excuse that she might believe. "Then I changed my mind, so I blew the candle back out and I decided to come back to bed. I didn't think I'd made enough noise to wake you, Mother, but I'm very sorry if..."

My voice trails off.

After a moment, I spot the skull next to the desk. It's hidden well enough, but part of its face is just about visible in the moonlight if one looks in the right direction. So far, Mother has kept her back to the desk, and I can only pray that she does not turn and notice what I have brought inside.

Suddenly she turns and limps back toward the door, pulling it open and stepping out onto the landing. Finally she closes the door again, having left the room without uttering a single word, but I do not dare relax, not yet. Instead, I remain frozen in place on the bed, terrified that she has gone to fetch a birch stick or something else she means to use against me. It is only when I hear her bedroom door bump shut that I finally realize she seems to have believed my story, or that at least she did not disbelieve it sufficiently to punish me.

Either that, or she is saving the punishment for morning.

Once I am absolutely sure that she is gone, I climb out of bed and retrieve the skull from its hiding place, and then I look around for some safer spot where I can keep it well out of sight. Finally realizing that there's only one option, I pull a chair next to the wardrobe and climb up, before carefully placing the skull where it cannot possibly be seen. I feel bad treating human remains in such a way, but I suppose it wasn't in hallowed ground anyway, so the top of a wardrobe isn't *that* much more disrespectful than a muddy grave in a patch of woodland.

"Good night," I tell the skull, before climbing back down and putting the chair in its usual place next to the desk. With that done, I head to bed and settle back under the covers, although my mind is rushing and it takes several hours before I'm finally able to sleep. Already, the first rays of morning sun are beginning to lighten the sky outside my window.

And then suddenly I am woken by the most dreadful scream.

MARY

"I SAW HER!" MOTHER screams, struggling to pull away from Father's arms and then tripping, falling to the ground and letting out a gasp of pain. "I saw her face!"

Startled as I stand in the doorway, I watch as Mother starts dragging herself across the floor of the master bedroom. Father is clearly just as shocked and confused, and he barely seems to know what to do with himself as he hurries around Mother and finally tries hauling her up. His efforts are in vain, though he tries several times.

"Get off me!" she shouts finally, pushing him away. "I felt her cold hands on my arm! I felt her, Gordon! I felt her, she was touching me and -"

Stopping suddenly, she spots me for the first time, staring straight at me with reddened, teary eyes. For a moment she seems utterly mesmerized by the sight of me, but then she turns away as if something about me has sent a shudder through her soul. She tilts her head,

156

and for a few seconds I think I once again hear a faint, whispered voice.

"You must pull yourself together, my dear," Father says as he helps her onto the edge of the bed, where she collapses on her side. "This is no way to behave, Eve." He hesitates for a moment, before turning to me. "Mary, your mother is not well this morning. She's going to need rest, and I must attend to her. Please, go downstairs and inform Mr. Carsdale that you'll be the only one requiring breakfast. Ask him to set something aside for me to eat later."

"But Father -"

"Go, girl!"

Realizing that I cannot argue, I take a step back and pull the door shut, but then I pause as I hear Father trying desperately to console Mother. I can hear the whisper, too, although Father is apparently oblivious.

"I had the most terrible dream," I hear Mother sobbing finally. "No, a nightmare. In this nightmare, I got up in the middle of the night and went to Mary's room. She'd been awake, she claimed she'd risen to attend to a need, but that she'd then changed her mind and returned to bed. I wanted to ask her what she'd really been doing, but I sensed another presence in the room."

"Eve, really, there's no -"

"I sensed it!" she hisses. "It was her, Gordon!"

"Who?"

"Don't act like an idiot. You know perfectly well who I mean. It was Marguerite! I felt her presence in the child's bedroom!"

Father sighs. "And how could it be her? She is

long gone, my dear, to a place from which nobody can possibly return."

"How can you be sure?"

"I saw her at the bottom of the grave myself. God help my soul, but I did. I saw her down there, and I myself helped fill that cursed pit with frozen soil. There was no way out."

"But after that..."

"After that there was nothing more of her. She suffocated in the dirt."

"And after *that*?"

"After that there was nothing," he continues, sounding tired now as I continue to listen from out on the landing. "My dear Eve, you spent all day yesterday talking about how the girl reminds you of her... I mean, how she reminds you of someone from the past. It's hardly surprising that you seem to have worked yourself up into a hysterical state. As a woman, you are far more prone to these distractions and indiscretions, but you must at least try to be logical. A feeling in a dream is hardly proof of anything. Are you, perhaps, entering your monthly cycle again?"

"And then I saw her this morning!" she stammers.

Again, he sighs.

"I did, Gordon! Just for a moment, I saw her standing at the foot of our bed!"

"You mean Mary?"

"I mean Marguerite! I swear, Gordon, that wretched woman was -"

Suddenly I hear a loud slap, and I instinctively

take a step back from the closed door.

"Perhaps that will calm your nerves," Father says firmly. "You must push these fears well away, my dear, or they will surely take root and you'll become as insensible and pathetic as your own mother. Is that what you want? To become one of those women who are pitied by all?" The bed creaks as he gets to his feet, and I sneak to the top of the stairs so that I'll be able to more quickly retreat once the door opens. "I'll leave you alone for a few minutes, Eve, to pull yourself together. And then I want to hear no more talk of Marguerite Alesi or figures from the past, and no more questions about matters that are settled. Do you understand?"

"Do you hear that, Gordon?" she asks.

"Hear what?"

"Just listen for a moment."

For a few seconds, the only sound from the room is the faint, continued whisper.

"I hear nothing," Father says finally. "You are to get yourself under control, and you are not to emerge from this room until you are ready to comport yourself properly. I shall ask you again, Eve. Do you understand what I am telling you?"

I wait, but Mother does not answer.

A moment later the door handle turns, and I take that as my cue to scamper quietly down the stairs. By the time I reach the kitchen, however, I hear Mother cry out again, and Father runs back to the room. I am starting to think that perhaps Mother is finally losing her mind.

***

"TAKE SOME VEGETABLES, MARY," Mother says calmly as we sit at the dinner table. "They're very important for your well-being."

Although the potatoes seem soggy to the point of having been overcooked, I set some on my plate anyway.

"Mr. Carsdale must have been very distracted in the kitchen today," I suggest, trying to make light of things.

"Mr. Carsdale is gone," Father replies.

I look over at him.

"Why?" I ask.

"We are in the process of searching for some more help," he continues, sounding exhausted and looking utterly distracted. "Your mother had to make do in the kitchen as best she could manage and..."

His voice trails off, and all of a sudden I cannot help but note that he appears rather pale.

"You ask a lot of questions," Mother says after a moment. "Child, you would do well to remember your place."

"Yes, Mother," I reply, looking down at my rather unappetizing meal. I never knew how much I relied upon Mr. Carsdale's cooking skills until they were gone. "I'm glad you're feeling okay, Mother."

"I just had a funny spell," she continues, although her head twitches again. "You know how it can be, Mary. Well, perhaps you do not, not yet. You're not a woman. It can be very easy for women to let their thoughts overpower them. One must not read too much into one's dreams, or one is liable to find them spilling out into the world around us. And then one must remind oneself that they really *are* just dreams, which can be quite exhausting. Fortunately, your father reminded me that I must stay strong, and that is -"

She flinches suddenly.

"And that," she adds finally, sounding a little breathless, "is what I am doing."

I look over at Father, but his head is bowed and he's simply staring down at his plate. Turning back to Mother, I cannot help but notice that she seems to be eyeing me with a great deal of suspicion. I think perhaps I preferred things when she was upstairs whimpering.

"I have pulled myself together now," she explains, "and overcome my delusions. As any strong woman must do. I know what is real and what is not. I recognize what is possible and what can only exist in fancy. Do you know, child, that for a short while this morning I actually came to believe in ghosts?" She smiles. "I even thought I saw one. Why, if I had remained in that fragile state, I might even believe I was seeing one at this very moment."

I wait for her to continue, but now she's simply staring at me.

Not daring to break eye contact, I nevertheless set my hands in my lap.

"But no," she whispers. "I am not seeing a ghost. What a ludicrous proposition. The dead do not return to this world, Mary. Where they go, I cannot say, but it is somewhere very far away. And they do not come back, and we would not hear them even if they called to us. Perhaps they *do* call to us, and perhaps in our weaker moments we might *think* we hear them, but we do not. Nevertheless, I do think they sometimes leave things behind, things that we might not immediately notice. Things that might somehow influence us. Does that make sense to your childish mind, girl, or are you not yet sufficiently developed?"

"I don't know," I reply, my voice feeling dry and choked.

"The dead are dead," she continues. "If you don't -"

Before she can finish, I hear a loud bump and I turn just in time to see that Father has slumped forward and slammed his head against the table. His face is resting on his plate, and I stare in horror as I see that he is no longer moving at all.

"Well, that's some auspicious timing," Mother mutters, as if she's not very surprised. "Now let me think, your father wasn't allergic to nuts, was he? Oh yes, he was. I suppose I should have left them out of tonight's meal."

Shocked, I push the chair back and get to my feet.

"Sit," Mother says firmly.

"But -"

"Sit!"

I hesitate for a moment, before slowly sitting back on the chair. My heart is racing and I can barely keep my thoughts straight.

"Draw yourself to the table," Mother continues.

I stare at Father's un-moving figure for a

moment, before pulling my chair closer to the table. I know Father can't be dead, I know that I must simply be missing something about this situation, but at the same time I am quite sure that Father would never partake in some kind of joke. I am filled with panic, yet I do not know what I should do next.

"Your father appears to have left the conversation," Mother says calmly. "Keep a stiff upper lip, Mary. This is not the time to let yourself get emotional."

Still staring at Father, I feel a shudder pass through my chest.

"But Mother," I stammer, "he..."

My voice trails off.

"What, dear? Whatever's the matter?"

"He... I mean, is he... Is..."

I hesitate for a moment longer, as I realize that Father has been face-down in his dinner for a couple of minutes now.

"Is he... dead?" I manage to ask finally.

"Well that depends on whether he can breathe gravy, doesn't it?" Mother replies, before reaching over and turning Father's face slightly, allowing me to see his dead, gravy-smeared face and the fragments of potato that are stuck to his wide-open eyes. "Oh dear. I do fear the worst."

With that, she lets his face press back against the plate.

"I suppose there will be some changes around here now," she continues, picking up her knife and fork and then immediately starting to cut into her meat.

"Your father was a good man, Mary, but he could be somewhat spineless. Now that it's just the pair of us, I shall need you to help out more in the house. Still, you're getting old enough for extra responsibilities, and I am sure I'll be able to find plenty of jobs for you." She pauses, and I see a flicker of something new crossing her face, as if she's perhaps not quite as calm as she's trying to appear. "Life goes on, my dear, and you must be very well-behaved. Is that understood?"

I want to ask what she means, but still I cannot stop turning back and looking at Father. And then, after a moment, I realize I can hear the whispering voice again.

"I should have done that years ago," Mother mutters. "Now eat up, dear. You have plenty of work to do after dinner, starting with the task of removing your father and -"

"No!"

Suddenly filled with the realization that I have to get out of here, I get up from my chair and take a step back.

"You're insane!" I stammer. "You've completely lost your mind!"

She tilts her head slightly.

"You're a murderer!" I continue. "You killed Father! You... you... You killed him!"

"Sit down, Mary."

I shake my head, before turning and hurrying toward the door. Racing up to my room, I make my way inside and then I stop as I realize that I'm not entirely sure what to do next. Thoughts are rushing through my mind, but finally I realize that I simply must go to town and speak to the police, and I must tell them what Mother has done. I have no idea how they'll react, but they have to at least come out here and investigate, which means that perhaps Mother will be hauled away for her crimes and I shall be sent to...

To where?

With Mother gone, I would be an orphan. Or alone in the world, at least.

Still, I have no choice. Turning, I head back to the door, only for it to swing open as Mother steps through. Gasping, I try to pull away, but she shoves me back until I slam hard against the wooden floor. Dragging myself toward the window, thinking that perhaps I can climb out and drop down into the flowerbed, I finally start to reach up, only for Mother to snap a cane across my back and send me slumping back to the floor.

"And what do we have here?" she mutters, reaching down and picking up the skull from next to my writing desk.

"Leave that alone!" I shout.

"My," she continues, taking a closer look at the skull as a faint smile crosses her face. "Hello again, Marguerite. How distressing to find that you have temporarily found your way back into the house."

With that, she drops the skull, letting it crash back down against the bare boards with such force that a section cracks away from one of the cheekbones.

"No!" I gasp, trying to crawl around Mother and make for the door. Before I can get even halfway across the room, however, she cracks the cane against my face, cutting open a seam of flesh and sending me falling back against the side of the bed.

Reaching up, I feel blood running down to my chin. I'm trembling now, terrified of what Mother might do next, and a moment later I see that a dribble of blood is already running from the end of her cane. As Mother steps closer, I flinch and put my hands up to cover my face, and then I try to curl into a ball as she slowly, creakily kneels in front of me.

"Fruit of my loins," she says calmly, as she leans so close that I can feel her hot breath against my face, "how am I going to make you see things my way? How am I going to set you on the straight and narrow?"

She pauses for a moment, as the whispering voice gets louder and louder in the air around us, and then finally she tilts her head as if she's heard something she understands.

"Ah yes," she purrs. "I have an idea."

PART FOUR
1906

AMY CROSS

EVE

"I THINK I AM getting much better at the piano now," Mary says happily as she spoons some more potatoes onto her plate. "You were right, Mummy. All I really needed was more practice. Thank you for telling me to keep at it."

"Not at all, dear," I reply. "It fills my heart with joy to hear you playing."

"I know I shan't ever be able to play in public," she continues, "but I still like to practice for my own amusement. Why, I can play for hours and hours each day without every growing tired or bored."

"It's good that you know your place," I tell her. "I'm so glad that you don't fill your thoughts with foolish ambitions. So many women these days seem to think that they need to become the equal of men, in order to achieve anything in this life. The truth is that women are born to a quite different role, and it is best that we stick to our own course. You and I, my darling girl, are happy just the way we are."

"You are right again, Mummy. I'm so glad that I have the benefit of your wisdom. I'm the luckiest girl in the whole world."

I watch for a moment as she starts to eat, and then I cut into my own meat. Mary has become a quite excellent cook over the past few years, better than I myself ever managed, and I am so very proud of her. Even now, she maintains perfect poise and posture as she sits at the other end of the dining table, and at the age of eighteen she has blossomed and become an utterly beautiful young woman. To my relief, her resemblance to Marguerite has even faded, and now I dare say she actually looks a little like me, and like Gordon too. I can only suppose that nature has finally taken its course.

"Might I play for you after dinner?" she asks eventually. "Please, Mummy? I don't want to bore you, but I would so dearly love for you to hear how I'm getting on."

"Of course, darling," I reply, unable to stifle a faint smile as I realize that life is so perfect now. "Nothing could give me greater pleasure than to hear my own dear daughter playing in the evening. I think, in fact, that this is what I have wanted my entire life."

Wetherley House is now the happiest house in the whole of England.

***

LATER IN THE EVENING, the sound of Mary's

playing fills me with joy as I step into the drawing room. Somehow, the music seems to drift effortlessly from room to room, almost as if it follows me, and I cannot help but smile as I make my way over to the bookcase and search for a specific volume. Finally locating one of Gordon's old books on gardening, I slip it out and start searching for the section on perennials, so that -

Suddenly I hear a loud banging sound, and I turn to look back through to the hallway.

Mary is still playing, but I am sure I heard someone at the front door. It's almost seven in the evening and I can't imagine how anybody would ever have business at Wetherley House at such a late hour. Indeed, it has been so long since we last had visitors at all, I had begun to think that we were never to be disturbed again. A moment later, however, the knocking sounds returns, and this time Mary abruptly stops playing.

Now the house is silent, but finally the knocking rings out for a third time, and it is clear that our unwanted visitor will not simply leave.

"I'll answer!" I call out, setting the book down and heading back into the hallway, from where I can see that there appear to be two figures outside. As I get closer to the door, I cannot help worrying that this disturbance might mean trouble. "Go to your room, Mary," I continue, as I reach for the latch. "I shall deal with this."

I wait until I hear Mary reaching the top of the stairs, and then I slide the latch aside and pull the door open. As soon as I do so, I'm startled to see my cousin

Muriel Cruikshank standing outside with her son George.

"Oh, thank goodness you're home!" Muriel says, bursting inside without even waiting for an invitation. "We're in the most frightful jam, Eve! You're a lifesaver!"

"What are you doing here?" I stammer.

"What are we *doing* here?" She lets out a long, pained sigh, as if she has just ended some awful tribulation. Turning to me, she bumps against the hall table, almost knocking it over. "Let me tell you, Eve, this is the last time I ever go on holiday beyond the confines of London. As soon as one gets away from the city, one enters a wild and savage land that barely deserves to be considered part of our fair England at all! It's quite astonishing, but the warnings were all quite correct!" Stepping past me, she sets her hat on the table and then sits on the nearest chair, which creaks under her considerable weight. "There are no trains past Colchester this evening," she continues. "Can you believe that? No trains at all. It's as if we're in the wilderness!"

"I'm sorry," I reply, "but I still don't -"

"We're stranded, Eve! Stranded, hundreds of miles from home! It's only by the grace of God that I recalled you had returned to Wetherley House, and I said to George that we would simply have to throw ourselves on your mercy."

"She did say that," George adds glumly.

"We need to stay the night," Muriel continues breathlessly. "I'm so sorry, Eve, but we desperately need you and dear Gordon to put us up. How is Gordon, by the way? Still a handsome devil?"

"I..."

Barely knowing where to begin, I stare at my cousin with a sense of utter astonishment.

"You don't have any food, do you?" she asks, before turning to George. "Darling, I need something to eat. You'll have to find me a morsel, so that I can eat while Eve and I catch up!"

George turns to me.

"I believe there is a public house in town," I say cautiously, "with rooms available on a nightly basis. I don't mean to sound unwelcoming, but I rather feel that you'd be more comfortable in -"

"With all those beer-drinking loudmouths?" Muriel roars uncouthly. "I'd say not! Whatever's given you that notion, dear Eve? I don't want to expose poor George to such horrible things."

"She doesn't," the boy adds forlornly.

"We shan't bother you too much," Muriel continues. "George and I are very quiet and polite house guests, and it's only for tonight and tomorrow morning. Or perhaps until Thursday at the latest."

"Thursday?" I gasp. "That's out of the -"

"Where's dear Mary, anyway?" she continues, turning back to her son. "You remember Mary, don't you? Perhaps not. After all, it *has* been a while and she's several years older than you." She turns back to me. "You and Gordon have rather hidden Mary away from the rest of the family, haven't you? She must be, what, eighteen years old now? Surely she's coming into her own and filling out nicely?" A leering grin crosses her face. "I dare say the local boys must be starting to sniff around, eh? Are you planning to marry her off any time soon?"

"I -"

"Of course, girls of that age can be so much trouble," she adds. "I hope Mary hasn't become too rebellious!"

This stream of questions is so shocking, and so rapid, that I honestly don't know where to begin. Muriel was always frightfully rude, but since our last encounter she seems to have become something from a caricaturist's most fevered dream. In fact, I had not notice before, but now I see that her left eye is rather bloodshot.

"You look shocked," she adds finally. "George, go to the kitchen and raid their larder. Find me something to eat, boy." Easing herself off the chair, which creaks once more, she steadies herself for a moment against the dresser. "My knees aren't half bad, Eve. Now, let's get started, shall we? What's been going on with you since the last time we met? I want to hear all about it!"

EVE

"THEY SOUND UTTERLY FRIGHTFUL," Mary whispers behind me, as I peer out through the crack in her bedroom door and listen to the Cruikshanks arranging themselves in the spare bedroom. "Mummy, they're not staying for long, are they?"

I open my mouth to assure her that they'll be leaving in the morning, but when I turn to Mary I immediately realize that I can offer no such reassurance. So far this evening, Muriel has ignored or perhaps not even noticed my subtle attempts to make her realize that she's not welcome, and I have had to accept now that she and her wretched son seem rather settled.

"How can they be related to us?" Mary continues. "They sound like pigs!"

"Every family must bear its burdens," I tell her, keeping my voice low so that the Cruikshanks won't overhear us. "Muriel and her spawn have always been rather raucous, which is why I have long tried to avoid having anything to do with them. Unfortunately, one cannot always avoid such people forever, and it seems that they have descended upon us for a short while. We must simply bear their visit with good grace and manners."

"Can't you throw them out?"

"They *are* family, dear."

"But -"

"You shall stay in your room," I add, trying to work out how exactly we are going to deal with this intrusion. "I do not want you exposed to them in any way, in case their uncouth manners rub off on you."

"I'm sure they wouldn't, Mummy."

"One cannot be too careful. You are to stay in here. Is that understood?"

Hearing footsteps outside the door, I listen to the sound of George running downstairs. He sounds like an absolute bull in a china shop, bumping against the walls and paying no mind to the fact that this is a restrained home. If he is like this when he is a guest, I cannot begin to imagine how he must behave at home. A moment later, however, I hear one of the floorboards creak on the landing, and I realize to my horror that Muriel must have emerged from the spare room.

"Eve?" she calls out as she approaches the other side of the door. "Are you in there?"

"Quiet!" I hiss to Mary, before slipping out onto the landing and pulling the door shut behind my back. "I trust that all is to your satisfaction, Muriel?" I ask, forcing a smile.

"Is young Mary in there?" she replies, reaching

past me to open the door. "I must see her!"

"I do not think so," I say firmly, pushing her hand away. "She is very tired and she has already prepared for bed."

"Oh, I don't mind that!"

"She's rather shy, too."

"Shy?" She chuckles. "I'll soon tickle all the shyness out of her!"

"I'd rather you didn't," I continue, bracing myself in case I have to physically fight her away from the door. Before I can say another word, however, I hear George thudding around downstairs, and a moment later there's a faint creak as another door opens. "What is he doing?" I ask, desperate to go to the stairs and look down, but not daring to leave the door to Mary's room unguarded.

"Oh, don't mind George," Muriel says with a grin. "He's just exploring the house."

"I'd rather he didn't."

"He won't break anything. He just got very excited when I told him you have a basement."

"Surely he's not going down into the -"

Hesitating for a moment, I realize with a sudden sense of horror that I can indeed hear footsteps pounding down the old wooden steps that lead into the basement. Racing to the stairs and their hurrying down as fast as my damaged legs can carry me, I rush after George and catch him as he reaches the bottom step, where the pool of light from the door above ends and the basement's darkness begins.

"You mustn't be down here!" I hiss, pulling him

back and forcing him up the stairs.

"I heard something," he replies, trying to push past me.

"Get up there!"

"Is someone down here?" he asks.

"Of course not!"

"But if -"

"Get out!" I scream, shoving him back so hard that he falls and lands hard on the wooden steps. "Right now! Get out of here at once!"

Clearly startled, he stares at me with a shocked expression for a moment, before suddenly bursting out laughing.

"Do you mean to mock me?" I stammer. "Why, I should -"

Before I can finish, I hear a faint scraping sound over my shoulder. Turning, I stare into the darkness, and I realize that the scraping sound is inching closer. I don't see anything, of course, but the air down here is so very cold and I'm filled with a sudden urge to get upstairs as quickly as possible.

"There *is* someone down here, isn't there?" George whispers, with a hint of awe in his voice. "There's -"

"Out!"

Manhandling him as best I can manage, I force him up the steps one by one, constantly struggling to keep him from craning his neck and looking past me. The child is most disagreeable, but somehow I manage to get him all the way to the door, at which point I give him one final shove and send him stumbling back. With that, I limp through after him and slam the door shut, before sliding the bolt across and taking a moment to get my breath back.

"Who is it?" George asks.

Turning to him, I see that he's already looking at the bolt, as if he means to go down again.

"Nobody," I gasp.

"But -"

"A dog."

"You have a dog?"

"Of sorts."

"And you keep him in the basement?" He furrows his brow. "That seems awfully mean."

"You don't know what you're talking about," I continue, taking a moment to straighten the front of my dress. "That dog, however, is the meanest and most vicious animal known to man, and it will tear the flesh from your bones as soon as look at you. Do you understand? If you go down into that basement again, you will end up as its next meal! If you're a sensible young gentleman, George, you will heed my words and curb your inquisitive nature."

He stares at me, and then slowly he starts to smile.

"Can I see it?" he asks.

I shake my head. Will this infernal child never learn?

"I want to see it!"

"It's not for seeing."

"Why not?"

"Because..." I try to think of an answer that will

satisfy him. "I just -"

"Did it do that to your legs?" he adds, looking down at my skirt just as Muriel comes down the stairs. "Is that why you're all crippled? Did the dog -"

Before I even have a chance to stop myself, I slap him hard across the face. He steps back, clearly startled, and then he runs sobbing to his mother.

"I'm sorry," I stammer, "he just... I shouldn't have done that, but I'm afraid I couldn't help myself."

"He's only curious, Eve," she replies as the boy clings to her. She runs her hands through his curly brown hair, and it's clear that she's very much on his side. "I don't use physical violence against George, as a rule. I don't believe in it."

"I shall endeavor to not strike the boy again," I continue, as George turns and stares at me with a venomous, teary-eyed glare. I swear, the child looks as if he utterly hates me, and although I am trying to make amends for my actions, I cannot help but feel that he deserves several more slaps.

"Why don't we get to bed, eh?" Muriel tells him, and George immediately starts making his way up the stairs, pulling his mother's arm so that she has no choice but to follow. "We'll be sharing the bed in your spare room," she tells me as she heads up with him. "There's no sense making two beds dirty, and besides, George gets nervous when he's not at home. Even in his own room, he sometimes needs me to get in with him."

"I'm sure," I reply, forcing a smile until they are safely out of sight. Once I've heard the door to their room bump shut, I unbolt the basement door and pull it open. Leaning into the cold air, I look down into the darkness, and I believe I can hear the faintest sobbing sound coming from far below.

Such weakness.

After shutting the door and making sure that the bolt is firmly across, I head up to Mary's room and slip inside. My dear girl is sitting at her writing desk, studying a book of compositions, as I walk over and place my hands on her delicate shoulders.

"He deserved that, Mummy," she tells me. "George is a wretched little swine. The look on his face when you slapped him was priceless."

"Yes, it was," I whisper, as the sobbing sound echoes in my thoughts for a moment. Finally, I reach down and kiss the top of Mary's head. "I'm so glad you thought so too."

"He'll go down again, you know," she adds.

"Will he?"

"A rotten little child like George? Oh yes, Mummy. You know he will. He'll go down into the basement again, except this time he'll be far more sneaky." She looks up at me with a faint smile. "What will you do then?"

***

"WETHERLEY HOUSE *IS* LOVELY," Muriel says as we sit at the breakfast table. "There's such a lovely atmosphere about the place. I noticed it as soon as we came through the front door last night."

"Thank you," I reply, supposing that she means

this comment as a compliment.

"Gordon looked rather rough this morning, though."

I start spreading some butter on a piece of bread, before stopping as I realize what she just said. Slowly I turn to her, and I watch for a moment as she adds sugar to her tea.

"Gordon?" I ask finally, feeling a little faint.

"You said he was off on business, didn't you?" she continues airily. "That was a naughty little porkie-pie, wasn't it? Still, he looked terribly gaunt this morning. You need to fatten the poor man up a little."

"What are you talking about?"

"Gordon." She grins at me. "I only spotted him briefly. I was in the bedroom with George and we had the door open. I happened to glance out toward the landing, and I saw Gordon walk right past. He didn't look in or say anything. He just headed toward the stairs and then, I suppose, he left the house." She pauses for a moment. "I didn't hear the front door go, but he *did* leave, didn't he?"

"I think you must be mistaken," I tell her. "Gordon was away last night."

"Well, I saw him at about half past eight this very morning."

I shake my head. "No. That's impossible."

"George saw him too. Ask him if you don't believe me."

Turning, I see that George is sitting obediently at the far end of the table, having finished his egg.

"I saw him," he says cautiously. "Mummy's

right. He did look *awfully* pale."

"I'm sure you must be mistaken," I reply, before turning to Muriel again. "Gordon is away."

"Perhaps he popped back for something, then," she replies, as she stirs her tea. "We definitely saw him. Where's young Mary, by the way? I still haven't set eyes on her since we arrived."

"She's in her room."

"But what -"

"Cramps," I add, hoping to end this infernal interrogation. "She is a woman now, you'll recall."

"Oh, it's her time of the month, is it?"

"Perhaps we should not speak of such things in front of the boy."

"George?" She laughs. "Oh, I have no secrets from him."

"It's true," George mutters. "She doesn't."

"And you'll be leaving today, I assume?" I ask.

"We must trouble you for one more night, actually," Muriel continues, as if the matter is settled and I have no say whatsoever. "Sorry, Eve, but the trains are a nightmare. Don't worry, though. I shall go into town today and arrange everything, and hen we shall be out of your hair tomorrow. I'm so grateful to you for putting us up like this, you've been an absolute life-saver."

"Another night?" I reply, feeling as if I cannot possibly stand having this woman in my home for even a moment longer. "Why not -"

Suddenly there's a creaking sound from upstairs. I look up at the ceiling, but the sound has already passed.

"That'll be Mary, I suppose," Muriel mutters,

before biting into a slice of bread. "I do hope we get to see her at least once before we leave," she adds, speaking with her mouth full. "We *are* family, after all. In fact, I think -"

"Excuse me for a moment," I say suddenly, getting to my feet and hurrying around the table.

Reaching the hallway, I stop for a moment and look up the stairs, listening in case there's another creak or any hint of movement at all. Hearing nothing, I nevertheless make my way up and head to the first open door, which leads into the spare room where Muriel and George slept last night. I pause again, before turning and looking both ways along the landing.

"Gordon?" I whisper. "Are you..."

My chest feels impossibly tight for a moment, before I realize that Muriel must simply have been wrong. Gordon is dead, and of that fact there can be no doubt. After all, I buried him myself. I just have to endure one more night with these intruders in my home, and then Wetherley House can get back to normal.

***

"WHATEVER IS THE MATTER?" I shout, stumbling out of my bedroom shortly after two o'clock in the morning, as screams ring out through the house. "What's that awful noise?"

"Where's George?" Muriel gasps as she emerges from the spare room. "What -"

"The basement!" I hiss, struggling as fast as I can manage and quickly limping down the stairs. Even before I get to the bottom, I know I shall find the basement door unlocked, and sure enough I see that it is hanging half open. Mary prophesied that the wretched child would go snooping again, and she was right.

The boy's cries are getting louder and louder, and Muriel pushes me aside as she races down to see whatever is the matter with him.

"What's he doing down there?" Mary asks.

Startled, I turn to see that she's standing right behind me.

"You should have locked the door," she continues.

"The lock is broken!" I stammer, as the horrid screams and cries continues. "I never thought it necessary! I never wanted visitors!"

"This'll be trouble," she whispers, keeping her eyes on the half-open door as Muriel cries out down in the darkness. "Can you hear their voices? Something truly wretched is happening down there." She hesitates, before turning to me with a faint smile. "I suppose that'll be the dog, won't it?"

Her grin widens.

"Woof woof," she adds.

"What am I to do?" I gasp, taking a step back as I hear fresh screams from directly below my feet. "Whatever am I to do?"

"Help!" Muriel shouts. "Somebody help us! Somebody -"

Suddenly she lets out a loud, guttural cry, accompanied by what sounds like a heavy impact against one of the stone walls.

With tears in my eyes, I listen to George's continued screams and cries. Perhaps it makes me a wicked person, but I can't help thinking that the best thing all round would be for the boy and his mother to simply never come back up from the basement. There would be questions, I'm sure, but nothing I couldn't bat away. And now, as George's horrendous gurgles continue to rise between the cracks in the floorboards, and as Muriel shrieks in sheer panic, I feel as if perhaps I should simply push the door shut, slide the bolt across, and make sure that the problem simply stays hidden.

So that's exactly what I do.

As I close the door, I hear a series of loud bangs on the steps, and I think perhaps someone is dragging something up. Sliding the bolt into place, I turn and lean back against the door before slowly slipping down to the floor. A moment later I feel somebody trying to get the door open, but of course the bolt can't be moved from the other side and I know that all the hammering and all the screaming in the world will be of no help. There are tears in my eyes, but I know that I am doing the right thing, and I also know that soon everything will be alright. I just have to stay the course and ensure that I do not weaken.

"How long do you think it'll take?" Mary asks, watching me from the other end of the hallway.

"I can't possibly say," I whisper, as fresh tears roll down my cheeks.

"Help us!" Muriel gurgles, banging her fists against the door and causing the wood to shudder behind my back. "For the love of all that's holy, let us out of here! Eve!"

"It might take a little while," Mary points out.

"I know."

"They're such screamers."

"I'm sure it'll be over soon."

"And then you'll have to go down there, Mummy."

I turn to her. "Will I?"

"Perhaps not," she continues with a faint smile. "Perhaps -"

Suddenly the door shudders with such force that I let out a yelp, and for a moment I worry that Muriel might find some way to force her way through. I swear I heard the wood crack slightly, but then there's another, louder bump followed by the sound of something clattering back down the steps into the basement. Falling, even. I flinch and hold my breath, and now I can hear some kind of rubbing sound, and I can't help but close my eyes and pray to God that this will all be over soon. Why would God want me to suffer through this agony, when he could bring peace back to Wetherley House any time he wanted?

Finally the screams end, although I keep my eyes tight shut as I hear occasional bumps from downstairs. In fact, I only dare open my eyes after twenty minutes or so, by which point the house has remained silent for quite some time. I am still trembling with fear, and I feel as if I shall never again have the strength to stand, but I know that I simply *must* go on. To do otherwise would be to display the kind of weakness that I so despise in others.

Slowly, therefore, I start hauling myself up from the floor, until eventually I am able to stand on my trembling, damaged legs.

"Now what, Mummy?" Mary asks from the doorway.

"Now I think it is bedtime," I whisper, turning and limping toward the bottom of the stairs.

"You're not going down?"

"No."

"Very well. Perhaps she will enjoy the bones."

Stopping halfway up, I look back down and see that Mary is grinning at me. At the same time, a gnawing, grinding sound is coming from the basement, and the wooden boards beneath Mary's feet are shuddering.

EVE

I CAN DO THIS.

Setting a pair of white gloves on my hands, I tell myself that I am far too strong to crumble. I have faced greater challenges in the past, and I shall most certainly get through this.

I take a deep breath, before turning and opening the front door, and then I flinch as I look out at the path that leads to the front gate.

I *can* do this.

***

THE WRETCHED TOWN IS always so busy. As I cross the street outside the local tavern, I cannot help but flinch as I spot several familiar faces looking toward me. It seems that the locals are always so very interested in the lives of the Carmichael family. Sometimes I wonder if they spend all their time gossiping behind my back.

There are far too many people in the world.

"Morning, Mrs. Carmichael," a trader says, doffing his hat as I pass.

I briefly make eye contact with him, before continuing on my way. The last thing I want is to talk to ruffians and laborers. I dislike coming into town at the best of times, and I would not be here today if a matter of great urgency had not come up. Fortunately Mr. Trin's glass factory is close by, and I'm able to quickly push the door open and slip inside. The interior is rather dark and gloomy, but at least here I am spared the looks and glances of all those foul people outside. I can hear voices in the next room, however, so I take a moment to compose myself before heading through another door and stopping again as soon as I see several men polishing a series of large glass panes.

"Impressive, aren't they?"

Turning, I find that Mr. Trin has emerged from his office.

"I know it probably just looks like glass to you," he continues, evidently proud of his work here and keen to share his achievements, "but a pane of that size is not easy to create, at least not cheaply. I've almost perfected the method and I believe that by the new year, we should be in a position to go into production."

"And this is why you had me come all the way here?" I reply, unable to hide my frustration. "Mr. Trin, if I wanted to admire a piece of glass, I could simply look through any window in my home."

"Step into my office," he says, gesturing for me to go through the door in the corner.

Sighing, I go into a small, cramped room that contains several overflowing desks. There is paperwork everywhere, along with design drawings and other assorted documents. The place smells rather foul, like a mixture of vinegar and something even more astringent, and I am minded to walk right out of here. However, it has been several months since I last came to check on the state of the business in which my late brother owned a share, and I suppose I should keep an eye on things so that this Mr. Trin fellow does not run everything into the ground. After all, the business is now half mine, and I have need of the income.

"I am working on another new technique," he says excitedly as he shuts the door and hurries around to the other side of the main desk. "I hope to produce sheets of glass that are just as large, but also much thinner. However, they must also be strong. Now, to this end I have developed -"

"I do not need to know the ins and outs," I point out, interrupting him. "Is the business financially viable?"

"Might I explain the bonding process that I think will produce best results?"

"How are the finances, Mr. Trin?"

He hesitates for a moment.

"I believe there will be a substantial profit by the end of the year," he says finally. "I told your late brother that I expected to be ready for production next year, but I think now we'll be ready a whole twelve months early."

"That is fine," I reply, "and -"

Before I can finish, I hear someone whisper in

my ear. Startled, I turn to see who has dared sneak up behind me, but all I see is the dingy corner of the room with nobody present. I turn the other way, filled with a sense of anger at the thought that somebody sees fit to trifle with me, but after a moment I realize that Mr. Trin and I really *do* seem to be alone here in the office.

"Mrs. Carmichael?" he says cautiously. "Are you alright?"

"The business is doing well, I take it?" I reply, turning to him. "And if -"

Suddenly the whisper returns.

"Who is that?" I hiss, turning once more but still seeing no sign of anyone. "Who keeps whispering into my ear in such a manner?"

I head over to the nearest desk and check that no fool is hiding on its other side, and then I turn and see that Mr. Trin is staring at me with a rather puzzled expression. I want to push the whisper out of my mind, but on this occasion I am sure I felt somebody's breath against my ear, and I am not minded to chalk the whole thing up to an excitable imagination. A moment later, I spot something rather unusual on a table by the window, and I wander over to take a closer look at what turns out to be a child's shawl.

"My wife and I are expecting again," Mr. Trin says nervously. "It's due in March. Twins and triplets run in the family, so we might be getting a real brood. We already have three girls, as you might recall."

"I do recall," I reply, "and might I add, they play rather too close to the house for my liking."

"They do enjoy the forest."

"Tell them to keep away from my land."

"Of course. I'm sorry if they've intruded."

"Your apology is accepted," I mutter, staring at the shawl for a moment before turning back to him. "I do not wish to be called into town again unless there is something very important for me to deal with. Is that understood? My time is valuable and I do not wish to be dragged away from my home just so that you can show off some pieces of glass."

"I'm sorry," he replies, "I just thought that you'd like to see how we -"

"Well, I wouldn't."

He opens his mouth to reply, but then he falls silent and I can tell that I seem to have made my point.

"I can have financial statements sent to you at the house," he says finally, "if that would suit your needs?"

"That would be fine. And if there is nothing else for me to be doing here, I think I shall take my leave. Good day, Mr. Trin. I wish you luck with whatever processes and other experiments you're carrying out here. Just don't forget that this is not a hobby. It is a business."

With that, I turn and head toward the door.

"Give my regards to Mrs. Cruikshank," he says suddenly.

I freeze in the doorway, before slowly turning and seeing that the wretched man is sorting through the papers on his desk.

"What did you say?" I ask.

He glances at me.

"I heard that your cousin, Muriel Cruikshank, was staying with you for a few days," he tells me.

"You heard that?"

"I believe she was in town before she went to your home. She spoke to quite a few people. By all accounts, she was rather excited to be seeing you again after such a long time."

"People... know she was staying with me?" I stammer, feeling a rush of panic as I realize that at some point I might face questions, once Muriel's disappearance has eventually been noted.

"That boy of hers is rather ill-disciplined," he continues. "Sorry, perhaps it's not my place to say so, but he was running around in the town square and making the most frightful racket. I honestly don't remember the last time anyone attracted so much attention. I'm afraid to say that people won't forget their brief visit in a hurry. I hope they're not causing too much trouble for you at Wetherley House, Mrs. Carmichael."

"I..."

Taking a deep breath, I quickly realize that I must not let my discomfort show.

"What happens at Wetherley House," I say calmly, "is none of your concern, Mr. Trin. Nor is it the concern of *anybody* in this parochial little town. If you hear any further discussions of the house, or of my visitors, I would kindly ask that you tell the local gossip-mongers to mind their own business and find some other topic for their tittle-tattle."

"Of course, Mrs. Carmichael."

Sighing, I turn once again to leave.

"Give my regards to your husband, though," he adds.

I turn and glare at him, and he quickly looks down at his papers again. Evidently he has realized that he should not be saying such things, and I can only hope that at least this will be the last time he troubles me in such a manner. For the third time, I turn and walk out of the office, although I manage only a few steps before I'm startled by the cries of several men. Looking across the workshop, I see that one of the large glass panels is beginning to topple, and sure enough it quickly falls to the floor and shatters.

"Careful, lads!" a voice calls out. "These things can kill, you know!"

"Oh dear," Mr. Trin mutters, hurrying past me and going over to see what's going on. "What happened? Was it the stress again?"

Sighing, I turn and head out of the building, and then I start making my way back out of town. People are watching me, but I keep my eyes focused on the road ahead. All I want is to get home and shut the door, and block the world out, and spend the rest of the day with my darling daughter. That is the only world that interests me now.

***

"I THINK I AM getting much better at the piano," Mary says happily as she spoons some more potatoes onto her plate. "You were right, Mummy. All I really needed was more practice. Thank you for telling me to keep at it."

Staring out the window, I watch the lawn with a growing sense of foreboding. Over the past few days, ever since Muriel and George's brief visit, I have felt unsettled, as if the world beyond the house is starting to shift and turn toward us. The delivery man came yesterday, and I know he sensed my unease. He, like Mr. Thin, made some casual comments about my visitors, and I fear I snapped rather in my haste to put him straight. Now, as I look toward the darkening sky, I feel certain that somebody or something is coming this way.

"I know I shan't ever be able to play in public," Mary continues, "but I still like to practice for my own amusement. Why, I can play for hours and hours each day without every growing bored or tired."

Why can't the world leave us alone? Why must anyone ever come to Wetherley House again? I would be so very happy to just spend all day, every day listening to Mary as she plays the piano. Instead, however, I know that the brutish world is plotting its next intrusion. Muriel Cruikshank and her wretched son were just the forward guard, the first incursion, but the world will send someone else soon, then more and more, until a rushing tide of visitors threatens to drown us and send our bodies into the depths.

"Mother?"

Startled, I turn to Mary and realize that she has been speaking and I have not paid attention. Her voice became a background drone, stifled by my own thoughts.

"Are you not enjoying our usual conversation this evening?" she asks.

"Of course, darling," I reply, trying to raise a smile. "Where were we?"

"I was asking if I might I play for you after dinner," she continues, clearly relieved that we're back on track. "Please, Mummy? I don't want to bore you, but I would so dearly love for you to hear how I'm getting on."

"I would like that a great deal," I tell her. "We must -"

Before I can finish, I flinch as I hear a loud banging sound coming from the basement. A moment later, the sound shifts and slams against the underside of the floorboards beneath my feet, with such brutal fury that I feel the vibrations against the soles of my feet.

"Perhaps I should play *now*," Mary says, already getting to her feet. "To fill the house with a more agreeable sound."

"Please do so."

Putting my head in my hands for a moment, I close my eyes and listen to the brutish thuds. After a few seconds, however, Mary starts to play the piano in the next room and I listen as the music starts drowning out the thuggishness that seems particularly determined this evening to break through. In fact, after a moment, I realize the banging sound has changed slightly, almost as if a piece of bone is being slammed against the wood.

Instinctively, I get to my feet and make my way to the doorway, where I stop so that I can watch Mary playing. It takes only a couple of seconds, however, for the thudding to follow me and once again hit the boards beneath my feet. Will that cursed noise never leave me alone?

"I shall play louder, Mother," Mary says happily, and that is exactly what she does, until the whole house is shuddering.

At least now I can no longer hear the bangs coming from the basement, although I can feel the vibrations no matter where I stand. The thing down there seems to be following me around the house.

***

AT LEAST THE CACOPHONY ends when night comes. Alone in my bed, staring up at the moonlit ceiling, I tell myself that I must enjoy these hours of calm. I dare not waste the peace by sleeping. Instead, I force all bad notions from my head and focus on the thought that I have got what I wanted, and that everything will be alright in the end.

Just a few hours later, however, the world intrudes yet again.

EVE

"GOOD MORNING, MRS. CARMICHAEL."

Ignoring the trader, I hurry across the street, storming toward the building that houses the infernal Mr. Trin and his glass-making business. I thought I had made him understand the other day that I do not wish to be disturbed, yet early this morning I received another message from him, telling me that I simply must come down here this morning. Evidently there is a matter of life and death for us to discuss, although I honestly find it difficult to believe that it could not wait.

Unless the man has developed a method for turning manure into gold, I shall consider this trip to be a waste of my valuable time.

Rounding the corner, I slow as I see that all bedlam has broken out in the vicinity of the factory. Scores of rough-looking workers are using joists and ropes to lift a series of large glass panes onto the back of a carriage, and the scene has attracted gawping spectators from nearby buildings. Some children are playing nearby, letting their laughter ring out across the town square as if they have no self-control whatsoever. I have half a mind to turn right around and march right back to Wetherley House, although after a moment I spot someone waving to me and I feel a shudder run through my chest as soon as I see the grinning face of Mr. Trin.

"I'm so glad you could come down," he beams as I reach him. "I know you said you didn't want to be disturbed again by business matters, but I really thought you should witness the proudest moment in our company's history."

"Are you a cretin?" I spit.

He turns to me, and now his smile seems a little frozen and uncertain.

"Dear Lord, man," I continue, struggling to keep from screeching at him, "did my words yesterday pass into one of your ears and straight out from the other? Do you think that I was speaking simply so that I could listen to the sound of my own voice?"

"But -"

"Glass!" I hiss, looking toward the latest large pane that is being lowered onto the pile. Several meters wide and several long, the pane is certainly large, and I can't help noticing that it's dangling rather precariously from the ropes that are being used to maneuver it toward the carriage. "You brought me down here so that I could look at glass? Again? Glass is something that one looks *through*, Mr. Trin. Not *at*!"

"I thought -"

"Did you?" I ask, turning back to him. "Did you really think, or did you simply let your excitement get the better of you? I am sorely tempted to believe, Mr. Trin, that you are a man of very limited intelligence." Sighing, I realize that he looks utterly crestfallen. "Evidently you have some ability when it comes to this particular line of business, but in other matters you must be sorely lacking."

Suddenly something bumps against me, and I turn to find that one of his three little girls has stumbled into my side.

"Dolly, be careful," Mr. Trin says, reaching out and taking her hand, before gently pulling her away from me. "You mustn't play too close to people."

"I'm sorry," the little girl says, staring up at me with a smile. "I won't do it again."

"See that you don't," I say firmly.

She narrows her eyes, watching me as if she's curious about some aspect of my manner.

"Can we play in the forest?" one of the other girls says as she comes over. At this rate, I shall soon be surrounded. "Please?"

"No," I tell her.

She turns to me, as her sister finally arrives and I find myself facing these three identical-looking children. They look to be no more than five or six years old, each wearing a rather fancy little white dress complete with unnecessary red ribbons.

"Mrs. Carmichael," Mr. Trin says after a moment, "I don't believe you've met my girls. This is Dolly, this is Molly, and this is Holly. Holly's the oldest, by three minutes. Dolly's the youngest by two."

"One and a half," the girl replies, evidently having the audacity to correct her father.

I open my mouth to tell Mr. Trin that I have no interest whatsoever in his sniveling little family, although for a moment I can't help but notice that these three girls make a rather unusual sight. For one thing, they honestly seem to be utterly indistinguishable from one another, and for another they're all staring at me as if I'm quite the most unusual person they've ever seen in their lives. Finally, all at once, the three of them look down toward my skirt, as if they're curious about my damaged body.

"Let me be perfectly clear," I tell them, "that you are not to play in the forest anywhere near my home. You are not to play within earshot of Wetherley House, in case your laughs and screams reach my property. Is that understood?"

The children stare at me for a moment longer, before two of them turn to their father as if they seek his answer. The third child, whose name I have already forgotten, continues to keep her eyes fixed on my dress.

"I'll make sure they don't bother you again," Mr. Trin says, sounding a little deflated as his workers continue to yell at one another.

"See that you do," I reply, "because otherwise -"

Suddenly feeling something tugging at my skirt, I look down and see to my horror that one of the little girls has crouched down and is trying to lift the hem so that she can see my legs.

"Stop that!" I shout, reaching down and striking

her across the face with such force that she falls back and immediately starts crying.

"Dolly!" Mr. Trin says, helping her up and giving her a hug. "You mustn't do things like that! It's rude!"

"I only wanted to see!" she bawls.

"I have had quite enough of this madness for one day," I say firmly, feeling as if these infernal children are going to drive me out of my mind. "Mr. Trin, if you call me back into town one more time on a matter of such trivial un-importance, I shall withdraw my support from this business venture entirely and leave you to go it alone. Is that clear?"

"Of course, Mrs. Carmichael. I'm sorry, Mrs. Carmichael."

"And the same goes for your children in the forest near my home," I add, as the three little girls hurry away to play nearby in the street. "I do not want to so much as hear their laughter drifting onto my land. I would consider that to be a gross invasion of my rights."

"I'll talk to them later," he continues. "They're such lively, happy children. They love nothing more than to play, but I'll find a way to make them understand."

"See that you do," I mutter darkly, "or perhaps I shall have to investigate the construction of one of Mr. Twain's electrified fences. If that's what it takes to keep intruders off my family's land, I don't see that I have a choice."

With that, I turn my back on his shocked face and begin to make my way along the busy street, slipping through the crowd of rabble. Behind my back, the loathsome workers are yelling at each other, but a moment later I hear that infernal whispering sound again. I stop and look around, but of course there's no sign of anyone. Still, the sound continues, and after a moment I see that the three young Trin girls are staring at me from the other side of the street. They're standing near the truck that's being loaded with glass panes, and suddenly one of the girls turns and calls out to her father.

"Daddy!" she shouts. "Who's the horrible woman who's whispering into Mrs. Carmichael's ear all the time?"

I turn and look over my shoulder, but there's still nobody. When I look back at the three children, I see that they're still gawping at me.

"Mrs. Carmichael?"

Realizing that a man has approached me, I turn and find that a police officer has come over.

"I'm terribly sorry to disturb you," he continues, his voice barely rising above the incessant whispering sound, "but I was planning to come out to Wetherley House later today and speak to you about a rather delicate matter."

"If it's about the Cruikshanks," I stammer, "I know nothing."

"Cruikshanks?" He furrows his brow. "No, Mrs. Carmichael, I think we're at cross purposes here. I need to talk to you about -"

"Watch out!" a man yells. "Move! Get out of the way!"

Suddenly there's a loud snapping sound nearby.

I turn and look. Before I even have a chance to blink, however, the uppermost pane of glass slides away from the rest at speed and shoots out from the back of the carriage, slamming straight into the three young Trin girls and slicing cleanly through their necks in just a fraction of a second.

As the blood-smeared pane finally smashes down to the ground, the girls' decapitated heads drop from their bodies and bump onto the cobbles, leaving the three bodies standing with blood spraying from the stumps of their necks. And then, one by one, the three bodies drop down on bent knees before toppling onto their sides and spilling more blood.

As screams ring out from the crowd, I stare at the three severed heads and see that each of the girls is still blinking. This continues for a few seconds, before first one falls still, then the second, and finally the third.

EVE

"IT SOUNDS UTTERLY HORRIFIC," Mary says, staring at me with an expression of pure horror. "All three girls? All at once?"

"I have never seen a scene like it," I reply, thinking back yet again to the awful accident I witnessed in town. Or rather, trying *not* to think back, but finding that the grisly image is lodged in my mind. I take another sip of water. "Mr. Trin became utterly catatonic. I can't imagine he'll get over it."

"And the girls were looking at you when it all happened?"

"I don't see what that has to do with anything."

"Of course not, I just..."

Her voice trails off for a moment, as if she still can't quite believe that such a terrible thing could have occurred. At the same time, there seems to be just the faintest trace of a smile trying to curl across her lips, as if she's struggling to keep her true feelings contained.

"It's just hard to believe that such a thing could be an accident," she continues finally. "It's almost tempting to think that the fates conspired, or some other force intervened. Still, I suppose that's not possible. God would never do such a thing, and I can't imagine that there's anything else in all of existence that would be capable."

"You must put such thoughts out of your mind," I tell her. "The triplets simply suffered a very nasty accident. Perhaps if they hadn't been so ill-disciplined and unruly, they wouldn't have been standing in such an unfortunate place to begin with."

"But -"

"If they had been in school, or studying verse at home, they would still have their heads."

"I hope you didn't say such a thing to poor Mr. Trin."

"At least they'll no longer be bothering us by playing near the forest," I add. "It's a terrible thing, but not every consequence is going to be negative." I pause for a moment. "Although I suppose something will have to be done about the business now. With Mr. Trin likely out of action, perhaps I shall have to sell it all off to the highest bidder. Still, there should be someone out there who'd be willing to take on all the new ideas Mr. Trin was coming up with. I'm led to believe that there's quite some degree of promise in his work. He claimed to be developing an exceptionally thin and sharp type of glass and, well, one way or another today's horrible accident at least proves that he must have been onto something."

"There is a man coming toward the front door."

"I'm sorry?"

Turning, I look out the bedroom window and see that Mary is right. A figure is indeed making its way along the path that runs from the distant gate, and something about the figure's gait give me pause for concern. As he comes closer, I realize that he is wearing a dark uniform, and finally I feel a sudden clenching sensation in my chest as I understand that this gentleman appears to be a police officer. Not just any police officer, either. He's the same uncouth ruffian who tried to speak to me earlier in town, and whose conversation I would have been forced to endure had the accident not occurred. It would appear that he's determined to try again.

"What does he want?" Mary asks.

Turning to her, I can see the fear in her eyes.

"You must get rid of him!" she says firmly.

"Wait here," I reply, getting to my feet and taking a moment to straighten the front of my dress. I take another sip of water, before setting the glass on the bedside table. "I shall see to this matter. I'm sure he's just performing his rounds and checking on all the houses in the area."

I turn and head toward the stairs, and then down toward the hallway.

"They don't do that, though, do they?" Mary asks.

Stopping, I glance back at her.

"He must be here for a specific reason," she continues. "Don't let him into the house."

"Quiet," I reply, keeping my gaze fixed on her for a moment. "I need you to be quiet."

"You don't have to worry about *me*," she says with a smile. "You know who you have to worry about. Keep that man out of this house."

Before I can answer, I hear a loud, brutish knocking sound at the front door. My chest tightens with fear and I turn to see that a jovial-looking policeman is already waving at me through the glass panel. I force a smile, hoping to set him at ease, and then I make my way over so that I can turn the latch. I still hesitate for a moment, worried about how I shall appear once I have to speak, but I quickly remind myself that I have spoken to such people before. I can do it again.

"Good morning," I say as I finally open the door. "What brings you to Wetherley House?"

"Good morning, Mrs. Carmichael," he replies, removing his hat in the proper manner. "I'm sorry to disturb you on this fine day, but we were rather unfortunately interrupted earlier by that terrible business in town."

"Indeed.

"As I was about to tell you," he continues, "a matter has arisen in London and I have been asked to come over and make sure that it's of no concern."

"London?" I cannot help feeling a flush of relief. "I have no dealings with anyone in London."

"Might I come inside for a moment?"

"Of course."

I step aside so that he can enter. I hate the intrusion, of course, but I know I cannot turn the man away. Of course, he somehow manages to step on not one but two creaking boards in succession, and I flinch as I imagine how loud those boards must sound in the basement.

"Do you know a Doctor Josiah Edge, M'am?" he asks as I shut the door. "Or rather, *did* you know him?"

"I beg your pardon?" I reply as I turn to him. I recognize the name, of course, even though I have not heard it uttered in many years. Nor did I ever wish to be reminded of that man again.

"A Doctor Josiah Edge of Marystone Street in London was found dead last Tuesday week, M'am," he continues. "Suicide by hanging, I'm afraid to say."

"How dreadful," I mutter, although my mind is racing as I try to work out why such news should be brought to my door.

"Doctor Edge left a note behind," he continues, "in which he blamed his failings on various factors. He seems to have been a rather bitter gentleman, if I'm blunt, and it was a very long note. More like a small pamphlet, really. Anyway, I'm told that most of it was a kind of ramble concerning the injustices of the world and the fact that his genius had not been recognized by his peers, but there was one section in which, well..."

He hesitates for a moment, as if he's worried about sounding indelicate.

"Well, M'am, in one section he speaks of you specifically. And of this house, actually. And of certain matters that I've been asked to clear up with you, on behalf of my colleagues in London."

"I can't imagine what I might have to do with this," I reply. My throat is so very dry now.

"Is your husband at home?"

"No. No, he's not."

"Do you know when he'll be back? It's just that I'm not sure I feel comfortable discussing the contents of the note with a lady such as yourself."

"If the note mentions me," I continue, "then I suppose it's only right and proper that you tell me what it says."

Even as those words leave my lips, I know that I do not mean any of them. The truth is, I am simply trying to sound normal and unconcerned, while my mind races and I try to think of some way to make this mean leave.

"Doctor Edge made certain allegations in his note," he explains, "about something that he claims took place here at Wetherley House eighteen years ago. The nature of these allegations is a kind of brag, actually. He seems to think that he took part in some kind of operation for which he should receive a great deal of credit. Now, I don't want to go into the awful particulars with you, seeing as how they're too offensive for the ears of a lady, but suffice it to say that my colleagues in London have spoken to a surgeon and asked for his opinion. He was shocked, but he did say that the operation described in Doctor Edge's note... Well, it might be possible for it to have been actually performed."

"And what operation is that?" I ask, trying not to show that I am on the verge of fainting with fear.

He pauses for a moment, watching me carefully. Does he see my discomfort?

"Do you have a daughter, M'am?"

"What of it?"

As soon as I have uttered those three words, I know how defensive I must appear.

"Is she at home right now, by any chance?"

"She is not."

"She's out, is she?"

"She is."

"With your husband?"

"Yes."

"And he is her father?"

"Of course."

He pauses again, and now it's clear that he's not entirely satisfied by my answers. After a moment he glances across the hallway, almost as if he heard something.

"Would you mind, M'am," he says finally, turning back to me, "if I took a little look around?"

"That would be most inconvenient," I reply.

"It's just," he continues, "Doctor Edge says in his note that he was paid to carry out an operation on a lady of French origin, by the name of Marguerite -"

"I really have no time for this," I say suddenly,

opening the door open and stepping aside so that he can leave. "I don't know what kind of house you think this is, but you can't barge in here with these wild accusations and these claims that have been dragged from the pages of a madman's journal. My husband will be outraged when he hears of this, and you'll be lucky if you keep your position. I would strongly advise you to leave at once, and you can tell your colleagues in London that I have nothing to tell them about this Doctor Edge individual. His claim to have somehow moved a child from one woman's body to another is utter, fanciful nonsense."

"It is, is it?" he replies, furrowing his brow.

"It is."

I wait for him to leave, but he still seems very concerned. A moment later, as if the fates themselves have conspired to turn against me, a heavy bump rings out from the basement beneath our feet.

"Are you alone in the house, M'am?" the police officer asks.

"I am."

"Are you sure about that?"

"I am."

"So there's not -"

"I am," I reply. "I mean, I'm not... I mean, I'm quite alone. Of that, I am certain."

"And if -"

Before he can finish, another bump rings out, and this time I once again feel the floorboard shudder. Looking down, I see that the same board runs under the officer's feet as well, which means that he might have felt it too. When I look at his face, in fact, I can immediately see that he is concerned.

"Would you mind terribly," he says finally, "if I took a look in your basement?"

"I think I would mind, yes," I tell him.

"And why is that?"

"This is my home. I don't want grubby men poking about here."

"Is there somebody in your basement, M'am?"

"I have already told you that I am alone in the house. Are you calling me a liar?"

"M'am, I -"

"Let him, Mummy."

Turning, I look toward the door that leads into the drawing room, but there's no sign of Mary. When I turn back to the officer, I see that he's eyeing me with even greater suspicion than before.

"You have to let him, Mummy," Mary's voice continues, emerging from the whisper that continues to scratch at my ear. "There's no other way now."

I open my mouth to reply, before realizing that perhaps I should not do so. Not in front of company.

"You have to let him go down to the basement," she continues. "Everything will be alright if you just let him go down to the basement."

"Alright, then," I continue, shutting the door again and then heading over to the basement door. "If you're so insistent, I suppose I shan't stand in your way."

My hands are trembling as I slide the bolt

across. I hesitate for a moment, trying to work out exactly how I shall deal with this situation, and then finally I pull the door open and feel the cold air against my face. As I turn to the police officer, I remind myself that I shall simply have to think on my feet this time, and that I have done so on numerous occasions in the past. Even now, as I wait for this irritating man to step past me and go down into the basement, I can already see that he is concerned.

"There's nothing down there," I tell him, hoping to goad him into seeing for himself. "This is all a terrible fuss over nothing, and I have plenty of housework to do, so I'd rather you looked around and left as quickly as possible. You've already been frightfully intrusive."

"I might come back later," he replies, "with -"

"Are you scared?"

As I say those three words, I hear a faint scratching sound at the foot of the wooden stairs. I doubt the police officer was able to hear, not from all the way over by the front door, but I most certainly know now that she is coming. My initial instinct, of course, is to slam the basement door shut and slide the bolt across, but I am starting to think that this wretched officer has no intention of going down to take a look. If he leaves now, he'll surely return later in the day with more of his kind, and then I shall have a real problem. If I can just deal with him before he has a chance to speak to anyone else, I might yet contain the situation.

A moment later, I hear another scratching sound, this time a little closer.

She's coming up the stairs.

"What *are* you waiting for?" I ask, keeping my eyes fixed on the officer. "You must do what you came here for. I have nothing to hide."

He looks at the open door, and I think that perhaps now he *does* hear the scratches.

"It's quite alright," I continue, pulling the door open all the way and, in the process, making sure that I stay well back. "You look a little pale. Please, tell me that you're not going to waste any more of my time."

As the officer continues to stare at the door, my darling Mary steps into view behind him.

"Oh Mummy," she says with a smile, "you *are* clever. I'm so proud to be your daughter. I hope that I'm like you when I get older."

"Are you *sure* you're alone in the house, Mrs. Carmichael?" the officer asks, his voice sounding so tight and nervous as the scratching sound gets further and further up the stairs. "There's no-one else here at all?"

Behind him, Mary's smile grows.

Glancing down into the dark basement, I'm shocked to see a pair of savage eyes staring back up at me from the gloom. I instinctively step back and move behind the door. My heart is pounding, but I know I have to do this. I can sort everything out once the officer has been dealt with, but for now I just have to make sure he doesn't cause any more trouble.

"M'am," he says finally, taking a step toward me, "I'm afraid you -"

Suddenly she screams and strikes, lunging up from the basement and clattering through the open door. I pull back as she bumps past me, and I must admit that I'm shocked both by the sight of her bloodied, naked body and by the foul stench of bodily fluids that immediately fills the air. She lunges at the police officer, but he stumbles back and into the dining room, quickly slamming the door shut so that she can't go after him, and now she's clawing frantically at the wood in an attempt to make her way through.

"This way!" I shout, running to the kitchen door and pointing through to the next room. "Go around, foolish girl!"

She turns to me, and for a moment I see pure hatred in her bloodshot, yellowing eyes. She stumbles this way, limping heavily on the stump of a right foot that she tried to gnaw off several years ago. Maggots are wriggling in her flesh, swarming from her legs all the way up to the side of her face. This is the first time I have seen her properly in the light for several years, and I must admit that the sight is entirely disquieting. Taking a step back, I reach for the letter-opener from the hallway table and I hold the blade up so that she'll realize I'm still in charge. She's still staring at me with those ravenous eyes, and I can't help but notice patches of fresh blood still smeared all around her mouth, left over no doubt from her encounter with Muriel and George.

"Not me," I say firmly. "Him."

Stepping closer, she snarls at me.

"Not me!" I shout again. "Never me! Him!"

She hesitates, before we both hear a bump from one of the other rooms. The police officer is evidently trying to find another way out of the house, and the creature quickly turns and limps through to the kitchen. More maggots are wriggling through the flesh and meat around her spine.

I hesitate a moment, not wanting to get too close to her, and then I start to follow. I can hear the officer attempting to force one of the windows open in the drawing room, but he won't have much luck.

"Stay back!" he yells suddenly, which I assume means that the creature has reached him again. "Dear Lord, what are you?"

Suddenly I hear the creature let out a horrific snarl, followed by several loud bumps from the drawing room and the sound of glass breaking. Evidently she has attacked him, and I step back against the wall with the letter-opener still in my hands, waiting for the inevitable sound of her finishing the man off. I'm already trying to work out how I shall deal with all the damage, and how I shall lure the creature back down into the basement once her work is done, but for now I simply have to wait and hope that this is over quickly.

And then, to my horror, I hear an agonized scream ringing out through the house.

Her scream.

Before I can react, the creature stumbles back into view and drops to her knees. Blood is spraying from the side of her neck and she's clutching desperately at the wound as if she hopes to somehow seal the flesh that appears to have been ripped open. I wait for her to get back up and go after the officer again, but instead she slumps down onto her hands and knees and starts crawling this way, as if she's trying to get back to the basement.

"What are you doing?" I sneer as she gets closer. "He's still in there!"

Grabbing an umbrella, I use the end to push her back. She lets out a pained snarl, but more and more blood is rushing from her wound and she seems to be weakening. I think I can even see fear in her eyes, and a moment later I spot movement in the next room.

Turning, I see to my horror that the police officer has staggered into view, holding a bloodied piece of glass in his right hand.

"What did you do?" I shout, filled with a sudden sense of outrage. "What did you do to her?"

He doesn't answer. Instead, he simply stares in horror at the creature as she crawls past me and tries to reach the basement's open door.

"No!" I hiss, stepping over her and pushing the door shut.

As I turn back to the creature, she lets out an agonized cry before rolling onto her side, leaving a thick, smeared trail of blood on the floorboards. Realizing that she's lost too much blood, I rush over and kneel next to her, but now I'm able to see that the cut in her throat has torn all the way through to the bone. Thick, dark blood is gushing out, no longer spraying against the walls but still emerging in a torrent. I want to help her, to find some way to make sure that she survives, but she's starting to shudder now and her whimpering sobs are becoming louder.

"For the love of God," the officer gasps, stumbling past us and hurrying out through the front door, "the stories about this place were true!"

I should go after him, but I cannot bring myself to leave the creature. Reaching down, I touch the side of her bloodied face as she lets out a series of pained, throaty gurgles. Her eyes, swollen and bloodied, have partially squeezed from their sockets, protruding more than halfway. Some of the hair on her head has been torn away, exposing patches where she appears to have dug her fingernails into her scalp, almost to the bone. When she opens her mouth and lets out another cry, I see that her tongue is twice the normal size and thick with protruding boils.

I shall think of a way to save her, and of a way to put all of this right. I know I shall. I just need a moment to come up with a new plan.

***

SEVERAL HOURS LATER, AS the evening sky begins to darken, a dozen police officers reach the front door and shout at me to move away from the bloody corpse. I can't move away from her, though. How could I leave her alone and naked and dead like this, with no-one to hold her?

After all, I am her mother.

EVE

Six months later

"YOU MUST SPEAK FREELY to me, my child," the priest says calmly, keeping his voice low as we sit facing one another in the cold stone jail cell. "Anything you tell me will be between us and the Lord."

"I do not need to speak to the Lord," I whisper, staring down at my trembling hands, trying to find some way to keep them from shaking. "He hears my thoughts, does he not? He knows what I believe in my heart, that I did nothing wrong. He will judge me accordingly."

"Were you offered the chance to visit Mary's grave?"

"Grave?"

I glance at him, and I can see the horror in his eyes. I am quite sure that nobody wanted to come and speak to me today, but I suppose all condemned souls must be offered counsel in their final moments. Still, this priest is doing a bad job of hiding his disgust, and I do not know whether to hate him or pity him. Before I can say anything, however, I hear a faint whisper in my ear. I turn and look across the cell, but there is no sign of anyone.

"Mary was buried in an unmarked plot in the churchyard," the priest explains. "No stone was erected. There was nobody to pay for one, either for her or for your husband. But if you had wanted to visit and -"

"No, I didn't need to visit," I reply, interrupting him. "What point would there be? I shall be seeing her again soon."

"The Lord will judge you, Eve," he continues. "You must know that."

"I do."

"And the things you did..."

His voice trails off for a moment.

"I have an answer for any charge," I tell him. "Just because a court of men could not understand what I did, that does not mean God will be so blind. He will see that every decision I made, every choice, was made out of love. Love for my family, love for -"

"You cannot be serious!" the priest splutters, his eyes filled with shock.

"I am very serious," I reply calmly.

"The things you did to that poor girl!" he continues. "At least your husband died quickly, but that girl..."

He hesitates, and I cannot help but notice that his fingers are continually picking at the cover of the bible he's holding. Evidently I am not the only one whose hands will not stay still on this cold and merciless morning.

"You tortured her," he adds.

"I disciplined her."

"They say you turned her into a savage."

"And how could I have done such a thing," I reply, "if there had been no savagery in her to begin with? Answer me that. Anything that I drew from her soul must surely have been put there by God, so -"

"Do not say that name!" he hisses, getting to his feet. "I am sorry, Mrs. Carmichael, but I fear I cannot do my duty here today. I am supposed to offer you solace, and to help you come to terms with your actions as you near God's judgment, but I simply cannot sit here and listen as you attempt to justify what you did to that girl."

"My daughter -"

"She wasn't even your daughter!"

"She most certainly was."

"Not according to the court records. You had her torn from the womb of her real mother and..."

He hesitates, before turning and heading over to the door, where the guard is already preparing to let him out. After pausing for a moment longer, however, the priest finally turns back to me, just as I hear the whisper in my ear. This time, having grown accustomed to this strange whisper, I do not even bother to turn and look.

I know I shall see no-one at my side.

"I was merely disciplining the child," I say finally. "That is all. Eventually she would have been ready to come back up into the main part of the house. I just needed more time and -"

Pausing suddenly, I think back to all the pleasant hours I spent talking to Mary, even though she was down in the basement. At the time, I supposed that somehow her soul was rising up between the floorboards and coming to join me, but now I am starting to wonder whether something else was with me in the house, something with its own mind. The thought chills me to the bone, so I quickly put it from my mind and think instead of the beautiful piano music I heard every night. *That* cannot possibly have been a figment of my imagination.

"I can offer you no solace," the priest explains. "I do not believe there is anything that can redeem your soul, Mrs. Carmichael. You kept that girl naked and cold in your basement for several years. The only thing I don't understand is why you would go to all the trouble of stealing somebody else's child, only to then mistreat her in such a monstrous manner. The court transcripts state that you wanted a perfect daughter of your own. In the name of all that's holy, then, why did you turn the girl into such an abomination?"

"I wasn't done with her," I point out. "I needed more time."

"Time?"

"She would have come around eventually. She would have become what I wanted."

He makes the sign of the cross against his chest.

"You cannot possibly understand," I continue. "I had the strength of the Lord in my heart. I knew that everything I did, I did in his full view. He could have stopped me, could he not, if I had been doing anything wrong? Therefore, I was in the right."

"Do you truly believe that?"

"With all my heart."

His lips tremble, as if he's on the verge of asking another inane question, but then finally he steps out of the cell just as two other guards arrive. I know that the time has come, so I get to my feet before they have to ask me, and I make my way across the cell. Their cold, ignorant eyes are fixed on me, but I have become accustomed lately to expressions of scorn on the faces of those around me. I do not expect any of those idiots to understand my actions but, as I am led away from the cell and along the dark stone corridor, I know full well in my heart that the Lord will understand completely. And as I see the noose awaiting me in the room at the end, I feel my resolve strengthen. The whisper continues in my ear, and I am certain now that it is the voice of God, telling me that I have no reason to fear my moment of judgment.

I did nothing wrong.

Once I am up on the platform, a silent, solemn man places the noose around my neck. The priest says a few words, before taking a step back and bowing his head.

I wait.

Any moment now, the trap door will open beneath my feet and I shall hang.

"The curse will not die with you," a voice whispers in my ear suddenly. A foul, rasping female voice. "I wanted her. I'm still owed a child, to use as my own body."

Before I can open my mouth to reply, the trap door opens and I fall. The noose tightens, and my neck is snapped.

I did nothing wrong!

PART FIVE
1996

HANNAH

HE TURNS TO ME and rests his face on the pillow and blinks a couple of times, and I can instantly see that something has changed. His eyes, white and bloodshot still, stare at me with some kind of fresh intensity, and it takes so much effort to remind myself that hope is gone.

He's not going to get better.

This is just another brief, cruel tease, like...

Like last Wednesday.

"Hannah," he whispers, through cracked and broken lips turned bloody by the cancer. "Listen to me."

"It's okay, Daddy," I reply, somehow managing not to cry and instead reaching over to wipe his forehead again, the way I've been doing for hours now all through the night. "You don't have to speak. Just try to rest."

"Listen to me," he gasps.

"You need to save your energy."

"Burn the house."

"Daddy..."

I pause, seeing the intelligence and clarity in his eyes, but telling myself that the patterns of his delusion have just shifted a little. How many times has the doctor told me that Daddy's mind is long gone? Enough times that I know I have to steel myself against hope, that's for sure. He has moments, of course, when he seems to be his old self, but those moments never last long and he always drifts back into delirium.

"Burn the house," he whispers again.

"Well, I don't think we're going to burn it, Daddy," I tell him, as I dab at his forehead again. "We all love this apartment. Katie and Johnny and me. You know we do, and anyway, I think your neighbors in the building would be a little unhappy if we tried to burn it down."

"Not this place!" he hisses, suddenly turning in the bed and reaching over, grabbing my arm with surprising strength. I can feel his bony fingers holding me tight, and he seems to be pulling me closer. "The other house! The house that has been in our family all these years!"

In the next room, Katie's still unloading the dishwasher and making a terrible racket, as I lean toward Daddy.

"Burn Wetherley House!" he gasps, and now I can smell his chemical breath, filled with the stench of all the drugs that have been pumped into his cancer-stricken body. "Promise me!"

"Wetherley House?" I reply, surprised that he should mention that place now. "Daddy -"

"Burn it!"

"I thought you sold it years ago."

"It's still in our family!" he gasps. "I could never bring myself to sell it on, in case someone else might inherit the curse! I thought it should just be left locked and abandoned, but now I realize I was wrong! You must burn that house!"

"Why, Daddy?" I ask.

He stares at me for a moment, as his bottom lip trembles, and then slowly he turns and looks toward the bedroom window. His eyes open wider than ever, even though I know he can't possibly see much anymore. Outside, the midnight air is calm. Somehow, impossibly, the whole rest of the world seems to be going about its business, even as my father is eaten away by this cancer.

"She'll still there," he whispers.

"What are you talking about, Daddy?"

"She's waiting."

"Who is?"

"I saw her once," he continues. "I went to the gate, shortly after I inherited the place. I was going to go into the house, but then I saw Evil Mary at one of the windows and I didn't dare. I stared at her, and she stared back at me, and I walked away."

"From Wetherley House?" I reply, struggling to work out how much of this story might be real, and how much is his dementia. "Why would there have been anyone at Wetherley House, Daddy? The place has been abandoned for years, hasn't it?"

"Mary!" he hisses, turning back to me. "Mary's still there!"

"What -"

"The only hope is to burn it down! Burn it and salt the land!"

"You need to rest," I tell him. "Daddy, there's nothing to worry about, you just -"

Suddenly he reaches up, grabbing my arm and trying to haul himself out of the bed.

"No, don't do that!" I say firmly, slipping free of his grip and placing my hands on his shoulders, trying to hold him down as he lets out a chesty groan. "Daddy, you're not well enough to be on your feet, so just stay down, okay? Daddy, the doctor told you not to try getting up!"

"I have to go!" he gasps. "I have to burn that house down!"

"Daddy, you're not thinking straight!"

He lets out a gasp of pain, and I help ease his shuddering body back down against the bed.

"You have to do it!" he groans. "Promise me, Hannah! Don't go inside! Don't ever go inside! Just make sure that house burns!"

"I've never even been to Wetherley House," I remind him. "You never let any of us go, remember? In fact, you told us it'd been sold. Daddy, you've never believed in stupid stories before, so why are you suddenly getting so agitated about the place? We can sell it if -"

"No!" he hisses. "Burn it!"

"It's just a house."

"That house has been in this family for generations," he continues, "but no-one has lived there in more than eighty years, not since the tragedy!"

"But -"

"She's been waiting! She's patient, Hannah. That house is cursed! Evil Mary is still there, waiting for someone to make a mistake and unlock the front door! I saw her! I swear to you, I saw her once from the road! You can't let anyone go there! I should have -"

Suddenly he breaks into a coughing fit, and I grab a bowl and hold it under his mouth. Thick slime runs from his lips, and he suffers convulsions for a few minutes before sighing as he leans back. Taking a wad of tissue paper from the nightstand, I wipe his chin.

"Where am I?" he asks suddenly.

"You're in bed."

"Where?"

"London, Daddy. You're in your flat in London. Remember?"

He turns to me, and I can see that his mind is getting clouded again. He stares at me for a moment longer, before letting out a faint sigh as he tilts his head back slightly.

"I want to fix that fence tomorrow," he continues. "Rip it out and start again."

I feel tears in my eyes as I realize that he's drifting off, back to a time when he was still big and strong, when he could do jobs around the place.

Sometimes I think it's better for him when he's like this, because he doesn't have to face the fact that his body is wasting away. I wish he could be strong again, although I've come to accept over the past few months that those days are long gone.

"I'll do that fence right this time," he whispers as his eyes slip shut. "Should've done it years ago."

"I'm gonna go check something, okay?" I tell him, slipping my hand away from his. "I'll be back real soon, but I'm gonna go take a look at one little thing, so wait right here." I turn to leave the room, before leaning back down and kissing him on the forehead. "I love you, Daddy."

Once I'm out of the room, I lean back against the wall and try to pull myself together. Sitting with Daddy can be tough sometimes, especially when he thinks he's young again. He rambles on and on, and I get the impression that his mind is constantly flitting between today and the past, between sanity and the delirium caused by his body shutting down. Still, I should be used to it by now, so I sniff back the tears and tell myself to get a grip. Finally I pull my cardigan closed and button it so that I won't be too cold, and then I make my way through to the kitchen. Sure enough, Katie is still hard at work, loading the dishwasher again now that she's managed to get it empty.

"This thing'd better have a good warranty," she mutters, "with all the use we're getting out of it."

"He was talking about Wetherley House again," I tell her.

She turns to me.

"He wants us to burn it," I continue.

"He does, huh?" She pauses, before grabbing a box of dishwasher tablets from the counter. "Seems drastic."

"He's very insistent," I continue. "I don't know what's wrong, but he was rambling on and on about all the stories. You know the ones."

"Evil Mary? Evil Mary, something like that?"

I nod.

"He's losing his mind, Hannah," she points out, leaning down and setting the dishwasher on. "I know you don't want to admit it, but it's true. He's drifting through his own mind, remembering things and imagining things and losing touch with reality."

"But when he talks about Wetherley House," I continue, "those are the moments when he seems most lucid."

"And you're an expert, are you?"

"You've never been to that place, have you?" I ask, heading to the window and looking out across London. From high up here on the fifteenth floor of the tower block, I can see the city's lights sparkling all around, and I watch for a moment as a train snakes its way toward Southfields station.

Suddenly Katie reaches past me and sets something on the windowsill. Looking down, I see an old, slightly rusty key.

"What's that?" I ask.

"What do you think? It's the key to the front

door of Wetherley House."

I turn to her.

"I think it's the only one, too."

"Where did you get it from?"

She smiles. "Dad's boxes."

"He always guarded this so carefully," I point out, picking the key up and turning it over in my hands. "You know, I looked the house up in some library books once, and I found a few mentions of Wetherley House. There are plenty of stories about the place."

"What's her name again? The woman who's supposed to haunt the place? Mary Carmichael?"

"She was real."

"Sure, but the story will have been completely exaggerated."

"I hope so."

"We can always go and take a look," she replies. "After -"

She pauses, and I know what she was about to say.

"You know what I mean," she continues. "I'm just saying, if -"

Before she can finish, the alarm on the counter starts screeching, indicating that Daddy's monitors have detected a problem. Katie and I exchange a worried glance before both running through to the hallway and through to his room. In the process, I drop the key, but I don't go back to pick it up.

"Daddy?" I call out, tripping and almost falling as I follow Katie into the bedroom. "Are you okay?"

"He's not breathing!" Katie yells as soon as she reaches the bed.

"Call the doctor!" I scream, racing over and seeing that Daddy is completely still. His eyes are wide open, staring up at the ceiling, and his mouth is hanging loose, but I check the side of his neck and there's no pulse. Looking over at the monitors, I see that the main screen is showing a flat-line.

"Jesus Christ," Katie mutters as she runs around to the other side of the bed, "don't do this to me now, old man. Do *not* do this!"

"Daddy, stay with us!" I shout, leaning toward him and kissing his cheek as tears roll down my face. The alarm is still sounding, filling the room with such a loud screeching noise that I feel as if my bones are shaking. "Daddy, do you hear me? Daddy, you have to stay with us!"

HANNAH

"YOU DO IT."

"No, you do it."

She sighs. "Hannah -"

"I'm not the one who wanted to come here in the first place!"

"You're the one holding the key."

I hold the key out to her.

"What are you so afraid of?" she asks. "It's just a house."

"Then you open the door," I reply, "and -"

Suddenly I turn and look back toward the dark country lane that runs past the house.

"I swear I saw someone out there when we arrived," I continue.

"Another ghost?"

"No, I think it was a man, standing in the

shadows. I think he was smoking a cigarette."

"This is the countryside," she replies. "People are weird in the countryside. I'm sure he wasn't a ghost. He was probably just some passing perv."

She sighs again, before taking the key and sliding it into the lock. She has to jiggle it about a little, but finally she manages to get it turned, and then she pushes the door open. Immediately, we both step back as we smell a strong, fusty stench coming from the hallway.

"Is that what ghosts smell like?" Katie asks, waving the smell away. "This place stinks!"

I open my mouth to reply, but suddenly I feel a shudder pass through my chest. I really, *really* don't want to set foot inside Wetherley House, and I'm thinking more and more that this whole trip was a huge mistake. I only came because Katie kept saying I was scared and I wanted to prove her wrong, but now that I'm here on the doorstep, I have to admit that I *am* scared.

"I saw her once," Daddy's voice says, echoing in my thoughts. "I went to the gate, shortly after I inherited the place. I was going to go into the house, but then I saw her at one of the windows and I didn't dare. I stared at her, and she stared back at me, and I walked away."

Looking back at the gate, I realize he must have meant one of the windows at the front of the house. I look at each of the windows in turn, but there's definitely no sign of any creepy, spectral figures. Daddy was a no-nonsense kind of guy, and it's hard to believe that even in his worst moments he could have imagined such a terrible thing, but I guess I have to stay focused and remember that there's no such thing as ghosts.

The legend of Mary Carmichael simply can't be true. And Wetherley House is just an empty house. Nothing more.

***

"IT'S LIKE SHABBY CHIC," Katie mutters as she runs a hand across the kitchen counter, "without the chic."

"Don't you think there's a weird atmosphere here?" I ask.

"I'm pretty sure that's mold."

"No, I mean..."

Sighing, I realize I can't put it into words. Still, as I turn and look around the kitchen, I can't shake the feeling that we're being watched. Or rather, not *watched* exactly, more that something here is aware of our presence. I guess I just built myself up into a lather on the way here, and when I turn back to Katie I see that she's grinning at me.

"What?" I ask.

Laughing, she shakes her head.

"What?"

"You actually look pale," she replies. "Do you realize that? It's like the color has actually drained from your face. Let me guess, you've read the ghost stories about this place a hundred times, maybe even more."

"I have not!"

"Then what's this?"

Reaching into her pocket, she takes out the grubby, tattered copy of J.R. Gayle's *100 Haunted British Houses* that I thought I'd lost.

"That was just for fun," I tell her.

"Oh yeah?" She starts flicking through, before stopping near the middle. "Wetherley House in Somerset -"

"You don't have to read it out," I say with a sigh.

"Because you know it off-by-heart?"

"Because you obviously can't take the idea seriously."

"This Mary woman sounds really crazy," she continues, turning to the next page. "According to Mr. Gayle, people have heard her screaming inside the house. Like, people have been passing on the road outside, and they've heard actual screams coming from the place. A couple of times the cops were even called out, but they never found any trace that anyone had broken in. Apparently Mary Carmichael didn't take too kindly to being left all alone here. They say she was completely insane by the time she died."

She turns to another page.

"I've got to admit, it's a slightly more convincing ghost story that some of the others in here. A young woman is tortured and brutalized by her mother, and then dies after attacking a police officer. The mother hangs, and the young woman's ghost haunts the house forevermore, roaming from room to room and never -"

Suddenly a loud, heavy bump rings out from upstairs, followed almost immediately by a second. I look straight at the ceiling and then over to Katie, and I immediately see a grin on her lips.

"Right on cue," she points out, setting the book down.

"Can we stay somewhere else tonight?" I ask. "I think there's a pub in town, they probably have rooms."

"Aren't you going to go and look?"

"We could get pub food. You like pub food."

"It was probably just a mouse or something."

"I bet they have steaks."

"Or the ghost of Mary Carmichael."

Grinning, she steps closer. I know she's trying to wind me up, but I also know that it'll probably work.

"Think how long she's been waiting for fresh victims," she continues, stopping right in front of me. "All those years, just drifting from room to room, looking out the windows and waiting for someone to open that squeaky garden gate. Do you think ghosts get bored when they're haunting empty houses? Or do you think they're kept busy by thoughts of revenge? Maybe Mary never lost faith, maybe she always knew that eventually some fool would enter the house again. She was insane when she died, remember. Out of her mind, slathering, almost an animal. So I guess her ghost is insane too. She's been so patient. It'd be a shame if she didn't get her reward."

I wait for her to continue, but now she's simply staring into my eyes, and her smile has faded.

"Oh, look at you!" she laughs suddenly, tapping the side of my face with the book, which she then thrusts into my hands. "Go up and take a look around. See for yourself that there's nothing here."

***

I START MAKING MY way up the stairs, and I feel my chest tighten a tad with each step. I feel the cold air, too, and I make a mental note to turn the radiators up later. The stairs creak a little beneath my feet, and the railing wobbles slightly as I hold tight to steady myself, but I force myself to keep going until eventually I reach the top. Looking along the landing, I see the wallpaper pattern fading into the dark distance, and I can just about make out one perfectly square window at the far end. Darkness has begun to fall outside, and there's a very faint pattern of tree branches casting their dancing shadow against the window's glass. Other than that, however, the scene is entirely quiet and still.

I can hear something, though.

A kind of scratching, rustling noise.

My first instinct is to call Katie and get her to come up with me, but I know I'd just end up being mocked. Better to show her that I'm not a complete mouse, I suppose.

Stepping forward, I reach down and touch the nearest radiator, finding it to be completely cold. I try to turn the valve, only to find that it's already on maximum, which I suppose means there must be something wrong with the radiator itself.

Great.

Cold and gloomy. Welcome to Wetherley House. I'm starting to understand why Daddy left the place empty all these years.

Reaching out, I press the switch on the wall, and the main light flickers to life above me. Now the landing feels less threatening, and I'm already a little relieved. In fact, the knot in my chest has begun to ease and I'm starting to think Katie will be somewhat justified when I get back downstairs and she mocks me for being so easily freaked out. I should go down right now and get it over with, but instead I linger on the landing for a moment longer, looking at the various closed doors and still hearing a very faint scratching sound that's so low, it almost isn't there at all.

But it is there.

I think.

I mean, I'm sure.

I think I am.

Whatever it is, though, it's quieter than the sound of my own breath.

Making my way over to the nearest door, I immediately realize that this is not the source of the noise. I head to the next door, but the sound seems not to be coming from there either. Checking more doors one by one, I have no better luck, until finally I reach the door at the farthest end of the landing. Turning slightly, I place my ear almost against the wood, and now I can tell with absolute certainty that something is indeed scratching on the other side.

Directly on the other side, in fact.

It's as if, as I listen, fingers are just inches away inside the room, scratching on the door as if somebody is trying to get out.

I lean closer, until my ear is pressed against the wood.

The scratching sound continues, and now I can tell that it definitely sounds like several small fingers trying to dig through the wood.

"Go on, pussycat," I hear Katie's voice saying. "Run."

I *want* to turn back, but I refuse to give my sister that satisfaction.

Keeping my ear against the door, I reach down and touch the door handle, holding it for a moment before slowly starting to turn it so that I can push it open.

As soon as the handle lets out a faint click, the scratching sound stops.

A moment later, I realize I've inadvertently begun to hold my breath, so I turn the handle all the way and then slowly push the door open a crack until I can see through to the gloomy room, where an old bed stands stripped and bare. I don't dare open the door all the way, not yet, but I already feel the icy air from the other side, and I take a moment to listen to the silence and reassure myself that the scratching has stopped. I suppose we might well have termites in the house, or the pressure in the room might have been disturbed in some way I don't really understand, or -

Suddenly the handle is snatched from my grasp

and the door swings open with such force that it lets out a loud bump as it hits the wall. Startled, I stare straight ahead into the room, but I see nothing and no-one ahead of me.

Just the room.

The room with the bay windows.

This must be the master bedroom. Or at least it was, back when the house was in use. Stepping into the room, I pick up an old, dirty glass from the nightstand and hold it to the light so that I can see the smudged fingerprints and lip marks. Whoever used this glass and left it behind, they must have lived here eight decades ago, and it's hard to believe that any traces could still remain. Making my cautiously across the room, I can't help looking more closely at the glass, squinting as I try to make out the smudged marks. One of them is definitely a fingerprint, or part of a fingerprint, and I suppose -

Suddenly, I see a pair of eyes staring at me from the other side of the glass.

Startled, I take a step back and lower the glass, but now I see only the gloomy room and the open doorway that leads onto the lit landing. I look around, finding myself quite alone, but I know that I saw two eyes a moment ago, and I know they were real because I saw them blink. They were old eyes, and I think they belonged to a woman.

I hold the glass up again, but this time I see nothing untoward and a moment later I lower the glass and place it back on the bedside table. Heading over to the window, I open the curtains and look out at the lawn. I don't really want to turn my back on the room, but I tell myself that I need to prove to myself that there's nothing here. Besides, the view from up here is quite beautiful, and I definitely want to go and take a long walk in the garden tomorrow, and maybe explore the forest at the far end. As I watch the evening light catching the tops of the trees, I tell myself that this house isn't really so bad, and finally I turn and look back across the room.

Of course there's no sign of anyone.

Swallowing hard, I tell myself that once again I'm letting my fears get the better of me.

I'm not an idiot and, despite what Katie might say from time to time, I'm not some timid little mouse either. In fact, I'm sick of being painted as the weak one in the family, and I'm starting to realize that it's time for me to show some strength of character. Heading back across the room, I step out onto the landing and reach back to pull the door shut, before deciding at the last moment that perhaps it should be left open slightly. After all, a house needs its air to circulate, doesn't it? Otherwise even the dust remains still. Pulling the door half shut, I step back and look through the crack, seeing the empty bed again. There's nothing in there and I don't need to be scared, and I'm not going to let this house get to me.

Taking a deep breath, I head along the landing, pushing each of the doors open along the way. When I get to the top of the stairs I reach out to switch the light off, before deciding to leave it on instead.

"That was a whole lot of nothing," I call out to Katie as I head down to find her. "I've left the door to the rooms open, just to air them out a little. We need to get someone to look at the radiators tomorrow, 'cause they don't seem to be doing anything at all."

Reaching the door to the front room, I smile as I see that she's sitting in an armchair by the fireplace, but then my smile fades as I realize that she's staring this way with a horrified, shocked expression.

"What?" I ask.

When she doesn't answer, I look over my shoulder, but all I see is the slightly gloomy hallway and the front door.

"It's late," I continue, turning back to her and making my way over. "I think I'm going to turn in for the night and get up early in the morning. I want to explore, and I want to get this place feeling a little more..."

My voice trails off as I realize that she barely seems to have noticed my return at all. Instead, she's sitting stock still in the chair and still staring at the doorway, as if something in the hall has really caught her attention. I turn and look again, trying to figure out whatever might be wrong, and then I look back down at my sister with a puzzled expression.

"I guess you're staying up, then?" I ask, before turning to head into the kitchen. "I'll just -"

Suddenly she grabs my wrist, holding me tight, but she's still staring at the open doorway.

"We're not alone," she whispers, her voice

trembling with fear and her eyes wide with shock. "There's another woman in the house."

HANNAH

"YOU'LL THINK IT'S STUPID," I mutter, holding the phone with one hand while I sift through decades-old papers with the other. Morning light is streaming through the kitchen window, and so far Daddy's paperwork is turning out to be quite a mess. I brought it all with me so I could get it done, but now I'm starting to think I'll need to hire a professional. "It's just... Katie started acting very strangely last night. She said she saw a woman in the hallway while I was upstairs."

"A what?" Johnny replies over the phone.

"I went upstairs to check a noise," I continue, holding up a sheet but finding that it's not the tax form I need, "and there was nothing up there, but when I came back down Katie looked as if she'd had the fear of God put in her. And when I finally got her talking, she said that just after I'd gone up, some woman had walked right past the doorway and had looked in at her for a moment before continuing through to the back of the house."

"Like a burglar?"

"No, not like a burglar. Like a..."

My voice trails off as I realize that I don't really want to say the word. Maybe I shouldn't have mentioned any of this to my brother at all.

"Are you sure you haven't got this the wrong way round?" he asks. "Shouldn't you be the one getting all spooked out, and shouldn't Katie be the one phoning me up to complain?"

"I'm not that easily scared," I reply, "and I'm not complaining either. I don't know, it's just..."

Again, my voice trails off, and this time I can't help thinking back to the eyes I saw staring at me from the other side of the dirty glass in the master bedroom. I've been carefully avoiding thinking about that, and about the scratching sound, and I quickly tell myself that they were both nothing. After all, I *can* be easily spooked. I'm just going to be strong from now on, and not let my mind run away with me.

A moment later, however, I hear a faint bumping sound from upstairs, and I have to admit that I feel a flicker of concern as I look toward the ceiling, only to quickly realize that it's simply Katie getting out of bed.

"So when are you coming?" I continue, forcing myself to focus on other things as I look back at the paperwork. "We need to tidy the place up a little and then get an estate agent to -"

"We're not coming."

I hesitate, feeling a flicker of annoyance.

"I thought we were all going to meet here," I remind him.

"Louisa and I have busy lives," he replies, and I can hear the tension in his voice. "We can't drop everything and come down to poke around in some dusty old house. We actually have things to be doing."

"And you're saying Katie and I don't have -"

"You know what I mean," he adds snappily. "You can spare the time and we can't. It's as simple as that. I'm not going to let Dad's death interfere with what I've got going on. I already had to take a morning off for the funeral last week -"

"Yeah, a whole morning," I mutter, rolling my eyes.

"- and Louisa's hardly in any state to travel given that she's in her thirty-fourth week, so it's already a really bad time."

"Sorry," I mutter. "If you want, I can ask Daddy to come back to life for a while and then die when it's more convenient for you."

"Don't get pissy with me."

"There's a lot of paperwork we need to get done," I continue, trying to change the topic. "I brought it to the house, I thought this would be a good chance for us to all look through it together."

I wait for an answer.

"You said you were coming, Johnny."

"I said we'd *try* to come."

"No, you said -"

"Don't put words in my mouth. I said we'd try!"

"No, you said -"

Sighing, I realize there's no point getting into an argument. I know full well that Johnny said he'd come and meet us here, but I also know that my brother never, ever admits when he's wrong.

"We could really use you here," I point out, this time not managing to hide the irritation in my voice. "Katie and I have done everything so far. You keep saying you'll help out, but nothing ever actually happens. The three of us are in this together."

"Just dust the place and get it on the market."

"You don't even want to see it first?"

"A rickety old house?" I swear, I hear him chuckle. "No thanks. It might be good for a laugh, but I'm not going to let any of this interfere with what I've got going on."

"And what exactly have you got going on? Being an ass?" I almost say.

Almost.

But somehow, I manage to hold my tongue.

"Dad didn't leave a will," I tell him with a sigh, "and from looking at the papers so far, it seems like his financial affairs are pretty complicated."

"We'll just sell the flat and the house, divide the money in three, and call it a day."

"Sell the -"

Pausing for a moment, I want to ask him if he's serious, but I already know the answer to that question. Johnny has no interest at all in our family's history.

"This house has been in our family for generations," I point out.

"So?"

"So we can't just sell it."

"Yes we can."

"But -"

"Okay, then," he continues, "buy me out. You and Katie, or just you, whatever, I don't care. Buy me out of my share with all that money you've got. Oh wait, you don't have two pennies to rub together, do you? So really, you can't afford to sit on a house that's worth half a million pounds and start pontificating about what other people should want. Maybe in some fantasy world it'd be nice if you could hold onto the house, but you can't, so let's not even get into this argument. Case closed, yeah?"

I open my mouth to tell him to go to hell, and that there's no way this place is worth half a million in its current state, but then I hear Katie coming down the stairs and I look over toward the door that leads into the hall.

"Katie?" I call out. "I think we need to talk about something!"

I wait, but she doesn't reply. A moment later I hear a clicking sound, followed by a bump as if she just unlocked the basement door.

"Katie?" I call out again. "What are you doing?"

"I'm too busy for this," Johnny says. "Don't go fussing around. Put the place on the market and get out of there, you don't need to turn it into a big job. And stop trying to make me feel bad for not coming down there.

There's a limit to my availability. I have a life, remember."

I can hear Katie down in the basement now, and after a moment I get to my feet and head across the room. Sure enough, when I reach the doorway I see that the door to the basement has been left open, although I can't imagine what Katie's doing down there with any lights on. I can definitely hear her, though, bumping about beneath my feet as if she's getting on with something.

"I want you to arrange for the house to be properly valued," Johnny says.

"I'll call you back."

"I also -"

Cutting the call, I set my phone down on the hallway table before heading to the basement door and looking down the steps into the darkness below.

"Katie?" I call out. "What are you doing?"

No reply.

All I hear is more bangs and bumps.

"The light doesn't even work down there," I point out, reaching out and pulling the string that's dangling next to me. When the light fails to come on, I pull the string again, just to be sure. "I don't think it's safe to be pottering about," I continue, "so can you come back up here? Or at least use a torch. What are you after, anyway?"

The bumps continue for a few seconds, followed by the sound of shuffling footsteps, and then finally I can just about make out a figure in the darkness at the bottom of the steps, staring up at me. I can't see Katie's face in the gloom, but at least she seems to have finally heard me.

"What are you doing?" I ask. "I just talked to Johnny and he's not being reasonable at all. I was thinking maybe you could talk to him instead."

I wait, but the figure is simply staring at me from the darkness. All I can really make out are her bare legs at the bottom of the steps, and the rest of her is shrouded in shadow. In fact, the more I look at her, the more I realize that she seems to be naked, and I can't imagine why my sister would be up and about like this.

"Katie," I continue cautiously, "can you call Johnny later and -"

Suddenly I hear a banging sound over my shoulder. Startled, I turn and see that the front door is opening, and a moment later Katie steps into view carrying half a dozen large bags of shopping that look set to fall from her arms at any moment.

"Little help?" she calls out, pushing the door shut with her butt.

I stare at her for a moment, my mind racing as I try to figure out what's happening, and then I look back down the steps and see that there's no longer anyone standing at the bottom. My heart is pounding, however, and when I turn back to Katie I see that she's already taking her shopping through to the kitchen.

"No help?" she gasps. "I got up early and went into town. Although I forgot oranges, so maybe you can pop back in later. Now are you just going to stand there, or are you going to help me with these bags?"

***

"THERE'S NO-ONE HERE," KATIE says as we stand at the bottom of the steps. She's holding her phone up as a flashlight, and I've got a kitchen knife in each hand for protection. "There's no other way in or out, either."

"I saw someone!" I say firmly, still watching the shadows carefully, waiting for something to come at us. "We have to call the police!"

"And say what? That we're being haunted?"

"Someone came down here! I thought you were in the house! I heard someone in your room, then I heard them coming down the stairs, and then I *saw* someone standing right here! She was naked! I didn't see her face, so I assumed it was you."

"Thanks."

"You know what I mean!"

"Hannah..."

"You saw someone too!" I continue. "Last night! You told me!"

She sighs.

"You were terrified!"

"I was exhausted! I was out of my goddamn mind thanks to not sleeping for two nights in a row, and driving all the way here!" She sighs again. "And that's exactly what's happening with you, except that you're too far gone to even realize it. I picked up some sleeping pills in town, and you're taking a couple and going straight to bed."

"I can't sleep!" I tell her. "We have to go to the police and -"

"There's no-one here!" she says firmly, before tapping the side of my head. Then she turns and walks across to the far side of the basement, using the phone's light to prove that we're alone. "There's only someone in your mind," she continues, before tapping her own head, "and in mine. We're two sleep-deprived women in a creepy old house. I mean, when we arrived last night, it was like the beginning of a horror movie. Do you realize how weird it'd be if we *didn't* go a little la-la? Come on, Hannah, don't make this any harder than it has to be. We need to work together instead of constantly arguing."

She comes back over and steps behind me, heading toward the stairs.

"But I saw -"

Before I can finish, she clamps a hand over my mouth.

"Don't say that," she continues. "Okay? When you say things like that, you make it harder for both of us. I'm the first to admit that I *thought* I saw something last night, but I'm also the first to recognize that I'm not thinking straight. You need to be the same. Now, promise me that you're going to stop yammering on about impossible things that you think you've seen and heard."

She waits for me to say something, but I simply stare at her.

"Promise me," she adds, "or by God, I will go

back into town and buy a goddamn gag to tie around your mouth."

She pauses, before moving her hand away from my mouth.

"I'd love it if this house was haunted," she continues. "That'd be great, because it'd mean that the little bumps and things in the corner of our eyes are something real. Frankly it might also make the house sell for a higher price. But there's really nothing. Come on, Hannah, we're both clinging to our sanity for dear life here. Let's help each other, instead of making things worse. Even if you think you see something, just keep telling yourself that it's all in your mind."

I open my mouth to reply, to tell her that I *did* see something, but finally I manage to hold back. Katie's a couple of years older than me, and she's always been the sensible one.

"That's better," she continues, before stepping past me and starting to make her way up the creaking wooden steps. "Now I suppose I should go and call our asshole brother and hear what whiny problems he's got today. I assume he's flat-out refusing to help in any way?"

Left alone at the bottom of the steps, I stare across the dark, bare basement and wait just in case there's any hint of movement. I keep telling myself that Katie is right, and I know that I'm exhausted, but at the same time I can't help replaying the events of the past twenty-four hours over and over in my mind, and I think that maybe -

"Oh no," Katie says suddenly, grabbing my hand and forcing me to follow her up the steps. "If you think I'm leaving you down here alone, you're straight out of luck."

HANNAH

"I'LL TAKE THE SALMON and cream cheese baguette, please," I tell the barman, as I set the menu down. "And a steak baguette for my sister. I'll be taking them home with me."

"They'll be ready in about five minutes."

"That's great. Thanks."

I smile as he heads through to the kitchen, leaving me alone at the bar. After a moment, however, I can't help looking at the large mural on the far wall, depicting a pretty terrifying-looking woman who appears to be strangling a man. The painting's kind of crude, but there's a house visible in the distance behind the woman, and it doesn't take a genius to recognize Wetherley House. Up near the ceiling, the name Mary Carmichael has been painted in big, blocky letters.

"That's her, you know," a voice says suddenly.

Turning, I see that the man sitting at a corner booth is watching me as he sips from his pint.

"I'm sorry?"

"That's her." He nods toward the mural. "And I know who you are, too. You're one of them that's gone up and opened the front door at Wetherley, aren't you?"

"My father owned the house," I reply cautiously, "and -"

"I know, I know." He takes another sip and then sets his glass down. "There are a lot of people around here who'd rather you hadn't done that."

"We're just airing the place out a little," I tell him, feeling distinctly uncomfortable and hoping that the baguettes will be ready soon, so I can leave. "We're going to put it on the market soon."

"Is that right?"

"My father died recently."

"I heard. We all heard. News travels fast around here."

Not really knowing what else to say, I look back at the mural. The woman looks totally bizarre and freakish, with wild, yellowish eyes. Her long black hair runs all the way down the front of her body, protecting her modesty, and there are flecks of blood on her hands. Frankly, she looks like a monster.

"You seen her yet?"

I turn back to the man. "Sorry?"

"Her." He nods toward the mural again. "Has she shown her face since you got to the house?"

"No," I reply, "of course not. She..."

My voice trails off for a moment.

"If you mean Mary Carmichael," I continue finally, "then no, she's dead. I had no idea people around here talked about her so much."

"What do you think it's like for us," he replies, "living in a town where we know there's something like *that* on our doorstep." He looks past me, toward the mural. "There's two types of people here. The first is the type that keeps well away from Wetherley House. Some won't even drive past the place, they don't even want to look at it or even hear it mentioned. Then there's the other type, the type that's willing to at least glance at the windows as they go along the road that runs into town from the east. You'd be surprised how many of those folk reckon they've seen a figure in one of the windows."

"I know about the ghost stories," I tell him.

"Oh? So you've been here almost a day, and you're already an expert, are you?"

"I didn't mean that," I continue, "I just... I know that people talk about Wetherley House. I know there are things that are supposed to have happened there and -"

"Supposed?"

"I mean -"

"It's all documented," he adds, interrupting me. "Eve Carmichael, and what she did to her daughter. How she turned Mary into a monster, and how Mary stayed in the house even after she died. When I was young, I even knew an old guy who'd been one of the coppers who went out there. He'd seen Mary's body with his own two eyes, and he said he'd never witnessed anything so awful. They found human remains in the basement, too. A woman and her son, relatives of the family. They'd been slaughtered, and most of the meat had been gnawed from their bones."

"I really don't think that -"

"I'll prove it to you."

Getting to his feet, he comes over and then steps past me, heading behind the bar.

"Just grabbing the book, Norman!" he calls out, and the barman yells something back from the kitchen. Turning to me, the man sets a cloth-bound book on the bar and opens it to the first page. "They took photos back in those days," he continues, turning to the next page, revealing an old black-and-white image of the house's hallway, with blood smeared on the wall next to the basement door. "Seen these before, have you?"

"No," I reply, "and I'm not sure I -"

Suddenly he turns to the next page, and I'm shocked to see a picture of the brightly-lit basement. There are dark patches all over the floor, and after a moment I realize that there's what looks like part of a human spine resting in one of the corners.

"There aren't real," I say firmly. "They can't be real."

"No?"

He turns to the next page, revealing a close-up photo of a shattered skull.

"These are the only copies known to exist," he explains. "Don't want them getting out for the public to gawp at, do we? We just keep 'em here and show 'em to anyone who doubts the stories about Wetherley House."

He turns the page again, and I let out a gasp as I see several pictures of a naked, bloodied body in the house's hallway. A thick mop of tangled black hair covers the girl's face.

"That's Mary, after she died," the man continues. "The monster herself."

"I'm sure she wasn't a monster," I reply, swallowing hard.

"No?"

He turns to the next page, and this time the body has been rolled over and the hair has been moved from across her features, revealing a horrifically gaunt face with large, wide-open dead eyes. The girl's mouth is open too, as if she died screaming. After a moment, I look at the mural and see that it's clear the painting was based on this photo.

"She was kept in that basement for several years before she died," the man explains. "By all accounts, she was a normal girl before that, but she certainly wasn't normal by the end. I mean, look at her. Even dead, you can tell there's madness in those eyes."

"I don't think you should be showing these pictures to anyone," I tell him.

"Oh, calm your britches," he says with a sigh. "They're used as a warning."

"But -"

"And then there's this last thing you need to see."

He turns to the final page, where there are two

photos.

"That's Eve Carmichael herself," he says, pointing at the picture of an austere-looking woman in a plain dress. "They took that after she was arrested. She was sent to the gallows not long after." He moves his finger across the page, toward an older photo showing a smiling, pregnant woman sitting on a chair with a man next to her. "And that is believed to be the only surviving image of Mary's mother, a French woman by the name of Marguerite. The fella next to her is her husband Robert. He died shortly after this picture was taken."

Staring at the photo, I can't help but note the happiness in the woman's eyes. She has one hand resting on her swollen belly, and the picture seems so hopeful and full of life.

"Do you see it?" the man asks.

"See what?"

"Look closer."

I turn to him. "I'd really rather -"

"Look closer!"

Sighing, I look back at the picture for a moment. Just as I'm about to tell the man that there's nothing untoward, however, I realize that as well as Marguerite and Robert, there appears to be a third face in the photo. Peering closer, I try telling myself that this extra face is just a smudge on the wall behind them, but deep down I can tell that this isn't the case. The face is faint and slightly blurred, but there's definitely someone standing with them in the room. Except that while Marguerite and

Robert are staring at the camera, the third face is looking down at the pregnant belly.

"See that blur?" the man behind the bar asks, pointing at a smudge in the air, covering part of the belly. "I reckon that's a hand."

"This is just a trick photo."

"From 1888?" He shakes his head. "We've had it analyzed. There's no trickery here."

"You want me to believe that you've found a ghost in the picture?" I ask, before realizing that his story is starting to fall apart. "That doesn't even make sense," I point out. "If the unborn baby is Mary, then who's the smudged ghostly figure supposed to be, anyway?"

"Well, that's the part we haven't figured out just yet."

Before I can reply, I hear a door swinging open, and to my relief I turn and see that barman coming through with the baguettes in a brown bag.

"Thanks for the ghost story," I mutter, taking the bag and turning to leave, "but I have to get back to the house now."

"We've been guarding that house for eighty years."

I turn and see that both men are watching me now.

"I'm sorry?" I ask.

"After the first stories started doing the rounds," the first man explains, "people started going out there. Thrill-seekers, people who wanted to see a ghost for themselves. So a few men in the town formed a kind of neighborhood watch organization to make sure the house was never deserved. Every single night for more than seventy years, there have been men out there at the edge of the property, guarding Wetherley House and making sure that no-one sneaks in. I myself joined the group back in the 1980's, and you can ask any of us who've been out there, we've all heard noises coming from inside." He pauses. "If you like, we can stay out there and -"

"No," I reply, shocked by the idea. "Wetherley House belongs to my family, and we don't need some random group of locals hanging around outside to keep people from going inside."

"You want us to stand down, then?"

"I want you to let us get on with sorting the house out in private," I tell him, feeling a little frustrated now. "My sister and I definitely *don't* want gangs of men hanging around outside. If we see anyone, we'll call the police!"

"But if -"

Without waiting for him to finish, I head out into the midday sun and then hurry along the street. Before I've managed more than a couple of steps, however, I notice that a woman seems to be watching me from a nearby doorway. I swear, sometimes I think this entire town is obsessed with Wetherley House.

Nearby, some children are playing a game. At first they seem like a welcome relief from the morbid atmosphere, but as I pass them I realize their song concerns a familiar subject.

"Evil Mary's gonna get you!" they call out, as one of them skips repeatedly over a rope. "She's gonna eat your throat!"

HANNAH

"I GOT THE ORANGES!" I call out as I step through the front door. "You won't believe some of the things people were saying to me, though. This man in the pub went on and on about the house. I brought something for lunch, though."

After setting the oranges in a bowl next to the door, I slip my shoes off and set the bag of baguettes down before stopping to hang my coat up. As I do so, however, I realize I can hear a voice coming from the kitchen, and I realize with a dull sigh that maybe another local has arrived to offer some wisdom. I appreciate all the words, but at the same time I was hoping for a break after my encounters in town. Besides, I'm surprised that anyone actually knocked at the door of Wetherley House; most people give the place a wide berth.

Making my way across the hall, I stop near the door and listen to Katie's voice.

"I don't think she would," she's saying, with a

slightly flat tone. "She's not like that."

I wait, but now the house is silent again.

"I'm not saying I can't try," she says suddenly. "I'm just saying I don't think I can count on her."

Wondering why my sister's visitor seems so quiet, I take a step closer to the door and see that Katie is actually sitting quite alone at the kitchen table. She's slumped slightly in the chair, which is unusual enough, but the strangest thing is that she's staring at the opposite chair as if she's hearing someone speak. I watch for a moment, convinced that Katie will – as usual – hear me and turn to make some dumb joke, but instead she simply continues to stare at the other chair as if something has caught her rapt and undivided attention. She certainly seems not to have noticed my arrival.

"Well," she continues finally, "I can try tonight."

And then silence once more.

"What should I do?" she asks after a few more seconds.

She waits, and then she nods.

"And if she won't go? She might not. She might insist on staying."

A pause, and then she nods again.

"Of course. It's not ideal, but -"

Suddenly she turns and looks straight at me, and for a moment her gaze is strong and angry before her features soften slightly and she sits up straight on the chair.

"What are you doing?" I ask, stepping into the kitchen.

"What are..." She pauses again. "What are *you* doing?"

"I just came back from town. I picked up the oranges, like you asked, and I got some baguettes from the pub." I glance around the kitchen, still convinced that there has to have been some kind of mistake. "Were you talking to someone?"

"No."

I turn back to her.

"Were you on the phone?"

She shakes her head.

"I didn't hear you come in," she tells me, with a faint smile. "What are you up to, sneaking about like that? You're so much like a mouse, Hannah. You should grow whiskers."

"I'm not a -"

I catch myself just in time.

"So have you got one of those in-ear phone things?" I ask.

She furrows her brow.

Stepping over, I look into one ear and then the other, figuring that she was on the phone with one of the hands-free devices I've seen other people use. Spotting no sign of anything, however, I look around the kitchen again before turning to see that Katie is staring at me with a new kind of intensity, almost as if she's studying my face with great scrutiny.

"I heard you talking to someone," I tell her.

"You're mistaken."

"Is this some kind of joke?" I can't help sighing as I head to the sink and pour myself a glass of water.

"I'm not up for jokes right now, Katie. I felt like everyone in town knew that I'm staying here at the house. There was this man in the pub who just came up to me and started talking about the place. He showed me a whole load of photos, and some of them were horrible. I'm pretty sure they must have been fake, though. I mean, they can't just keep them there at the pub and get them out to scare people." I pause for a moment. "At least there'll be no more strangers in the road outside the house. I found out what that was all about and I put a stop to it."

Setting the glass down, I turn and see that Katie's still staring at me.

"You're being weird," I point out.

"Am I?"

"You know you are. Stop trying to freak me out."

She hesitates, before looking back over at the empty chair. I swear, for a moment it feels as if she's hearing someone speak. Finally, however, she turns back to me.

"Why don't you go to your room?" she asks.

"Sorry?"

"You look tired. You look like you need some sleep."

"I *do* need some sleep."

"I have pills that'll help."

"I'm not a big fan of pills."

"But they'd be good for you."

She pauses, before getting to her feet and heading over to the counter, where she grabs a bottle of pills and turns to hold them out toward me.

"You'll sleep really well with these," she continues.

"I think I might just take a walk," I reply, ignoring the bottle as I head to the back door. "Tire myself out the natural way, you know?"

Struggling for a moment to get the key to turn, I finally manage to open the back door. A bit of a breeze has picked up in just the few minutes since I got home, and the tops of the trees are swaying at the far end of the lawn, but some bracing weather isn't going to put me off. My mind is racing and I feel like I need to get out of myself a little.

"I won't be too long," I continue, turning to see that Katie is still standing next to the counter, still holding the pill bottle out as if she expects me to change my mind and take a few. In fact, she seems almost stalled, as if she can't believe that I've turned her down. "The baguettes are in the hallway," I tell her. "Don't worry about waiting for me. I think I just need a few minutes to get my head straight before I do any more of that paperwork."

I wait for a reply.

"Okay," she says finally, although she sounds very uncertain.

"And whatever you're up to," I add, "can you cut it out when I get back? I'm not in the mood for games, Katie. And tonight, I really need to go over some of the papers with you. So can you please try to be acting normal by the time I come back inside?"

I wait for her to answer, but she simply stares at

me. Finally, giving up for now, I turn and head outside.

***

BEYOND THE HOUSE, BEYOND the lawn, beyond the first line of trees, the forest is so beautiful. The ground is uneven, though, so I reach out to steady myself against the trees as I pass, and I can't help noticing that their bark is cold and damp to the touch. Ankle-high grass looks as if it's swallowing my feet and the treetops are rustling high above me, almost as if they're welcoming me to the old family house.

And asking, maybe, why I never came here before.

The truth is that Daddy never let any of us come. We heard whispers about Wetherley House, and we had an inkling that it was a key part of our family's history, but Daddy never spoke to us about it directly. So we had to piece things together. Katie heard a fragment and Johnny heard a fragment, and I heard a few things, and from there we figured out that there was this house in our family that nobody wanted to visit anymore, where something very bad happened long ago.

I always knew I'd get to visit one day.

I just wish it could have happened while Daddy was alive.

When I reach a little stream that meanders through the house's grounds, I crouch down and try to see my reflection in the water. I don't really have much luck, but after a moment I take a stick from the ground and use it to move a few pebbles. This entire scene feels idyllic, and I'm really starting to wonder whether there's any way we could keep the house in the family. Maybe if I could persuade Katie, we could pool our resources and -

Suddenly hearing footsteps behind me, I turn and look the way I just came. Katie must have come out here after me, but there's no sign of her. I wait, convinced that she'll suddenly appear from behind one of the trees, but then I tell myself that I must be mistaken.

I look back down at the water, and immediately I hear several more steps hurrying this way.

Getting to my feet, I look all around, but all I see are the trees and – far off in the distance – the lawn and the house. Still, I know that I heard steps, even if I can't spot anyone right now.

"Hello?" I call out. "Katie, is that you?"

I wait, but now the wind is a little more chilly.

"If that's you, Katie," I continue, "you're in a really funny mood today, aren't you? Is there no -"

Before I can finish, I spot a hint of movement in the distance, and I realize I can just about make out Katie in the house's front room. Squinting, I'm able to tell that it's definitely her, which at least means that she's shaken herself out of that daze that kept her talking to herself in the kitchen. Making a mental note to keep an eye on her so that I can be sure she's coping okay with Daddy's death, I watch as she walks past one of the windows and disappears from view, and then I spy her through the hallway window. A moment later, to my surprise, I see that she's unbolting the door to the basement and going down the stairs.

What the hell is she doing in there?

I take a step forward, figuring I should go and find out, but suddenly something slams into my right hip with such force that I spin and thud down against the mulchy ground. Letting out a startled, pained gasp, I feel the fabric of a coarse skirt brushing against my face, and then I turn just in time to see a little girl running away between the trees, quickly disappearing deeper into the forest.

"Hey!" I yell. "What was that for?"

Hauling myself up, I dust some dirt and grass from my shirt.

"Hey!" I call out again, even though I can no longer see the girl. "I'm sorry, but this is private land! You can't play here!"

I wait, but now there's no sign of the girl at all, and the only sound comes from the rustling canopy high above. Still, there's no doubt that she was here a moment ago, and the fabric of her skirt was harsh and bristly, leaving a very faint itching sensation on my cheek.

Picking my way between the trees, I set off after the girl, although I don't really have much hope of finding her. I can already see the fence up ahead, marking the end of Wetherley House's land, and I imagine the girl has climbed the fence already and run off into the vast forest that stretches past the edge of town. Almost slipping a couple of times, I finally reach the fence and lean against one of its rickety posts, which immediately leans alarmingly. Steadying myself again, I look out at the forest and wait for a moment, just in case the girl shows herself, and then I turn to head back.

Startled, I find that three little girls are standing just a few feet away, on either side of a tree, watching me. They're wearing identical pink dresses, and they're each staring at me with the same calm expression.

"Hey," I say as I step back, bumping once more against the fence. "Do you realize this is a private garden?"

The girls glance at one another, before turning back to me and nodding in unison.

"This fence marks the garden," I continue, tapping the top of the nearest post. "It's fine to play out there in the forest on the other side, but in here it's kind of off-limits, if you know what I mean. Sorry, I just don't even know if it's safe to be here."

"We just wanted to look at the house," the girl on the left says, causing the other girls to giggle.

"I'm sorry?"

"We wanted to scare ourselves," the second girl explains.

"Well, I understand that," I tell her, "but you have the whole rest of the forest to -"

"There's no-one in that part," the first girl says, interrupting me.

"There are people in this part, though," the third girl adds.

"Huh." Staring at them, I can't help feeling a little freaked out. "So you guys are triplets, right?"

They pause, before the first girl finally nods.

"That's cool," I continue, trying not to come across as some kind of dull adult killjoy. "The thing is, I really need to ask if you could stay on the other side of the fence. Sorry, I know that might be boring, but we just can't have people we don't know playing on our property. My father died the other day and we're still kind of figuring the property out. There's no -"

"Can we go to the stable?" the third girl asks.

"The what?"

"The stable? It's -"

Suddenly the second girl nudges her.

"It's not there anymore," she whispers to her sister.

"What isn't there?" I ask.

All three of them turn to me.

"The stable," they all say.

"I don't think the house has a stable," I tell them, before remembering the wooden posts near the main building, which I guess could once have been some kind of outhouse. "I don't really know what was here before."

"There was a beautiful stable," the first girl says. "We used to come close when no-one was around and look at the horses."

"So do people sneak out here a lot?" I ask, unable to shake the feeling that these girls seem very calm and composed for kids who can't be more than six or seven years old. "At night, maybe?"

"At night?" The first girl's eyes open wider than ever, as if I've said the most shocking thing. "Why would anyone come out here at night?"

"We're not idiots," the second girl points out.

"The men aren't watching the house anymore," the third girl adds. "They've gone away. The ones who were guarding it."

"So they let you three come here?" I ask cautiously.

Two of the girls shake their heads, while the third simply continues to stare at me.

"Okay," I say, forcing a smile as I realize that they've got their own little game going on here, and that it's one I'm never going to understand. "I'm going to have to ask you to play on the other side of the fence. I'm sure you think I'm being really boring, but my sister and I don't even know if it's safe here. We wouldn't want one of your falling and hurting yourself. Do your parents even know that you're here?"

The girls stare at me for a moment, before suddenly stepping forward and walking either side of me. Turning, I feel a flash of relief as they start climbing over the fence.

"I'm sorry," I continue. "Please don't think I'm being mean."

"We don't."

Once they're over the other side, they turn and look back at me.

"How can you live in that house?" the first girl asks. "Aren't you scared?"

"There's nothing to be scared *of*," I reply, figuring that they must have been spooked by the same ghost stories that I've been told. "It's just a house, and the only people there are my sister and I. If you want to come and knock on the front door some day, we might be able to find a few biscuits and some glasses of milk. But please, don't play out here all alone, okay?"

I wait for one of them to speak, but now they're

just staring at me again.

"We should go now," the second girl says suddenly, turning to one of her sisters. "I don't like it here."

"I don't like it either," the first girl replies.

"I can feel her now," the third girl adds. "Can't you? She's much stronger than before."

"Who is?" I ask. "What are you talking about?"

"I think my sister might be right," the first girl says matter-of-factly. "Anyway, we don't want to upset you. Being at Wetherley House is your decision."

"We're sorry we disturbed you," the second girl adds. "We'll try not to do it again."

With that, all three of them turn and start tramping away through the forest.

"Feel free to knock on the door!" I call out, stepping over to the fence and resting my hands on one of the wooden boards. I don't want to be a complete grinch. "Just stay out of the forest, okay?"

Two of the girls keep walking, but the first stops and turns to me with a faint smile.

"We don't want to interfere," she says calmly. "We just wanted to watch."

"Watch what?"

She shrugs.

"Well," I continue, figuring that they're just messing with me, "I'm sorry you didn't get to see anything."

"We didn't say we didn't see anything," she replies. "We could see her inside your house. She was sitting at the kitchen table with that other woman. You were in the room too. Didn't *you* see her?"

I open my mouth to reply, but I've got to admit the kid has done a pretty good job of freaking me out. Before I can say anything, she turns and hurries after her sisters, and I'm left standing alone at the fence as a cold wind blows against my back and the treetops rustle high above. In fact, the bad weather seems to be picking up a little, and I'm starting to think that maybe I've been out here long enough.

Once the three freaky girls have disappeared into the distance, I turn and head back to the house.

HANNAH

"OH THEY KNEW EXACTLY what they were doing," I say with a smile as I wrap some more spaghetti around my fork. "Those three girls were trying to freak me out on purpose. They did a pretty good job, too."

Eating a mouthful of bolognese, I glance over at the other end of the dining table and see that Katie has barely touched her dinner. Night has fallen outside and I can see my own reflection in the window over her shoulder.

"They can't have been more than eight," I continue, "but these days kids hear all sorts of things, don't they? They probably know all about Wetherley House, and they thought they could scare me. There was something really weird about them. I invited them to come knock on the door some time, but I really hope they don't."

Again I wait for a reply, and again Katie seems almost to be in a trance, staring down at the tablecloth as if she's in another world.

"So what were you doing in the basement?" I ask, deciding to try another tack.

"I wasn't in the basement," she replies suddenly, looking straight at me.

"Earlier. While I was out in the forest. I saw you go down there."

She shakes her head.

"I did," I continue, unable to stifle a faint smile. "I saw you open the door and go down the steps, Katie. What's so fascinating down there?"

"I didn't go to the basement," she replies.

"Katie, I saw -"

"I didn't go to the basement," she says again, and this time there's a hint of defiance in her voice, as if she wants me to shut up. "Are those men gone now?"

"Men?" I pause, before realizing she means the impromptu neighborhood watch team that has apparently been keeping intruders out of Wetherley House for decades. "I think so. They said they'd stop if we wanted them to, and I didn't leave much doubt there."

"Good," she says firmly.

"I didn't know you felt so strongly," I mutter, looking down at my food. I can somehow tell that she's still watching me, and sure enough I look up after a moment and meet her gaze. "Fine, don't tell me about the basement," I continue. "I mean, even if you wanted to go down there, it wouldn't actually matter, would it? If you enjoy spending time in a dark, empty room, then I guess you should knock yourself out."

I wait for her to reply, to maybe throw some

witty or snippy comeback at me, but she simply looks down at her food as if she's lost in her thoughts. I want to say something, to ask if she wants to talk about Daddy, and I'm starting to think that maybe Katie's struggling more than I'd realized. I know I should probably just leave her alone and let her tell me if she wants to talk, but after a few seconds I realize that I can't possibly leave my sister in such an awful state.

Getting to my feet, I head around the table and reach down to give her a hug.

"I'm going to bed," she says suddenly, slipping out of the chair and hurrying to the door, leaving her plate almost completely full.

"Katie -"

"You should go to bed too," she adds, not even looking back at me as she heads out into the hallway. A moment later I hear her walking up the stairs, and finally her bedroom door swings shut.

Left standing alone in the dining room, I can't help struggling as I try to figure out what just happened. There's a part of me that wants to go up and knock on Katie's door, but at the same time I feel I should probably leave her alone and let her come to me when she's ready. She always talks about how she and Daddy weren't particularly close, although I know that deep down she might be using that explanation as a kind of defense mechanism. Still trying to work out how I can help her, I head through to the hallway and hesitate at the bottom of the stairs, before forcing myself to accept that she might need some space.

She knows where I am.

Turning to go back to the table, I suddenly see that the basement door has been left slightly open. I'm sure it was bolted when I came back from my walk in the forest, but when I wander over and pull the handle I find that the door creaks open all the way. I immediately feel the cold air against my face as I peer down the wooden steps into the darkness. I want to just shut the door and slide the bolt back across, but after a moment I see that the cord hanging from the light switch is much shorter than before, as if Katie has been fiddling with it. I reach out and give it a pull, and to my surprise the light comes on at the bottom of the stairs.

"Huh," I whisper, before figuring that I might as well check what else she's been doing. Making my way down the stairs, which creak and in some cases even seem to flex slightly under my weight, I finally get to the bottom and see that Katie seems to have been very busy in the far corner.

Heading over to take a closer look, I find several knives and trowels on the cracked concrete floor. I crouch down and peer at one of the rotten wooden timbers that runs vertically from the concrete and toward the main part of the house, and while most of the wood is dark brown, there's now a lighter patch where Katie seems to have been scraping through the rot as if she's been looking for something. To my surprise, I realize that there seems to be some movement deep in the wood, and when I lean even closer I see to my utter disgust that several yellowy-white maggots are wriggling in the cracks.

"Gross," I mutter, watching one particular

maggot as if makes its way across the surface of the wood.

Looking further up the wooden post, I see half a dozen more maggots, and I'm starting to realize that Wetherley House might have a much more serious problem than I'd realized. I guess Katie has been down here taking a closer look, and maybe she didn't want to worry me by telling me what she'd found. A moment later, feeling something wriggling on my right hand, I look down and see that somehow a maggot has found its way onto my flesh around one of my knuckles.

"Get off!" I hiss, flicking the maggot away before getting to my feet.

Looking up toward the ceiling, I'm shocked to see several more maggots on the wood, and sure enough another quickly falls down, landing in my hair.

"No, don't do that!" I gasp, stepping back and frantically running my fingers through my hair, trying to find the stowaway. My mind is already filled with horrific thoughts of the maggot wriggling into my ear and making itself at home, so I'm relieved when I finally feel the little critter and pull him free.

Still, as I head back to the stairs, I can't help running my fingers through my hair again and again, just in case any more maggots fell down.

"This is the most disgusting thing in the world," I stammer as I hurry back up to the door. As I get to the top, I pull the cord to switch the light off, and then I step out into the hallway, only to find that Katie is waiting for me.

Startled, I step back against the wall.

"It's disgusting down there!" I point out. "What are all those maggots doing? Do we need -"

Before I can finish, I see that there's a large black bin-liner on the floor, next to Katie's feet. The bin-liner seems to be moving slightly, accompanied by a rustling sound, and I'm shocked to see a couple of maggots near the top. Stepping closer, I peer inside and see thousands and thousands of maggots wriggling in a huge swarm. Some have managed to make their way to the edge of the bin-liner, and a couple have fallen onto the floor.

"Did you scrape all of those out of the wall?" I ask, taking a step back and turning to Katie. "What the hell is wrong with this house?"

"You should go to sleep," she replies calmly.

"Did you call someone?"

I wait for a reply, but she simply stares at me.

Checking my watch, I see that it's almost 10pm.

"It's too late tonight," I continue, trying not to panic too much, "but tomorrow morning we have to call someone to come and take a look at this. Why didn't you mention it sooner? The whole house could be infested! We might have to have the place torn down!"

Unable to stop staring at the bag of maggots for a moment, I finally turn and push the door shut before sliding the bolt across.

"And you have to get that bag out of here," I tell her, grabbing the free newspaper from the table and rolling it up, before trying to use one end to knock a few maggots escapees back into the bag. "Katie, are you listening to me? We have to nip this infestation in the bud as quickly as possible." I manage to get most of the maggots into the bag, but a couple fall onto the bare floorboards and I use the rolled-up paper to squash them. "I hate doing this," I continue, "but we can't let them get anywhere else. For all we know, they could already by in the walls all around us. I'm not squeamish, but I really don't like this!"

Realizing that Katie hasn't said anything while I've been talking, I look up and see her towering above me.

"This is serious!" I hiss. "We have to get on top of the problem!"

I wait, but she doesn't reply. She's still just staring down at me.

"It's okay," I continue, setting the paper aside and getting to my feet before brushing myself down just in case any more maggots are on me. "I'll sort it tomorrow. I'll call someone. Can you just do me one favor? Can you get rid of that disgusting bag? And make sure you dump it far away from the house."

She opens her mouth as if she's about to say something, but she still seems strangely zoned out.

"Okay, then," I say, figuring that she's in no fit state to help, "I'll get rid of the bag, shall I?."

"You should go to sleep," she tells me.

"Sure, after I've done this." Heading over to the dresser, I start searching through the drawers for a pair of gloves I can use while I take the disgusting bag of maggots outside. "I'm gonna need a long, hot bath when I'm done, though. I swear, it's gonna be a while before I don't feel like I've got maggots on me somewhere. You haven't seen any upstairs, have you?"

Reaching up, I run the fingers of my left hand through my hair again, just in case there are more maggots. Hearing a floorboard creak behind me, I figure Katie has finally snapped out of her daze and is coming over to help.

"Have you seen any gloves around here?" I ask, turning to her. "I'm sure -"

Stopping suddenly, I find that she's right behind me, and she's holding the bag of writhing maggots. Some of the maggots are already on her hand and wrists, but she doesn't seem to have noticed.

"You should go to sleep," she tells me, her voice trembling slightly.

"Katie -"

Before I can finish, she suddenly lifts the bag up and places it over my head. I let out a cry as thousands of maggots tumble across my face and through my hair, but Katie grabs my shoulders and turns me around before pulling the bag tight around my neck. I try to push her away, only to find that her grip is too tight, and a moment later she forces me down onto my knees. As more and more maggots wriggle all around my head, I realize that I'm already starting to run out of air. Filled with panic, I start desperately gasping, only to inhale hundreds of maggots that quickly fall down the back of my throat, while more are already wriggling into my nose and ears.

"Help me!" I scream, as I taste the foul, bitter maggots. I try to push Katie away, but she's holding me tighter than ever and I'm already barely able to breathe.

Reaching up, I try to rip a hole in the front of the bag, but the material is too strong. I can feel the maggots wriggling beneath the plastic, covering my face.

"It's like I told you," Katie says yet again, her voice sounding muffled outside the bag. "Mary wants you to go to sleep."

AMY CROSS

PART SIX
1996

AMY CROSS

JOHNNY

"I'M TOO BUSY FOR this," I tell Hannah as I head across the kitchen. "Don't go fussing around. Put the place on the market and get out of there, you don't need to turn it into a big job. And stop trying to make me feel bad for not coming down there. There's a limit to my availability. I have a life, remember."

I pause to pour myself a glass of water. Hannah's really getting on my nerves right now with her constant demands, and I'm sure she's going to whine on and on about how I'm not being supportive and how I'm causing problems and how I need to think of the family. All the usual bullshit. She doesn't understand the pressure I'm under now that Louisa is coming close to term. Hannah and Katie don't know what it's like to have responsibilities.

"I want you to arrange for the house to be

properly valued," I continue after a moment.

"I'll call you back."

"I also -"

Suddenly the call cuts out.

"Huh?"

I look at the phone's screen, and sure enough she hung up on me. Feeling a flicker of irritation, I try calling her back, but this time she doesn't even deign to answer. Usually it's incredibly difficult to end a conversation with Hannah, but this time she seems to have suddenly decided that something else was more important. I'm half-minded to send her a message, telling her to show me some more goddamn respect, but a moment later I hear Louisa coming through from the front room and I turn just in time to see my heavily pregnant wide waddling into the kitchen.

"Hey, you shouldn't strain yourself," I tell her. "I can fetch anything you need."

"How about a pair of new ankles?" she gasps, leaning against the counter as she runs a hand over her belly. "The only thing I need right now is to get off that sofa and actually walk around. Junior's really kicking this morning. How did the call go with Hannah? I thought she'd keep you on the line for at least another hour."

"She's being her usual self," I mutter as I start checking the mail. "Sentimental. Indecisive. Annoying. She doesn't seem to understand that Wetherley House is a bloody goldmine. I know there's history attached to the place, but it's not *our* history. It's time to let someone else take over."

"Who's that woman?"

Turning, I see that Louisa is looking out the window. Heading over to join her, I immediately see that there's a woman standing at the far end of the road, seemingly staring at our apartment.

"Beats me," I mutter. "Some local nut-job?"

"She's watching us."

"You can't tell that from here. She's just standing around. She's probably waiting for a taxi."

"No, she's looking right at us. Can't you feel it?"

Reaching up, I pull the cord that brings the blinds down.

"There," I say as I peck her on the cheek and head back to the mail. "Is that better?"

"Why would she be watching *our* apartment?" she asks, peering between the slats of the blinds. "She's still there, Johnny. You have to go out there and tell her to go away."

"It's a free world, honey," I mutter, separating the mail into one pile for bills and another for junk. "If some random woman wants to stand a few hundred meters from our apartment and stare at the world around her, I can't stop her."

"I want you to go and make her leave."

"Yeah, right."

"Johnny!"

Turning, I see that she actually seems serious about this.

"You want me to go out there into the street," I

say, unable to stifle a faint smile, "and approach some random woman? She might be a psychotic ax murderer for all I know. Or a drugged-up hobo. Forget about her, she's probably already wandered off by now."

She turns and peers back out between the blinds.

"No," she says after a moment. "She's still there."

"Then she'll leave soon."

"She's staring right at this window, Johnny."

"No she's not. Your eyesight isn't *that* good, honey."

"I can feel it. She's looking right at us."

Sighing, I glance at Louisa again. She's still looking out the window, and I can't help thinking that she's letting her hormones get the better of her. I knew stuff like this might happen during the pregnancy, but I didn't think it'd manifest in this kind of extreme paranoia.

"I'm not going out there," I tell her after a moment. "I'm not going to approach a random stranger and accuse her of watching our apartment. No way. I'm not doing it."

***

"THIS IS RIDICULOUS," I mutter as I make my way along the bright street, heading toward the corner at the far end where the woman is still standing. "Why the hell did I agree?"

Stopping for a moment and waiting for a break

in the traffic so I can cross the street, I glance over my shoulder and see that Louisa is peering out at me from the window, still watching between two slats in the blinds. I force a smile and offer a little wave, but she doesn't respond and to be honest she's starting to look just a little crazy. These pregnancy hormones really seem to be doing a number on my usually-sane-and-reasonable wife, but at least I know it'll only last a few more weeks. Once the baby pops out, she'll simmer down.

Finally I get a chance to cross, so I hurry over to the other side of the road and make my way toward the far corner. As I get closer, however, I see that there's no longer any sign of the woman, and I feel a flash of relief as I realize that maybe I'm not going to have to confront some random stranger after all. Still, I head all the way to the corner and stop in the exact spot where the woman was standing earlier, and I make a real show of looking around in case there's any sign of her. Hopefully this should persuade Louisa that I've done my best. Turning to look back at the apartment building, I squint as I try to spot my wife in the window, but my eyesight isn't good enough.

"So that was a complete waste of time," I mutter, as I start heading back toward the building. "Not an overreaction at all. I should *always* go running around in the street, chasing after fu-"

Suddenly a brief scream rings out nearby, and I immediately look toward the apartment. When the scream returns a moment later, I realize I recognize

Louisa's voice.

Racing across the road, dodging the traffic as horns blare at me, I run toward the building. A couple of concerned onlookers are already at the front door, but I push them out of the way and swipe my key-card before rushing into the foyer and up the steps. I can hear voices shouting at the top, and Louisa is yelling my name over and over again. Sheer panic sends me bounding up the stairs three steps at a time until finally I reach the door to our apartment.

"Out of the way!" I shout at the idiots who are trying to get inside.

Unlocking the door, I hurry into the hallway and immediately hear Louisa sobbing in the kitchen. Running through, I spot her crumpled on the floor, leaning against the wall in the corner and shivering as tears stream down her face.

"What's wrong?" I ask as I run over and kneel next to her. There's no sign of blood. "Is it the baby? Did something happen with the baby?"

She tries to speak, but she's trembling too much and all I can do for a moment is put my arms around her and hold her tight.

"It's okay," I continue, kissing the side of her head. "I'm here. Everything's okay. I just need you to tell me what happened and -"

Suddenly she lets out another cry and clings tight to me. Turning, I see that a couple of our neighbors have reached the doorway, and now they're watching us with expressions of concern. We don't really know our neighbors at all, but frankly I can't blame them for being a little worried right now.

"It's alright," I tell them. "Everything's under control. Thank you for coming to check, but you can go home."

"Should we call someone?" one of the elderly men asks.

"Absolutely not. Please just leave."

As they turn and head away, I look back at Louisa and see that she seems genuinely terrified.

"Come on," I continue, wiping tears from her face, "just tell me what upset you. I won't make fun, I promise. I just need to know. Was it something to do with the baby?"

"It was that woman!" she blurts out.

I can't help sighing.

"It was her!"

"What about her?"

"I was watching you out the window," she stammers, "and I saw you go over to her. What did you say?"

"I didn't say anything. She wasn't there."

"You were standing right next to her."

"No, I got the street corner and there was no sign of her anywhere."

"You were right next to her!" she hisses. "Johnny, you were next to her and she was looking at you, and then..."

Her voice trails off, as if she's remembering something awful. Already, I can see fresh tears welling in her eyes.

"Okay, let's skip the part on the street," I tell her. "What happened next? What made you scream?"

"I lost sight of you for a moment," she continues, "and when I saw you again, you were alone on the corner."

"That's right. I was alone."

"I thought you'd told her to go away. I was relieved, I thought it was over, but then..."

She pauses, and now she seems close to another full-on breakdown.

"But then what?" I ask.

"Then I turned around," she whimpers, "and I saw her right there!"

She points past me. Turning, I realize she means the doorway that leads through to the hall.

"You saw a woman standing inside our apartment?" I mutter, starting to feel just a little worried about my wife's mental state.

"She was there!" she hisses, her finger trembling as she continues to point. "I don't know how she got in, but she was staring at me and she didn't leave until you started unlocking the front door. You must have seen her! She was naked and old, and so thin, and there were..."

Her voice trails off for a moment, and then I notice that she's wriggling her fingers.

"Maggots," she continues, "like... Thousands, all in her flesh..."

I look over at the empty doorway for a moment,

before getting to my feet. Louisa clings to me, not wanting to let go, but I gently ease her hands away.

"I'm going to double-check that there's no-one else here," I tell her. "Will that make you feel better?"

"I'm not crazy!"

"No-one's saying you're crazy."

Well, I guess that's true. I mean, I haven't *said* that she's crazy. As I spend the next few minutes checking the rest of the apartment, however, I can't shake the feeling that Louisa could do a slightly better job of keeping herself together. She's a smart woman, she shouldn't be letting her hormones affect her like this, and I've got this horrible dull feeling in the pit of my belly as I start to realize that the final few weeks of her pregnancy might be a little tricky. Finally, getting back to the kitchen door, I see that at least she's managed to get up off the floor and sit on a stool at the breakfast bar.

"There's no-one else here," I tell her, as she dabs at her eyes with tissue paper. "There was never anyone else here."

JOHNNY

One week later

"THAT MUST BE IT," I mutter, leaning down and peering out the window as I drive the car slowly along the street. "Wetherley House. Doesn't look bad, does it? Must be worth a few quid."

"Great," Louisa mutters, her voice tense with irritation and travel sickness. "Can you stop this thing? I think I need to puke again."

"Nearly -"

"Johnny, now!"

Sighing, I hit the brakes just as Louisa opens the door. Stumbling out of the car, struggling to move with her huge pregnant belly bumping against the frame, she steps toward the back of the vehicle and leans down, and a moment later I hear her gagging slightly. I can't help rolling my eyes as I take the keys from the ignition and get out of the car's other side, and to be honest I'm slightly amused by Louisa's constant insistence that she's still suffering from morning sickness. She's ready to pop in a couple of weeks, so she should be well over that phase by now. It's all in her head.

"Why did I let you talk me into this?" she gasps, standing up and leaning against the side of the car. "I must need my head examined."

"It's not my fault," I reply, taking my phone from my pocket and bringing up Hannah's number, before tapping to call. "If either of my bloody sisters would actually answer when I ring them, this could all have been sorted out days ago. After all the grief Hannah gave me over the phone, I can't believe they didn't bother to show up for Dad's funeral."

"Remind me to give them a piece of my mind," she groans.

"Still no answer," I continue, as I cut the call and try Katie. Wandering away from the car, I swing the gate open and make my way along the path that leads to the house, but I've got to admit that so far this whole scene looks rather unpromising. The windows are all dark and there's no sign of life, so I'm starting to think that my initial theory might have been correct after all. Hannah and Katie simply did a runner and never bothered to tell me. They can be so childish sometimes. I guess they think they're teaching me some kind of lesson, but in truth they're just making me more and more pissed off.

"It's me," I say as soon as I'm put through to Katie's voicemail. "Listen, enough's enough, okay? If you're not mature enough to actually speak to me, you could at least send me an email letting me know what's going on. This place looks like it could fetch a nice sum on the market, so we just need to get on with the process." Glancing back toward the car, I see that Louisa is bent double again. "And don't think that this trip was easy, either. In case you'd forgotten my wife is more than eight months pregnant. You're putting us through a lot of unnecessary stress."

I look at the house.

"I'm right outside. Are you in there?"

I wait.

Finally, sighing, I realize that Hannah's probably laughing at me.

After I've cut the call, I make my way up the steps to the front door. I try the handle, not really expecting to have any luck, but to my surprise the door swings open and I step into a gloomy hallway. Hearing a buzzing sound, I look over at a nearby table and see a bowl filled with rotten oranges. A dozen fat flies are circling the fruit, with several more crawling all over the rind and the wall. Grossed out by the stench, I wave the flies away and grab the bowl, quickly carrying it outside and tipping the oranges into the bushes. Fortunately, most of the flies go buzzing down after their prize, and I set the bowl on the steps as Louisa finally lumbers this way along the path.

"Anything?" she asks.

"No, but they very usefully left the house unlocked. God knows what they were thinking."

"Is anything missing?"

"How would I know? I've never been here

before in my life."

"Even though it's been in your family?"

"I told you, it was left empty for years. Some kind of family superstition about bad things that happened here. Dad never liked to talk about it much. Or, in fact, at all."

"And you thought the house had been flogged off years ago?"

"I reckon the old man was planning to do something with it, but then the dementia took over." Sighing again, I step back into the hallway and wander to the foot of the stairs, taking a look up toward the landing. "It's a nice enough place, but you wouldn't catch me dead here. It's so far from everywhere, and it's not exactly modern."

Reaching out, I grab the railing and give it a firm shake, and sure enough the wood creaks loudly.

"Nice wallpaper," Louisa mutters, running her hand across the wall before taking a torn section of paper and pulling it away. "I think you'll have to put it on the market as a fixer-upper. Still, someone somewhere'll absolutely love to get their hands on a country house like this. Someone with time and money could spend years making this a pretty decent home." She turns to me. "How much do you think it's worth?"

"A million, maybe."

"That much?"

"Could be. It comes with a fair spread of land. Split three ways, a million'd be more than three hundred grand each. Not bad for a day's work."

"Think what we could do with that money," she

replies, leaning back against the wall and placing a hand on her swollen belly. "We could go on the holiday of a lifetime. We could go on a cruise!"

"With a baby?"

"No, silly. We'll wait 'til a few months after the birth, and then my parents'll look after the kid while we go off for a couple of weeks. We could go to the Bahamas or Bermuda, somewhere really warm. God, after carrying this weight around for eight months, I think I deserve to be pampered. And the baby wouldn't know we were gone."

"I just need to make my sisters see sense first," I mutter, before cupping my hands around my mouth as I look back up the stairs. "Hannah! Katie! Where are you? Come on, we need to talk about this place!"

"This is creepy."

Turning, I see that Louisa has opened a door nearby. Leaning through into the darkness, she seems engrossed for a moment by whatever she's found.

"Looks like a basement," she continues finally, as she starts stepping through.

"Careful!" I call out, hurrying over and grabbing her arm.

"I think you're right," she replies, stepping back as a creaking sound rings out. "I don't much fancy those stairs."

"Where the hell are my sisters?" I mutter, heading to the next room and looking through into the old kitchen. "I know they're not at home, so I assumed they were still here, pottering about and coming up with dumb schemes. Instead, they seem to have vanished off the face of the planet."

"I wish," Louisa mutters under her breath, followed by a loud bumping sound.

"What are you up to back there?" I ask, heading through to the hallway.

"That was you, wasn't it?" she replies.

"I thought it was you."

"Whatever it was," she continues, "it sounded close. Must be a ghost. That settles it, then. There's no way we're staying here for even one night. Either we set off home right now, or at a push we can check into that homely little pub we passed as we drove through town. I'm going to take a wild guess and assume there's not much in the way of luxury in this part of the world. God, I'd kill for a bath."

"We can manage one night in the house," I point out, before turning to see the expression of extreme, *extreme* disinterest on her face. "Or maybe you're right. We could just try the pub."

JOHNNY

"SO NO-ONE'S SEEN THEM since last week?" I ask, as I hand the barman some money for the drinks and food. "Did they not even come into town for supplies?"

"One of them came in, one time," he replies, setting the money down and then sliding an overflowing pint glass toward me. "All I know is there was a lot of talk in town about them going out to Wetherley House, and for a few nights we saw lights out there in the distance. Then eventually we stopped seeing the lights, and we just assumed they'd gone home. Some of the locals weren't too happy."

He fetches a bottle of soda from the fridge and brings it over.

"Have you tried calling them?"

"I have," I reply, bristling at such a dumb suggestion. "Well, thanks for your help. We -"

"The men who used to keep an eye on the place -"

"That's fine," I add, interrupting him before he has a chance to waffle on again. "I don't need a potted history."

"But if -"

"You don't know an estate agent around here, do you? I want to get started on listing the house. I'm also going to need to hire a cleaner. Do you know anyone in town who could do the job for a reasonable rate?"

He hesitates, as if he's not entirely sure that he wants to answer.

"Is that a no?" I ask. "Seriously? I didn't think people out in the countryside could afford to be so picky about the jobs they take. What's wrong, is city money no good in these parts?"

"You're welcome to put a card up on the noticeboard," he continues, "but I wouldn't go expecting too many people to call you. There aren't many from round here who'll be keen to go up to that house."

"Let me guess. Because it's haunted?"

"You need to speak to Daniel Langton," he adds, grabbing a piece of paper and scribbling a phone number down. "He spoke to your sister last week, I believe. He also knows some people who'd maybe be interested in buying the house and land from you. They've been talking about nothing else, non-stop, over the past few days. I'll be honest, they'd be doing it so they could tear the place down, and they might not be able to reach the market rate. Last time they were in here chatting away, it sounded like they'd been able to pull together about two hundred grand, but at least -"

"The house is worth four or five times that."

"Only if you can find a buyer."

"I don't think that'll be a problem."

"If you'll just accept their offer," he continues, "they'll do the right thing by Wetherley House. It's high-time the place was bulldozed. Someone has to think about the future, and about what happens to people who go near that land." He hands the piece of paper to me. "Call Dan Langton. He'll offer you as much as he and his friends can, and that'll be the end of the house. They'll take all the risks."

"If they want to make an offer," I reply, picking up the drinks but ignoring the paper, "they'll be able to do so through the estate agent. But two hundred isn't going to cut it. We're selling that house for as much as we can get. It's been in my family for generations and as far as I can tell, it's given us nothing but grief. It's about time the bloody place gave us something back. We're owed."

***

"ARE YOU WORRIED ABOUT them?"

Staring out the window in our little room above the pub, I can't help watching the darkness in the distance. If anyone had switched on any lights in the house, if anyone had so much as lit a match, they should be just about visible from here. But there's no sign of anything. After a moment I turn to Louisa and see that she's lumbering through to the bathroom, getting ready for bed.

"Hannah and Katie?" I reply. "No, of course not. They're grown women, they can take care of themselves. I just wish they could stop messing around and at least let me know what's going on. It's typical of them to leave all of this in my hands. I'm starting to think..."

My voice trails off for a moment.

"Starting to think what?" she calls back to me from the bathroom.

"I'm starting to think I need to reduce my sisters' involvement in my life once the baby comes."

Taking a deep breath, I feel a rush of relief that I've finally managed to get those words out. I've been feeling bad about the idea for a while now, but the truth is that I don't want my child to be exposed to the madness of my family. If Hannah and Katie are going to continue to pull dumb stunts, then maybe they're better off being kept at a distance. I have every right to cut off parts of my old life that no longer contribute in a positive manner.

"Thank God," Louisa says after a moment. "I've been thinking the exact same thing."

"You have? So it's a deal?"

"What do you think your sisters'll say?"

"Oh, they'll complain about things either way," I mutter, turning and looking back out at the darkness beyond the edge of this crumby little town. "They're both so emotional and hysterical, and that's the last thing

I want to have around our kid. You might have noticed that my family tends to be dramatic. We need to be practical and -"

Suddenly Louisa lets out a scream. Turning, I hurry to the bathroom and make my way inside, only to find that she's standing back near the sink and staring in horror at something on the floor. I don't see anything wrong at first, but finally I realize that there's some kind of wriggling *thing* on one of the tiles. Stepping closer, I crouch down to get a closer look.

"Is that a maggot?" I ask.

"Oh God, it was on my leg!"

I look up at her. "Seriously?"

"It was on my leg, Johnny!" she shouts, clearly in a state of panic. "I was just about to brush my teeth, and then suddenly I felt something tickling and -"

She lets out another shriek and starts brushing her legs frantically, and sure enough another couple of maggots fall down onto the tiles and immediately start wriggling.

"Where are they coming from?" she asks, climbing into the empty bath and stepping back against the wall. "What the hell kind of place are we staying at, Johnny? I told you we shouldn't have stayed here! We should never even have come in the first place! I want to go to a Radisson or a Hilton!"

"It actually looks fairly clean to me," I mutter, looking around the bathroom.

"Well they certainly didn't come from me!" she yells. "I want to leave right now!"

"I know, I know." Grabbing some toilet roll, I pick up the three maggots and drop them into the toilet before flushing them away. "We're here now."

"So?"

"So let's make the best of it."

"You owe me!"

I look up at her.

"For making me stay in a place like this," she continues, through gritted teeth, "you owe me a luxury spa weekend. At least! This whole hotel, this whole *town*, is cursed or haunted or something!"

"Are there any more maggots?"

"I don't think so," she replies, still checking her legs. "This place is seriously creeping me out. I had the most horrible nightmare earlier when I was taking a nap, just after we checked in, and now I've got bloody maggots over me!" She climbs out of the bath, although she's still looking around as if she expects more maggots to show up. "I had this nightmare about a woman sitting on top of me. You know the woman I saw in our apartment last week? It was her again."

"The one you *imagined*."

"She was digging her fingers into my belly and telling me that our firstborn child is going to be hers."

"Sounds melodramatic," I point out, double-checking the grouting in case any more little critters show up. "I think you should be fine now."

"It felt so real, too," she continues, turning to finish removing her make-up in the bathroom mirror. "She told me I'd married into the wrong family. She told me that every firstborn in *your* line is cursed to get taken away, because of something that happened years ago. Her voice was so horrible and shrill, it's like she was taunting me. I kept telling myself she wasn't really there, I kept trying to focus on the fact that the whole thing was just in my head, but that didn't make it any easier." She takes some cotton pads from a packet next to the sink and starts wiping her eyes. "Elizabeth Caulstone."

I head over to the door. "Who?"

"That was her name. In the nightmare. She told me, or somehow I just knew it. I don't remember. It was the freakiest thing. I think she was some kind of witch who got messed up with your family a long time ago."

"Oh, I'm sure she was. Door open or closed?"

"Closed."

After pulling the door shut, I head to the bed and flop down, grabbing my phone and trying yet again to call my sisters. They still don't pick up, and Hannah's goes straight to voicemail while Katie's at least rings for half a minute before the same happens. I've left more than enough messages over the past week, so this time I don't bother. I simply toss my phone aside, lean back with my hands behind my head, and try to think about all the things Louisa and I can do with our share of the money once we've sold Wetherley House.

This is our chance. We're going to be rich. And if my sisters don't come back to claim their share, we'll get the whole lot.

***

"WHAT THE -"

Sitting up in bed, in the darkened room, I look toward the door and see that there's a shadow at the bottom, as if someone's standing outside. A moment later, I hear the knocking sound again, and this time Louisa lets out a groan as she sits up next to me. Still feeling groggy from sleep, I realize someone must have been knocking for a while.

"Seriously?" she asks. "It's just after midnight. What the hell do they want?"

"Wait here," I mutter, climbing out of bed.

"Where else would I go?" She sighs. "If it's a bunch of drunks from the pub downstairs, I'm going to call the police."

Heading over to the door, I take a moment to make sure that my pajamas are properly buttoned and then I slide the bolt across, opening the door just a little. To my surprise, I find that there are three local-looking men outside in the brightly-lit corridor.

"Mr. Cruikshank?" one of them asks.

"It's midnight," I point out, figuring that they must have wandered up here after staying down in the pub for a lock-in. "For God's sake, can't you people leave us alone for five minutes?"

"We need to talk to you," the man continues. "My name is Daniel Langton, and I'm part of a group that would very much like to buy Wetherley House."

"It's not on the market yet," I tell him, "but once I've -"

"We can offer you two hundred and fifty thousand pounds."

"And what do you expect me to do in return?" I ask. "Laugh in your faces?"

"Please, Mr. Cruikshank, we only have so much, but we've pooled our resources and we just need you to listen to us. It's very important that Wetherley House is torn down."

"My wife and I are trying to sleep."

"I spoke to your sister last week, right here in the pub. It was after she ignored me that I realized we needed to buy the house from you, fair and square." He holds up a small cloth-bound book. "These photos might help you to -"

"I don't want to see any photos," I tell him.

He starts opening the book, but I snatch it from his hand and toss it back toward the top of the stairs.

"I don't want to see any goddamn photos!" I say again, more firmly.

"I'm begging you," he replies, "please listen to what we've got to say."

"Tell them to sod off!" Louisa whispers behind me.

Sighing, I step out into the corridor and pull the door shut, so as to keep from disturbing her.

"Wetherley House will be put up for sale," I tell the men, all of whom look like dirty yokels with barely two pennies to rub together, "but there's a proper process to go through and I'm afraid the house will go to whoever makes the highest bid. I'm not a charity. I've got a family to support."

"You can't let the house continue," this Langton guy replies, his voice filled with tension now. "We all thought that maybe once it was empty, after the last business with old Mrs. Carmichael, that'd be an end to it all. That's why we guarded it at night, to make sure no-one went inside. But even though it's stood up there for decades, all locked up, it's started to..."

His voice trails off.

"It reaches out," one of the other men adds finally.

I turn to him.

"It does!" he continues. "It reaches out, or the thing in it reaches out, and it tries to make certain things happen. It tries to influence events so that people'll go back there. The right people."

"What the bloody hell are you on about?" I ask. "Listen, I'm tired and -"

"It's never been empty," the third man says suddenly. "Not really. After Mrs. Carmichael was hung, Wetherley House was locked up and left alone by your family, but there's still been something there ever since. On the nights I've been out there, I've -"

"You trespassed?" I ask.

"We never set foot on the property," Langton tells me. "We just had three or four men stationed around the perimeter, to make sure thrill-seekers and ghost-hunters never got through. We caught a few each year, too. The thing is, I suppose we thought that if we could keep the house undisturbed, if we could isolate whatever's inside, no-one else would get hurt." He pauses for a moment. "Looks like we were wrong. She found a way to reach out and bring people here regardless."

"We should've just burned it to the ground," one of the other men mutters.

"And you'd all have served nice lengthy jail sentences if you had," I point out.

"That would have been worth it."

I can't help laughing. These madman seem so painfully earnest, it's almost as if they actually believe the bullshit they're peddling. I can only assume they're trying to spread ghost stories in a pathetic bid to lure tourists to their rubbish little town.

"You have to take this seriously," Langton says firmly. "There's been so much pain and suffering at Wetherley House over the years. So many people have died there, in such horrible circumstances, and -"

"So do they all haunt the place?" I ask. "Or is it just one of them? I've got to be honest, it sounds as if you haven't really thought this through very well. I mean, if several people died at the house, then surely their ghosts should be bumping into one another all the time, instead of just this Mary bird."

"It doesn't work like that."

"So how *does* it work?" I continue. "If you're the experts, why don't you tell me?"

"We always kept our backs to the house," one of the other men says. "When we were guarding it, I mean. We never dared look at the windows. May God have mercy on our souls, but we all turned our backs, except..."

"One man looked once," Langton adds. "He saw a figure at one of the windows, staring right back out at us. We believe her name is Mary Carmichael. Or Evil Mary, as she's better known these days. Nobody who goes into that house is safe."

I can't help sighing. This is ridiculous.

"Your family will never be safe for as long as Wetherley House stands," Langton continues earnestly, "and the shadow of that place will hang over this entire town. For the love of God, man, we all have a common interest in getting rid of the house as quickly as possible. If you don't agree now, the cycle will go on for another generation. She'll be doing things, she'll be twisting the fates of men in an attempt to get what she wants. And what she wants is first-born children from your family."

"Oh, pull the other one," I reply, pushing the door open and stepping back into the room. "It's got bells on."

"Listen to me!" He puts a foot in the way as I try to shut the door. "You have to -"

"No, you listen to me, Worzel!" I hiss, shoving him back out into the corridor. "If you bother us again, I'll call the police. Is that understood? This is none of your bloody business, and do you want to know something else? After the way you've shown up like this tonight, I wouldn't sell Wetherley House to any of you lot, not even if you could scrape together a vaguely respectable bid. This whole situation is pathetic, and you'd better not darken our door ever again." I start to shut the door, before pulling it open again so that I can add one final point. "Oh, and if anything happens to the house, like a fire for example, I'll know exactly where to send the police."

With that, I slam the door shut and take a deep breath, before turning and seeing that Louisa is sitting on the bed still, but at least she's put her phone aside. Instead, she's looking through some kind of pamphlet.

"Did you hear all that bullshit?" I ask, as the men's footsteps slink away from the other side of the door. "I guess you've got to give them credit for trying. I can understand children believing in this Evil Mary rubbish, but grown men? It's insane."

"She was real," Louisa whispers, with a hint of fear in her voice. "The woman in my dream, the woman I saw at the apartment... I found this on the bedside table. Evil Mary is based on a real person!"

Great. My wife has finally lost her mind.

JOHNNY

"I STILL DON'T WANT to hear it," I say firmly as I park the car at the front of the house and immediately start climbing out. "You're just working yourself up into another bad state."

"Will you at least listen to me for two minutes?" Louisa asks, getting out the other side with that goddamn pamphlet still clutched in her hand. "Mary Carmichael -"

"Enough!" I reply, almost shouting as I turn to her. "You've been trying to tell me this since last night, but I'm still not interested. You're starting to sound like those mad bastards from the pub. I don't want to hear it."

Realizing that I'm maybe being a little tough, I head around the car and place my hands on Louisa's shoulders. "I'm all for a good ghost story, but I'm worried that this stuff is getting too real for you. Now we have a plan this morning, and that plan involves taking photos and checking the place out and trying to decide how we go ahead with a sale of the house. Let's stick to that and try not to fill our heads with talk of this woman you've found online."

She sighs.

"If we don't get to work," I continue, "we might have to stay another night in that grotty pub. You don't want that, do you? If we get on, we might even make it to a Radisson or a Hilton by nightfall."

"Can I just tell you one thing?" she asks.

"I'd rather -"

"She was horribly abused by her mother. She became a monster."

I can't help sighing. Taking the pamphlet, I take a quick look and see that it's just some kind of home-brewed concoction, complete with lousy clip art. Figuring that I need to make a point, I rip it in half and then rip the pieces again, before letting the whole mess fall to the ground.

"Maybe you should have stayed at the pub today," I continue. "You need to rest, and clearly Wetherley House isn't very good for your state of mind."

"I *need* to be here," she replies, taking her Polaroid camera from the seat and standing next to me, then holding the camera up to take a picture of us together. "Say cheese, honey."

Before I have a chance, she takes a photo and I'm briefly blinded by the flash. The camera immediately starts whirring and then spits out a small white piece of card.

"Cute," I tell Louisa as she starts wafting the card in the air, trying to get the image to develop faster, "but I think for the job today, you need to use the digital camera. It might be less expensive."

"Just having some fun," she tells me, swapping cameras and then starting to make her way toward the house. "You remember fun, Johnny, don't you? It's what we used to have before real life got in the way." She stops, staring at the front door, and for a moment she seems transfixed by the sight of the place. "I think you need to sell Wetherley House as quickly as possible," she adds finally, turning to me. "Get rid of it. There's something about this place that I just don't like. Get it out of your family. And I should warn you. If I spot even one more maggot, I'm gonna scream like a bitch."

***

"THERE'S A FUNNY SMELL in some of the rooms," she says a short while later, as she comes through to the kitchen. The floorboards creak under her feet. "Do you know what I mean? Kind of fusty and... I don't know, exactly. Wrong."

"I found this," I reply, turning and showing her the purse I just discovered on top of the fridge.

"Whose is it?"

Opening the purse, I show her Hannah's various bank and ID cards.

"Why would she have left those behind?" Louisa asks, coming over to join me next to the sink.

"She wouldn't," I point out, feeling a flutter of concern. "I haven't found anything of Katie's yet, but if Hannah left all her stuff here, what's she been doing for the past week?"

327

"Are you worried? Do you think we should call the police?"

I hesitate for a moment, looking at the purse, before setting it down.

"Not yet," I say finally. "I think *something's* going on, but I still wouldn't put it past my sisters to be staging this for my benefit and I refuse to fall for their little stunt. Maybe Hannah wants me to get worried, so she can make some kind of point about the importance of family."

"She wouldn't go this far, surely?"

"She might, if she got a real bee in her bonnet." I pause again, trying to figure out exactly what kind of bullshit Hannah and Katie are trying to pull here. At least Louisa has an excuse for acting strangely, since she's full of pregnancy hormones, but my sisters are just being childish and immature. "The best thing to do," I continue finally, "is just to take plenty of photos for the estate agent, to give him an idea of what he's dealing with, and then we'll get the hell out of here. If my dumb-ass sisters want to play games, that's their business, but you and I have actually got a life to live."

"Is Hannah really this nuts, though?" she asks. "I know she can be difficult, but I never had her down as someone who'd pull this kind of stunt. If anything, she's the opposite. She's always so serious."

"Just get on with taking photos," I reply. "You know, it wouldn't surprise me if my sisters and those crazy locals have teamed up to lower the price-tag on Wetherley House." I pause for a moment, as the idea starts making sense. "In fact, that actually -"

"Jesus Christ!" Louisa shouts suddenly, grabbing my arm and stepping back as she stares in shock at the window.

Turning, I see that there are three figures in the distance, just beyond the line of trees that marks the start of the forest. Squinting, I realize with a flash of relief that it's just three little girls wearing whitish-pink dresses, although to be fair their appearance is more than a little disconcerting. They look like they've straight straight out of a history book.

"Bloody hell," Louisa continues, a little breathless as she steps closer to the window, "those little assholes almost made me jump out of my skin! What are they doing here?"

"Probably just kids from the town," I mutter, already heading to the back door. "I'll tell them to scram."

As I unlock the door, I hear the sound of the Polaroid camera. Glancing over my shoulder, I see that Louisa has taken a photo of the girls through the window.

"Well, they *do* look pretty weird," she points out, setting the card and the camera down and then getting back to work with her digital camera, taking pictures of the fittings in the kitchen. "Don't be too mean, honey. They're just children. You should probably tell them to stay off the property, though. You never know what's around, and you don't want to be liable if one of them slips and gets injured. If their parents smell money, they'll probably go crazy. You know what country people are like."

Heading out onto the lawn, I look toward the trees, but now there's no sign of the girls. I shield my eyes from the sun as I look all around, but now the little brats seem to have vanished, and I can only assume they must have headed back the way they came. I hesitate a moment longer, just in case they show up again, but fortunately they really seem to have disappeared. Still, the mere sight of the three little freaks was enough to give me the willies, and I can't help hoping that they steer well clear of the house from now on.

Once I'm back in the kitchen, I find that Louisa has headed upstairs, and I can hear her bumping about in one of the bedrooms as she takes more photos. Just as I'm about to go and join her, I spot the fully-developed Polaroid on the counter and I wander over to take a look. When I pick the photo up, however, I find that something seems to have gone wrong with the image. The girls' bodies are clear enough, but their heads are so blurred that they're barely visible at all.

"Huh," I mutter, setting the picture down before heading through to find Louisa.

JOHNNY

"SO WHAT DO YOU think?" I ask several hours later, as we stand in one of the bedrooms and look at the panels I've pulled from the wall. Darkness has begun to fall outside, and the lack of electricity in the house means the place is becoming gloomy as hell. "Are we done here?"

"At least we won't have to come back tomorrow," Louisa points out, before wincing as she places a hand on her belly.

"Something wrong?"

"Just a few pains," she mutters. "Mustn't grumble. It's nothing I can't -"

Before she can finish, there's a loud bumping sound from out on the landing, and a moment later the door slams shut. Startled, I stare at the door for a moment before turning to Louisa and seeing that she too looks a little concerned. Of course, her fear just reminds me that this whole situation is ridiculous, and I sigh as I force myself to relax.

"Just the wind," I tell her as I head across the room and reach out to open the door. Before I can grab the handle, however, I realize I can hear another sound coming from the landing, as if something is moving on the other side of the door. I pause, listening to a series of slow, shuffling clicking sounds that seem to be edging closer.

"I need to sit down," Louisa says, sounding a little breathless as she eases herself onto the stool I brought up earlier. "Are you okay?"

Without answering, I continue to listen to the creaks and clicks until they stops right outside this room. I know the idea is absurd, but for a moment I genuinely feel as if there's someone just on the other side of the door, just a few inches away. And then, as if to add to that sensation, I realize that something seems to have started scratching against the door's wood.

"Johnny?" Louisa continues. "Do you mind if we get going? I'm not feeling one hundred per cent right now."

I can't tell he about this. She'll freak and overreact.

"Johnny?"

I reach for the handle, but my heart is pounding and I can't shake the feeling that someone's out on the landing. I keep telling myself to get a grip, and reminding myself that I'm not paranoid like my wife or sentimental like my sisters, but at the same time I can't quite bring myself to open this door. It's almost as if a kind of faint fear is rippling up through my chest, spreading hundreds of little fingers through my body in an attempt to warn me that no matter what else happens, I mustn't let myself see the face that's staring at me from the door's other side.

"Get a grip," I mutter to myself, even as I feel cold sweat on my brow. "Just get a goddamn grip."

"Johnny?"

I try to grab the handle again, but I feel more certain than ever now that someone is waiting for me. And then, just as I think that I might be able to find the necessary strength, I spot something moving near my feet. Looking down, I see that a couple of maggots are wriggling through the gap at the bottom of the door.

"Johnny? Honey?"

"Stop!" I hiss, pressing my shoe against the maggots and squashing them into the floorboards, only for another to immediately wriggle into view.

"Johnny, sweetheart, please, I need help."

"Wait," I whisper, watching as a couple maggots appear.

I can hear someone breathing on the other side of the door.

Leaning closer, I press my ear against the wood, and now I'm more certain than ever that someone is taking slow, regular breaths just a few inches away.

"Johnny!" Louisa shouts. "For God's sake, help me!"

"Wait!" I hiss, trying to hear the breathing more clearly. I don't know why or how, but deep down I'm absolutely certain that the person on the other side of the door is a woman. Each breath she takes seems to draw me closer, but at the same time I can't quite bring myself to turn the handle and open the door.

"Johnny, the baby's coming!"

Suddenly feeling a hand on my arm, I turn and find that Louisa has struggled over to me. She starts to fall, but I manage to grab her arms and hold her up before supporting her as we struggle to the bed in the corner. Lowering her down, I look back across the room and see that there are patches of clear liquid on the bare wooden boards, and then I turn back to Louisa just as she lets out a low, pained groan.

"It's too soon!" she hisses, leaning back on the bed. "We have to get to a hospital!"

"I'll call an ambulance," I reply, fumbling for my phone but then seeing that I have no signal. I try to call 999 anyway, but the call won't connect. "It's okay," I continue, tossing the phone aside as I try to figure out what to do next. "I'll drive you! Can you make it to the car?"

"Do I have any bloody choice? I'm not giving birth in this dump! Just -"

Suddenly she lets out another pained groan.

"Hurry!" she gasps. "I need an epidural!"

Helping her up, I support her weight as we make our way to the door. At first I don't even think about the sounds I heard a moment ago, although I remember just in time as I pull the door open. To my immense relief, there's no sign of anyone out on the landing, so I lead Louisa slowly toward the stairs, while struggling to keep her from collapsing. We practiced for this moment, we even rehearsed the drive to the hospital, but somehow we never prepared for her to go into labor in a haunted house in the goddamn countryside.

"You just have to get to the car," I tell her. "Everything'll be fine."

"Hurry!"

By the time we get to the top of the stairs, I'm starting to worry that she'll never be able to make it as far as the hallway, let alone the car. We take each step slowly and carefully, and Louisa lets out a series of agonized groans as we make our way down toward the hall. I can barely support her properly, but I know we have to get to a hospital as fast as possible. The baby's not due for at least two weeks, and I don't have a clue what to do if it starts coming here at the house. Maybe I should have gone to those classes after all.

"Not much further now!" I gasp. "Just -"

Before I can finish, the step under my left foot shatters and my leg drops through. Stumbling, I grab the railing and try to hold myself up, but I let out a cry of pain as I feel a sharp section of rotten wood rip straight through my ankle and lower leg. Louisa has to support herself for a moment as I try to pull my leg free, but the wood is pinning me in place and even the slightest movement is enough to send a searing pain through my foot.

I try again, but I think the wood has torn all the way through to the bone.

"What's wrong?" Louisa asks, her voice tense with pain. "Johnny, are you okay?"

"Just give me a moment!" I hiss, trying to push through the pain as I turn slightly, hoping that I'll be able to somehow unhook myself. I can feel blood running down my leg, and my foot is dangling in the void beneath the stairs, having broken through to the basement steps.

"Johnny, hurry!" Louisa groans, before stumbling forward and starting to inch down toward the hallway. "I can't give birth here! Jesus Christ, I need a hospital!"

"I'm coming!"

I try yet again to twist my leg free, before realizing that there's no way I can avoid the pain. I hesitate for a moment, trying to gear myself up for the inevitable agony, and then I start counting to three under my breath.

Suddenly a hand grips my ankle from below. I freeze as I realize that icy fingers are reaching up from beneath the stairs – from the basement steps below – and are now holding me tight. As the fingers tighten their grip, I panic and pull back, tearing my leg free from the hole and slumping against the steps. I can see dark patches of blood glistening in the fabric of my torn trouser leg, and after a moment I look at the hole in the broken step.

I can't see a hand down there now, but I know what I felt.

"Johnny, quick!" Louisa yells from the hallway. "I can't have my baby in this hellhole! I need drugs!"

I take a moment to check my damaged leg, and when I pull the fabric of my trousers aside I find that there's a thick, deep gash running almost all the way up to my knee. Figuring that I'll have time to worry about that later, however, I haul myself up and start limping down the stairs, determined to get to my wife.

"I can't believe this is happening," she stammers as she starts to unlock the front door. After a moment, she turns to me. "Johnny, we can't -"

Suddenly she freezes, staring at me with an expression of pure horror.

"I'm okay!" I hiss, limping down another step but having to stop to get my breath back. I can feel more blood running from the wound on my left leg and I'm starting to get a little light-headed, but I have to hold myself together so I can drive to the hospital. "Just give me a moment. Just -"

"Don't turn around!" Louisa shouts, stumbling back against the door. "Johnny, get over here!"

"What is it?" I ask. "Honey -"

Before I can get another word out, I realize I can hear breaths over my shoulder. I start to turn, before feeling a sudden rush of cold air against the back of my neck.

"Don't look!" Louisa hisses through gritted teeth, as she reaches out to me with a trembling hand. "Get over here now!"

"What -"

"Run!" she screams, her voice trembling with fear. She's not looking directly at me. Instead, she's looking at something that's right behind me, and tears are starting to fill her eyes. "For the love of God, Johnny, move!"

I flinch slightly as I feel the cold air moving across the back of my neck. I want to reach out and take

Louise's outstretched hand, but at the same time I feel completely frozen to the spot, as if I can't move from the foot of the stairs, and a moment later I feel two ice-cold hands touching my head, one on either side of my face.

"No no no no no," Louisa whimpers, dropping down to her knees as she stares at me with tear-filled eyes. "Johnny, please..."

"Johnny what?" I ask, as the cold hands grip me tighter and start burning into my flesh. "Louisa, what's happening to me?"

"No, please," she sobs, still holding one trembling hand toward me. "Johnny, sweetheart, come to me! Please, just come here..."

I try to step forward, but now the icy hands on my head are holding me in place. It's as if the freezing fingers are somehow reaching deep into my body, chilling every bone and leaving me unable to move. I clench my teeth and try again, before letting out a faint groan as I find that the effort is too much. No matter how much I try to pull away, my bones seem frozen in place and all I can manage is to push my muscles futilely.

"Louisa," I gasp, "get out of here. Whatever it is, get out of here with the baby..."

"Johnny!" she screams. "No!"

"Get out of here!" I shout. "Whatever this thing is, don't let it -"

Suddenly my head is twisted round with such force that I feel a sickening crunch as my neck snaps. The very last thing I see, as my head is turned until it faces backward, is a pair of dark, rotten dead eyes staring at me from a leathery face.

It's my sister Katie, and she's smiling.

HANNAH

I CAN HEAR A baby crying.

Opening my eyes in the dark, I stare straight ahead into the void and listen to the far-off sound of a newborn baby. I don't know exactly where the sound is coming from, but the child seems to be screaming as if he or she is in agony. I instinctively try to step forward, before suddenly realizing that in fact I'm flat on my back. My next instinct is to reach up, but my hands quickly bump against some kind of rough rocky surface that's just a couple of inches above my face. I push, but the surface – whatever it is – feels very firm and secure.

Taking a deep breath, I feel a kind of dry powder at the back of my throat. I start coughing, but this space is too small for me to turn onto my side and really try getting the powder from my mouth properly. Instead, I push up against the rocky surface again, albeit with no more luck than before, and then I reach my hands out, trying to figure out where I am and how I got here.

It's almost as if I've been buried somewhere.

Suddenly the fingers of my right hand brush against a different kind of surface. Something wooden and rough, with splintered pieces sticking out. As I move my fingers across this new surface, I feel gaps where several planks are joined together, and finally I realize I can feel the sharp ends of nails poking down into this narrow space in which I find myself. I try to haul myself closer to the wooden section, so that I can investigate further, but as I do so my right cheek catches against another nail that's poking down, and I let out a faint gasp as I feel my flesh rip.

Maggots.

In a flash, I remember the bag of maggots that Katie placed on my head. I remember drowning in a mass of their wriggling little bodies, and I remember frantically breathing hundreds of them into my mouth and nose as I struggled to get free. At some point I dropped to my knees, then onto my side, but I remember how the bag was held so very tightly. I was suffocating, and Katie seemed determined to kill me, and then I must have passed out. I don't remember anything else after that moment, not until I woke up just now.

I stay quiet for a moment, listening to the sound of the baby in the distance.

"Hello?" I whisper finally, although I doubt anybody can hear me. "Help..."

Even those two simple words cause my throat to

catch. Dry and painful, my entire mouth feels as if it has not been used for several days, and after a moment I realize that I'm so very thirsty. I try again to move through the darkened space, this time taking extra care to avoid any more of the nails that are poking down, and finally I manage to maneuver myself under the wooden boards, which I think might be the underside of a set of floorboards. I press my hands against the wood and this time I feel the boards flex just a little, accompanied by a very faint creaking sound.

"Help me!" I gasp, pushing again, unable to apply too much pressure until finally I turn slightly and push my shoulder up against the wood. Leveraging the narrow space for a little extra grip, I start pushing as hard as I can manage. I feel as if I'm running out of air under here, and panic is starting to spread through my body, but I know I have to keep trying. I push harder and harder, until I feel as if my shoulder is about to break, and then I push some more until my entire body is straining. Even then I keep going, determined to get out of here and -

Suddenly the board gives way slightly, and I let out a gasp as I slump back down. Frantically pushing the board again with my hands, I find that two nails have come loose, allowing me to lift the board just high enough to see the legs of a table with several chairs arranged nearby. I immediately realize that I'm under the floor in the kitchen, which is a section of the house that has no basement underneath.

Pushing the boards again, I manage to force one

end a little further open and then I reach through in an attempt to gain a little better purchase.

A moment later I slip slightly and the board comes thudding back down. One of the nails slices straight through my outstretched hand and I let out a pained cry before clamping my other hand over my mouth.

I have no idea who's up there and who might be able to hear me, but I know I have to stay as quiet as possible. Maybe Katie -

Hesitating for a moment, I realize I'm scared of her.

My own sister.

Reaching up again, I push the board, and finally the nail slides up and out of my hand. I pull the damaged hand closer and examine it in the light. Although I see a bloodied hole just beneath the knuckles of my index and middle fingers, I quickly find that I can still move the hand properly, despite the searing pain. Pushing on the board yet again, I use my shoulder to force it open further, and finally I hear a snapping sound as the other end comes away. Setting the board aside, I'm able to force another one free, at which point I manage to clamber up and then roll onto my back.

I'm out.

I'm on the kitchen floor.

The room is dark and I can see the night sky outside the window, but at least I'm out of that claustrophobic little hole under the floor. The baby is still screaming somewhere in the house, but for a moment all I can do is wait to get my breath back as I stare up at the ceiling.

The child is up there somewhere.

The master bedroom, maybe, or the spare room at the top of the stairs.

Either way, I have to go and help. Even though I feel incredibly weak, and despite the pain in my hand, I struggle to my feet and start limping toward the door. My hips are hurting, most likely because I was immobile down there for so long, but I know I can't let pain stop me now. Wincing, I make my way through to the hallway and then I turn toward the stairs.

There's a body on the floor.

A man, slumped at the foot of the stairs. I don't know how, but I can tell immediately that he's familiar, so I limp closer until I see the side of his face and a jolt of shock bursts through my chest.

"Johnny?" I gasp, stumbling over to him and dropping to my knees. "Johnny, what the hell are -"

Before I can finish, I see that his eyes are wide open and glassy, and that his neck has been left resting at an impossible angle, almost twisted entirely to the side. Reaching out, I press two fingers against the side of his neck, and I immediately feel that his flesh is still and icy cold.

"Johnny," I continue, "wake up. Johnny, please!"

Grabbing his shoulder, I roll him onto his back. As I do so, I see that his head lolls back as if all the bones in his neck are shattered.

Letting out a brief cry of shock, I pull back and bump against the door as the baby continues to cry upstairs in the dark house.

Johnny's dead eyes are staring toward the wall now, and I know without a shadow of a doubt that he's dead. Still, I can't process that information, and tears start running down my face as I stare at my brother's body. For the next few minutes, all I can do is sit sobbing on the hallway floor, and every few seconds a brief rush of hope fills my chest as I try to think of some way that he might be okay. The hope quickly dies each time, only to come rushing back just a moment later.

Eventually I'm stirred from shock by a set of bumps from one of the rooms upstairs.

"Katie?" I whisper, hoping against hope that my sister will suddenly appear and tell me that everything's okay. That this is some kind of trick, or nightmare. "Katie, what's happening?"

The only response is a series of faint gasps, seemingly coming from the landing.

"Katie?"

Stumbling to my feet, I take care to not even look at Johnny's body as I limp to the stairs and start crawling up on all fours. Barely finding the strength to keep going, I notice after a moment that there are patches of thick blood dried on some of the steps, along with fresher-looking, redder smears. About halfway up, one of the steps has collapsed, and as I get closer I feel cold air from the basement. Every muscle in my body is aching, screaming at me to turn back, but that poor child sounds so upset.

I have to help.

"Katie!" I call out, struggling past the broken step and continuing to haul myself upstairs, getting closer and closer to the sound of the crying baby. "What are you doing?"

I almost slump and fall several times, but finally I grab the edge of the railing and pull myself to the top. Letting out a cry of pain, I turn and look along the landing, and I immediately see that there's a bloodied human figure dragging itself toward one of the doors. My first instinct is to call out, but suddenly I realize that the figure isn't Katie at all. It's another woman, and she's leaving a fresh trail of smeared blood on the floor as she pulls herself forward. And then, just as I'm about to call out to her, she suddenly turns to me. Her face is bloodied and battered, with thick swollen bruises, and one of her eyes looks to have been split open. Matted hair is stuck to the blood on her torn forehead and his bottom lip is trembling, but I still just about recognize her.

"Louisa?" I stammer, struggling to my feet and leaning heavily against the wall as I limp toward her. "What's happening? How did you get here? Why -"

Suddenly she lets out a pained moan, something that sounds more animal than human. In the process, thick black blood dribbles from her mouth and several teeth splatter down onto the wet floorboards. Her moan becomes louder, until one side of her lower jaw detaches altogether and a spray of blood hits the floorboards.

"What happened to you?" I ask as I reach her

and drop back down onto my knees. "Louisa, we have to get out of this house. Have you seen Katie?"

She groans again, and now I can see that tears are mixing with the blood on her face. She reaches out to me and grips my arm with a trembling hand, as if she's trying to use my body to haul herself up, but she's clearly too weak.

"Who did this to you?" I continue, trying not to panic. "Louisa, I found Johnny, he -"

The mention of his name brings another cry from her lips, this time one that sounds more pained and twisted. Her whole body shudders as she grabs my shoulder, but she seems unable to lift herself up and instead she starts pulling me down to toward the floor.

"Why is there a baby crying in the house?" I ask, struggling to stay up. Looking along toward the door at the far end of the landing, I realize that the baby seems to be on the other side of that door. "Louisa, whose baby is that? Why's it in this house?"

I pause for a moment, listening to the child's continued cries, before looking back down at my sister-in-law as she tries yet again to haul herself up.

"Louisa, who does that baby belong to? Where did it come from?"

She stares up at me, and for a few seconds I see fear and pain in her remaining good eye. And then, slowly, she starts to roll onto her back. As she does so, thick patches of dried blood start to pull away from the bare floorboards, and I realize with a growing sense of horror that her entire belly has been torn open. Not only that, but the gaping wound has begun to dry and stick against the boards, and now thick strands of rotten, pus-covered flesh are being torn away as she lets out a whimpering cry and rolls all the way onto her back, revealing the bloody, hollowed out hole where she's been ripped open.

As I stare in horror at the wound, and at the edges of her shattered ribs, Louisa lets out another agonized cry.

"I'll get her," I stammer, pulling back before getting to my feet and turning to look toward the farthest door. I can't even understand how Louisa is still alive, but she must have dragged herself all the way up here in search of her child. Now, limping toward the door, I realize that there'll be time to figure out the truth later. That poor little girl sounds utterly terrified and I just have to get her out of here.

She's all that matters.

Reaching the door, I try the handle but find that it's locked. Turning my shoulder against the wood, I try to smash my way through, but when that doesn't work I drop to my knees and peer through the keyhole. I immediately spot a wriggling little form on the bed by the window, and then a moment later someone walks past the other side of the door.

"Who's in there?" I shout, banging my fists against the door. "What are you doing to her her? Katie, is that you? What are you doing?"

Suddenly something comes wriggling through the keyhole, blocking my view. I pull back just as a thick fly buzzes out, brushing my face before it flies away. There's a strong smell in the air, as if something's rotten, but all I know right now is that I have to find a way to get into the bedroom and save the girl. I slam my shoulder against the door a couple more times, but I can already tell that I'm never going to be able to break through.

Pulling back, I try to work out how else I can get into the room.

"I'm coming," I whisper, as the baby continues to scream. "I'm going to -"

Before I can finish, I hear a loud, gurgled scream from over my shoulder. Startled, I turn just in time to see that Louisa has somehow not only hauled herself up from the floor, but is now stumbling straight toward me. I stare at her for a moment, and then I duck out of the way just as she throws what's left of her ravaged body against the door. The wood starts to split, and she steps back before trying again, then again and again, each time with more furious anger. She's smashing her own body apart, but at the same time she's also managing to break the wood around the handle, and finally I watch in horror as she lets out one more cry and cracks the door open.

As splinters of broken wood fly through the air, Louisa's ravaged body slumps down to the floor. Her head hits the boards and bounces slightly, and then she falls still with dead eyes staring toward the wall. The force of the impact sent her intestines unraveling through her ripped belly and slopping out onto the wooden floorboards.

Stumbling past her, I make my way into the room and start limping toward the bed. I look around, and now there's no sign of anyone else in here, so I hurry to the bed and look down at the wriggling, screaming baby. Hundreds and hundreds of flies are crawling all over her body.

"It's okay!" I gasp. "I'm going to get you out of here!"

I reach down toward her, but there are flies buzzing all around me and a moment later I spot a set of rotten human remains slumped in the corner, covered in flies and maggots. Horrified by the sight, it takes me a moment to recognize the shoes and tattered dress that the body's wearing, and finally I look at the bugs that are eating the remains of the face.

"Katie?" I whisper, realizing that I've finally found my sister. For a moment I can only stare at the hollow sockets of her eyes. I want to go over and try to help her, but I know it's too late.

The baby.

I have to save the -

Suddenly something brushes against my shoulder, bumping me forward. I spin around and look across the room. At first I only see Louisa's corpse on the floor, but then I realize that there's a patch of darkened air in front of the door, barely visible through the swarm of flies. The more I stare at that patch, the more it seems to resolve itself and form a human shape, and after a few seconds I realize that I can see a pair of eyes staring straight back at me from beyond the flies.

"Who are you?" I ask, filled with fear. "*What* are you?"

Instead of responding, she simply continues to watch me.

"What do you want with my family?" I continue, as I remember Dad's last words from his deathbed. "Are you Mary? What did any of us ever do to you?"

As I wait for her to make her move, I can't help looking at the rest of her body. She's naked and painfully thin, with bloodied wounds around her wrists as if at some point she was held in shackles. There look to be wounds in her belly, too, as if she was stabbed at some point, and maggots are wriggling in thick nests between sections of exposed bones.

"What did my brother do to you?" I sob, as fresh tears run down my face. "What did his wife do to you? What did my sister ever do to you? What did -"

Suddenly I gasp as she takes a step forward, directly into the swarm of buzzing flies. I instinctively move to block her way, so that she can't get any closer to the screaming baby. Reaching down, I brush as many of the flies away as possible, before turning to look at the rotten woman.

"You can't actually touch her, can you?" I continue, my mind racing as I try to figure out why she hasn't killed me already, and why she hasn't hurt the girl. "You hurt the others, you killed them, but..."

Hesitating for a moment, I start to realize that I

might have got that a little wrong.

"No," I whisper, "*you* didn't hurt them. That's why you needed my sister, isn't it? You used her, you got her to do these things for you. You made her kill the others, and you made her bring the baby up here, but you can't actually do it all yourself, can you?"

She takes another step forward, and this time she lets out an angry, sneering groan. The flies are still buzzing all around her, and I have to wave several away as they try to land on my face.

"You'd have done it by now if you could," I continue, before looking over at Katie's crumpled, rotten body. "You used her. That's what you do, isn't it? You use people, you manipulate them and you make them do things for you. But you do that because by yourself, you can't actually do very much at all."

She steps closer and hisses again, and more flies swarm from her mouth.

"You can't have her!" I shout, determined to stand my ground even though she's now only a couple of feet away. The baby is behind me, and I know I just have to keep her safe and then get her out of this house. "She's not yours. Whatever you're angry about, whatever someone might have done to you, it's nothing to do with her! Do you understand me? You've been tormenting this family for years, haven't you? That means that whoever made you angry, they must be long dead by now. It's time for you to leave us alone, Mary!"

I wait, hoping against hope that she might disappear, but instead I find myself staring into her cold, dead eyes. After a moment, however, I realize that she's not looking directly at me. Instead, she seems to be looking past me, toward the bed where the baby is crying.

"You can't have her!" I say firmly, finally realizing that I can't wait any longer. "If you want to try, you're gonna have to come through me first!"

Suddenly she steps forward. Before I have a chance to react, she walks straight through me. I let out a gasp as I feel a crunching, nauseating pain rippling through my flesh and passing quickly from the front of my body to the back. For a fraction of a second I'm frozen in place, before finally I feel the ghostly figure walking out the back of me, and I stumble forward before dropping to my knees with flies landing and crawling all over my face. The pain is immense, and when I look down at my hands I see that veiny black cracks have formed beneath my flesh and are now spreading through my body even as I watch them grow.

I try to cry out, but as the cracks continue to spread I feel as if my body is starting to freeze.

Slowly, I manage to turn and look at the bed, and I see that the ghostly woman is leaning down toward the little girl. More and more flies are crawling all over the girl now.

"Leave her alone," I whisper, barely able to get any words out at all.

The girl is screaming louder than ever.

"Leave her alone," I gasp again. "Don't touch her! Don't you dare touch her!"

I try to warn her again, but I'm starting to become breathless and I swear I can feel the cracks spreading through my chest and filling my lungs. For a moment, all I can do is stare in horror as the woman leans closer to the girl, as if she enjoys making her scream.

"Stop" I hiss, finally forcing myself to turn and reach onto the bed. Grabbing the girl, I pull her away and then force myself up, stumbling toward the door with the screaming child in my arms.

Before I've managed even a couple of paces, a large chunk of broken wood shoots up from the floor and slams into the side of my head. I almost duck out of the way in time, but the wood still clatters into me and I almost trip as I hurry out to the landing.

"It's going to be okay," I stammer, holding the girl tight as I make my way toward the top of the stairs. "You're not -"

Suddenly I cry out as another piece of wood hits my shoulder from behind. I stumble and bump against the wall, but I keep going and finally I start limping down the stairs. The boards are creaking and straining under my feet, and the railing shudders slightly when I try to support myself, but I can see the front door ahead and I know I have to keep going. At the same time, my limbs are becoming stiffer with each and every step, and I'm not sure how much longer I can stay on my feet.

A moment later one of the steps collapses beneath me, but I manage to grip the railing and hold onto the baby at the same time. Stumbling down the last few steps, I reach the hallway and hurry to the door, only to find that it's locked. I try pulling a couple of times, before realizing that I don't have time to break it down. Grabbing an old clock from one of the tables, I turn and throw it at the window, shattering the glass and then immediately starting to climb through.

Stray shards catch my arms and rip the flesh, but I focus on making sure that the baby doesn't get hurt. Once I'm through and out on the other side, I stumble across the grass and limp as quickly as possible toward the gate in the distance. I don't know how long this women can follow us, but hopefully we might be safe as soon as we're off the house's land. My legs almost buckle beneath me several times, causing me to stumble, but somehow I keep going while forcing myself to not look back.

I left the key inside, but it's too late to go back for that now.

When we reach the gate, I clamber over with the baby in my arms and finally I step onto the grass verge at the side of the road. I know we have to keep going, but in a moment of weakness I turn and look back, and to my horror I see the ghostly woman standing just a couple of feet away, on the other side of the gate. As soon as I see her eyes, she leans forward and screams, and I immediately stumble back a few paces until I'm in the middle of the road.

"Leave us alone!" I shout, with tears running down my face. "You can't have her! You'll never have her! Leave my family alone!"

She screams again, but it's clear that she can't leave the property, so I turn and start limping along the pitch-black country road. There are still some flies buzzing around us, as I hold the crying baby closer and whisper to her, telling her that everything is going to be fine. The pain in my limbs and chest is immense, crackling through my body with every step, but I have to keep going and I can see the lights of the town now, a couple of miles ahead. If I can get there, maybe I'll be able to find help and warn people about the house.

I don't know how long I spend walking, but after about an hour I hear a faint rumbling sound nearby, and I turn just in time to see the lights of a car coming up behind me. My legs finally buckle and I drop down onto my knees, clutching the baby. The car's headlights get closer and closer before stopping a few feet away, and a moment later I hear one of the doors opening.

"Are you okay?" a man calls out, hurrying toward us. "What are you doing out here in the middle of the night? I could've hit you!"

"Help!" I stammer, holding the baby out toward him.

He takes the girl, and I immediately slump down against the tarmac. I'm shivering and filled with pain, and I can see scores of thick black veins running through my shaking hands.

"What happened to you?" the man asks. "What the hell's wrong with your skin?"

"Help her!" I gasp, looking at the little girl as she continues to scream in his arms. "I got her away. I don't know how, I don't know why she let us go without more of a fight, but you have to make sure she's okay!"

"What's your name?" the man continues, still holding the girl as he takes his phone from his pocket. "I'll call for help. Can you tell me your name?"

"Hannah," I try to reply, but I'm shaking so much that the word barely leaves my lips.

"Okay, Hannah, I'm going to call for an ambulance, and I'll call the police too. Is this your baby?"

"She's my..."

For a moment, my throat seems to close entirely, and I can't get any more words out.

"Niece," I manage finally, as I feel my heart suddenly pounding harder and harder in my chest.

"Okay, and does she have a name?"

"She -"

Before I can finish, I remember a day at Johnny and Louisa's flat several months ago, when they were discussing baby names. They were going to call the child Ashley if it was a boy, but for a moment I don't remember what they'd chosen for a girl. After a few seconds, however, it comes back to me.

"She..."

I watch the girl's crying face for a moment.

"Rosie," I manage finally, as I feel my thudding heart suddenly come to a halt and stop beating. I'm dead. "Her name is Rosie."

PART SEVEN
TODAY

ROSIE

"ROSIE!" TOBY SHOUTS. "RUN! Rosie, you have to get help!"

Staring into the woman's dark, dead eyes, I feel trapped for a moment, as if I can't possibly look away. Finally, however, Toby's continued gasps of pain start shaking me from this inaction, and I look down to see him trying desperately to crawl away.

Reaching down, I grab his arms and start dragging him toward the door, while not daring to look back at the woman. I have no idea what's going on in this house, but I can figure it out once we've made it outside. As soon as I reach the landing, however, I see that the woman is now standing at the far end, blocking my way to the stairs. With panic rushing through my chest, I immediately drag Toby into the nearest room and then slam the door shut, before running around to the other side of a large dresser and pushing it so that the door can't be opened.

"You have to get out of here!" Toby hisses as he tries to sit up, only to slump back down.

"What the hell was that thing?" I ask, dropping onto my knees next to him. As he looks up at me, I see that the maggots are all gone, but that his face is still covered in tiny burrowed holes, most no larger than a pinhead. Reaching out, I run a hand across his cheek, feeling the holes against my fingertips. "Please tell me it was a trick. Please, Toby, tell me you set this all up as some kind of stunt."

"What are you doing?" he gasps, as I continue to feel the damage to his face.

"Who was that woman?" I ask, pulling my hand away.

"It must be her," he replies, looking toward the blocked door. "It must be Mary Carmichael. Maybe she's even the one who somehow got the key to me. She's real!"

"Don't lie to me!" I shout.

"Do I seem like I'm lying right now?" he stammers, trying once again to sit up and this time just about managing. At the same time he clutches one side of his chest, as if he's in pain. "I went into the room, and suddenly she was just there," he explains, still struggling to catch his breath. "I swear to God, I've never felt my heart jump with fear like that before, but when I saw her..."

His voice trails off for a moment, as if he's

reliving the moment.

"So many flies and maggots," he continues. "I could feel them inside me and -"

Suddenly he lets out a cry and starts furiously scratching at his face and chest, trying to rip his shirt away.

"Get them off me!" he screams. "Get them out of me!"

"They're gone!" I shout.

"Help!" he shouts, tearing his t-shirt and starting to dig his fingernails into his bare chest. Tears are rolling down his cheeks now, dribbling into the holes all across his features, and he's starting to sob. "I can feel them!"

"They're gone, Toby!"

Letting out a gasp, he slumps back against the wall and lets his hands fall to the ground. Already, he's managed to scratch thick cuts in his flesh.

"I can feel them," he whimpers. "I swear to God, I can feel them inside."

"Please tell me this is a joke," I say after a moment, still watching the door. "Either you've set it up, or someone else is messing with us, or -"

"That was Mary Carmichael!" he says firmly. "It has to be! All the stories about this place are true, about Mary's ghost haunting Wetherley House. Evil Mary's real!"

"Why?" I ask. "Why would she try to kill us?"

"According to the story, Mary was horribly abused by her mother. She was chained in the basement and -"

"I saw that!" I say suddenly, remembering the words I saw scratched into the wall when I was down in the basement. "She wrote her name hundreds and hundreds of times!"

"She was down there for years," he continues. "They say that by the time she was found, she was more animal than human. They found traces of human meat in her gut. She'd been beaten and tortured by her own mother for years, except that it turned out that the woman wasn't even her mother at all. Mary had been torn from her real mother's womb and raised by some crazy bitch named Eve Carmichael. And now Mary haunts the place, and she's determined to take every firstborn child in each generation of that family."

I open my mouth to ask if he's serious, before realizing that the story doesn't make sense.

"Why would she do that?" I ask.

"Because she's insane!"

"I still don't get it," I continue. "Even if I buy the idea of ghosts, why would someone like Mary come back and try to cause more pain, after she'd been freed? It just seems so cruel and pointless." I pause for a moment, trying to figure this mess out, as I hear a series of creaks coming from the other side of the door. "Wait, how old was Mary when she died?"

"I don't remember. She was born in 1888 and she died in 1906, so -"

"Eighteen," I whisper, thinking back to the horrific creature I just saw in the other room. "That woman wasn't eighteen. No way. She was more like eighty!"

"What do you -"

"There might be a ghost here," I continue, as I feel a strangely fuzzy feeling running through my head, "but I don't think it's..."

My voice trails off as I realize my thoughts are starting to fade away. No matter what I try to think of, it's as if every thought in my head is slowly sinking into the depths of my mind, and other thoughts are starting to take their place. I blink a couple of times, and I swear I can hear loud voices shouting now in the distance and I can smell smoke in the air. I look around, in case something's on fire, and then I slump back against the wall.

"Rosie?" Toby gasps, crawling over to me and placing a hand on my arm. "Are you okay? We have to get out of here."

"She wants me," I whisper, as the realization hits me. "I don't know how I know, but I can feel it. She wants..."

The words fade away, and for a moment I don't even remember what I was saying. I have to really struggle to get my thoughts back at all.

"She wants *me*," I continue, filled with fear as I realize that some other mind seems to be creeping into my head, like mist rolling across a moor. "Why me?"

No matter how hard I try to fight back, someone else's memories are curling through my mind, and I'm barely aware of the room or the house or Toby anymore. Instead I'm remembering a place I've never been, and sounds I've never heard, and at the same time I can feel a sense of fury rising through my chest.

Anger.

Real anger.

A kind of anger I've never known.

Toby's calling my name, but his voice is echoing in the distance. He's unimportant now.

Instead of being in the house, I'm suddenly outside in a muddy street with rickety wooden buildings all around. Rain is pouring down, splattering into the mud with shocking force, and I'm shivering in soaked clothes as I see angry faces staring at me from nearby windows. From nowhere, I'm filled with a sense of fear that seems to twist out through the veil of anger, as if I know that I'm hated, and finally I stagger back until I bump against the wall of a wooden house.

"Witch!" a voice hisses, and I turn to see a furious woman emerging from a nearby door. Before I can react, she pushes me hard and sends me falling back, and I land hard in the mud. "You're not welcome in my home!" she shouts. "Why don't you do us all a favor and leave this town in peace?"

I want to ask her what I've done, but instead I start screaming at her, warning her that she'll pay for laying a hand on me. The voice isn't mine, yet it's coming from my mouth as I get back onto my feet, and I'm filled with a sense of fury that I've never felt before.

I want to kill her.

I want to kill all of them.

And then everything changes.

Suddenly I'm naked and warm, and I realize I'm in some other room. Torches are burning in metal holders on the walls, and after a moment I find to my horror that I'm riding someone, and I can feel a man inside me. Looking down, I see the leering features of a fat old man staring up at me, and I feel his rough hands reaching up and squeezing my breasts. Except that when I look down in horror, I realize that they're not *my* breasts at all. Instead, they're large and swollen, with thick red and purple veins running through the pale flesh, and the nipples are large and firm. Looking down at the rest of my naked body, I see that it's the body of an old woman, yet I can feel the man's hands gripping me and tugging on me. Between my legs, his engorged manhood is buried deep inside me. There's no pleasure. Only pain.

"You're a nice young thing, aren't you?" he gasps, spraying white spittle from his lips. "Don't worry, I'll keep you safe. Just so long as you make sure my wife never finds out about this!"

Before I can scream, I hear a door swinging open, and I turn to see several men storming into the room with a group of women right behind them.

"There she is!" one of the women screams, pointing at me. "I told you! She's a witch!"

"Get her off me!" the man shouts from between my thighs, and he pushes me away as he scrambles off the bed. Naked and sweaty, he stumbles toward the door and then turns back to look at me with an expression of pure disgust. "She's hideous!" he yells. "She wasn't like that a moment ago!"

Again, I want to cry out and ask them what's happening, but instead I start laughing. I can't stop, not even when several other men come over and clamp metal shackles around my wrists. They drag me off the bed, not even bothering to cover my naked body as they haul me through the doorway and into the filthy street, where I'm pulled cackling through the mud as crowds jeer at me from all around. I can hear them calling me a whore and a devil and an abomination, but there's one word I hear more than all the others combined, spat at me with vitriol and hatred.

"Witch!"

"She fooled me!" the man from the room shouts, having dressed himself now and hurried out after me. "She changed her appearance! I thought she was my wife!"

"That's what witches do!" another voice yells, and then that word rises up all around, as if everyone in town is chanting it in unison.

Letting out a cry of pain as I'm dragged through the mud, I twist and try to pull free of the shackles, but their ragged metal edges are already digging deep into my wrinkled flesh. The harder I pull, the more my skin is gouged away, leaving rivers of blood running down as far as my shoulders. I cry out, my voice sounding so old and pained, and all around me the crowd jeers and boos until finally we reach the edge of town and I'm shoved forward. As I land, a boot slams into the back of my neck and forces my face into the mud, and for a moment

I think they might be planning to drown me.

When the boot eventually lifts, I roll onto my back and spit out mud, while the crowd continues to yell. A few seconds later rocks start hitting my naked body, and I curl into a ball while covering my face with my hands. Still they pelt me with their rocks and stones, and while some hit and bounce off harmlessly enough, others crack into me and cut my flesh. For several minutes the onslaught builds and builds, until finally a voice calls out and people stop throwing things at me, although one or two rocks still land and I don't dare uncover my face.

"We are not barbarians!" the voice says firmly. "This woman might very well be a witch, but -"

"Witch!" several other voices shouts.

"We are not going to execute her!" the first voice continues. "She'll be cast out of our town, with the mark of a witch upon her back so that no other innocents might be fooled by her. If she tries to ingratiate herself in any other towns, they'll see her for what she is. And that's the end of it!"

A chorus of boos and jeers begins to ring out as I'm hauled from the ground. My arms and legs are so painful, I feel as if I'll never be able to walk again, and I'm dragged quickly through the mud as people continue to yell at me.

And then everything changes again.

All I hear now is the rustle of leaves in a breeze, and I realize after a moment that I'm flat on my back in a ditch, staring up at a blue sky. A moment later I hear footsteps coming closer, and finally a woman steps into view, staring at me with an expression of pure shock.

"Are you alright?" the woman asks after a moment, before stepping a little closer.

She's beautiful, and her belly is swollen. I try to reach toward her, but I can barely move my arm at all. I can see the pity in the woman's eyes as she edges closer, and I can feel a ripple of hope in my heart. Although I try to call out to her, to beg her to help me, all I can manage is a faint, guttural groan that I doubt she can even hear. Still, she's starting to make her way through the long grass, as if she actually means to help me.

"Please," I try to gasp, "don't leave me here!"

"Marguerite, no!"

Suddenly a man grabs her by the arm, holding her back.

"Leave her!" he continues.

She turns to me. "But -"

"She's beyond help," he adds, staring at me with the same disgust I saw in the eyes of the people in town. "Look at the poor wretch. There's nothing anyone can do for somebody who's that far gone."

"She's in agony," the woman points out, and now I can hear that she has a strong French accent. "We can't just leave her like this."

"We can and we must."

I try again to call out to them, to beg them for help, but I don't have the strength.

"Besides, she's diseased," the man continues. "Look further along, my dear. Others have died down there. It happens sometimes. These peasants get thrown out of their towns and villages for one reason or another, usually something criminal that they've done, and they end up wandering the countryside until they can no longer manage for themselves, and then they end up like this. You cannot tell me, in all honesty, that such things do not also happen in France."

"I'm sure they do," the woman replies. "It's just that I have never witnessed them."

"There is no need for you to witness this."

He guides her away, and I can hear them still talking as they leave me here to die. I try again to get up, then again, and finally I feel fresh anger bursting through my chest. Although I still feel so painfully weak, I force myself up and start crawling through the grass, until I see that there's some kind of old-fashioned carriage parked nearby. The man looks to be feeding one of the horses, so I crawl toward the rear of the carriage, where the woman is settling into her seat.

Although I'm weak and in pain, I can feel a sense of pure fury rising through my body as I clamber to my feet and start climbing up the side of the carriage The woman seems lost in thought, to the extent that she hasn't even noticed me yet, and finally I reach for her. I almost fall, but I manage to push myself forward until I brush against the woman's arm, at which point she turns to me and cries out.

"She'll be taken from you!" I hear myself screeching, with the same horrific voice from before. "You left me to die and now a child will be taken from your family, so that I can live again and -"

Suddenly a blast knocks me away the carriage, and I crash back down against the muddy ground.

ROSIE

"NO!" I SHOUT, LEANING forward and covering my face with my hands. "Stop!"

I can feel an intense, splitting pain in my head, but after a moment my own thoughts seem to rush back into my mind and the pain begins to recede. Lowering my hands, I find that although those experiences felt so real, I'm back in a room at Wetherley House, with the dresser still pushed against the door. A moment later I feel someone touch my arm, and I gasp as I turn and find that Toby is right next to me. His face is still covered in tiny holes.

"Are you okay?" he asks. "You looked like you zoned out for a moment."

"She tried to get into my head," I stammer. "She *did* get into my head! I saw... I think I saw memories from her life. She's some kind of witch! She wants my body!"

"Your -"

"She think it belongs to her," I continue, trying desperately to figure out why she would have chosen me. After a moment, I start to realize that this whole night has been far more than just a coincidence. "She made it happen," I whisper, before turning to Toby again. "My car breaking down, and then you spotting me at the side of the road... What were the odds of those things happening and delivering us to this house tonight?"

"I only -"

"*She* did it!" I say firmly, as I think back to the face of the French woman I saw a moment ago. "She must think I'm part of the family she hates, or..."

My voice trails off for a moment as I try to work out what's really happening.

"Or maybe I *am*," I whisper.

"Your family?" He pauses. "I thought you were adopted?"

"I was! I was found in the middle of the road late one night, with my aunt. She died before she could tell anyone what had happened, and I was put into the foster system. I never managed to find out much about my birth family, but the man who found us that night said that my aunt Hannah was rambling about being chased by someone." I pause for a moment, my mind racing as I try to put it all together. "Toby, is this house anywhere near a town called Ambershot?"

"Ambershot? Yeah, it's a couple of miles away.

Why?"

"That's where I was found," I stammer, feeling a shudder pass through my body as I realize that it's all true. "When my aunt ran into the road, she must have been taking me from this house!"

"What are you talking about?" he asks. "It'd be way too much of a coincidence for -"

"It's not a coincidence!" I say firmly, getting to my feet and looking over at the blocked door. "The creature in this house must have reached out and arranged things so that I'd end up back here. She must have been so patient, waiting twenty years for another chance. She thinks she's owed a new life, and she wants a body from my family. If I was born in this house, that'd explain why she thinks I'm owed to her."

"That's insane!" Toby points out.

"*She's* insane," I reply, as I realize I can hear more creaks coming from the other side of the door. "She's a witch, too, and she cursed my family a long time ago. We have to get out of here before she tries to get into my head again. I don't know if I can force her out a second time."

I make my way over to the window and look out at the moonlit lawn. I try to pull the window open, figuring that maybe we can climb out and run, but the damn thing is bolted shut. After trying a couple more times, I turn to Toby.

"You're supposed to be the expert on these things," I point out. "How do we get away?"

He shakes his head.

"I thought you'd researched the -"

"I never actually thought I'd see anything!" he shouts, clearly starting to panic as he gets to his feet and keeps his eyes fixed on the door. "A few bumps, maybe some creaks in the night, but not *this*! This whole thing is insane! It was just supposed to be a bit of fun! I didn't think Mary was real!"

"She's not Mary," I whisper.

"What do you mean?"

"You were right about there being something in this house, but it's not Mary Carmichael. It's something else. Something older. This whole thing is my fault, she -"

Before I can finish, I feel another rush of nausea in my chest. Stepping back against the wall, I start seeing more images in my mind's eye, and for a moment I feel as if I'm getting dragged back into another memory that was never mine to begin with. Somehow I manage to push the sensation away, and then I make my way across the room and start frantically pulling the dresser away from the door.

"What are you doing?" Toby stammers.

"She just tried to get into my head again," I tell him, gasping as I struggle with the dresser's weight. "We can't stay here."

"But we can't go out *there*!"

"She's dead, Toby!" I point out, as I finally get the dresser moved. "Blocking the door didn't stop her anyway. It just made us feel safer."

With that, I pull the door open and find to my

relief that there's no sign of the ghostly woman on the other side.

"She's not like this all-powerful thing," I continue, stepping out onto the cold landing and looking both ways. "Think about it. If she could just take what she wants, she'd have done it by now. Something's holding her back, or forcing her back, or making it harder for her in some way. I don't understand it, but we have to take advantage and make a run for it while we still can." I turn to see that he's still in the room, as if he's scared to come out. "Staying in there isn't an option," I point out. "At least if we try to run, we have a chance."

"Where is she?" he asks, with tears in his eyes.

"I don't know, but it seems like each time she tries to get me, she has to retreat for a moment. This might be our only chance."

I wait for him to accept that I'm right, but he still seems terrified. Hell, I'm terrified too, but it's not like we have a choice.

"Toby, come on!" I hiss, reaching a hand out toward him. "You're not safe in there!"

"I don't want to see her again!"

"Neither do I, so let's get moving!"

He hesitates, but finally he comes over to the doorway. I reach out and grab his hand, pulling him onto the landing and then leading him toward the stairs. He stumbles a couple of times, clearly ailing, and I struggle to keep him from falling to the floor.

After just a couple more paces, however, we

pass another open door and I hear a sniffling, sobbing sound. Turning, I'm startled to see that there's a different woman sitting on the bed, weeping as she looks down at her own bloodied belly. Her hands are trembling, and after a moment she looks up and stares at me with tear-filled eyes. As soon as I see her face properly, I realize that I recognize her from that flash of vision I experienced earlier.

"Have you seen her?" she whimpers, with a strong French accent. "Have you seen my baby?"

"What the hell is that?" Toby asks, his voice tight with fear.

"Just keep moving," I reply, turning and leading him to the stairs. "There are ghosts here, but we only have to worry about the witch."

As we start making our way down, I can't help looking around for any sign that we're being followed. I know the naked old woman won't let us go without a fight, but so far she seems to be holding back. When we get to the bottom of the stairs, I look toward the front door, but I immediately feel an overwhelming sense of fear. I blink, and for a fraction of a second I see the outline of the naked woman, as if she's waiting for us to try to go out that way. Instinctively, I start to lead Toby toward the kitchen, figuring that we have to try the back door instead.

"I need to rest," he groans.

"We're going out the back way!"

"I can't walk..."

"Trust me!"

"Rosie -"

"Trust me!" I say again, pulling him along as I look back at the front door. He's barely walking at all now, and I almost have to drag him the last few steps. "She's waiting for us there. I can feel it. I can -"

"There's another one!"

Turning, I look toward the open basement door, just in time to spot a hint of movement in the darkness. Sure enough, a figure is slowly coming up the steps, making a steady creaking sound as it emerges into the moonlight. After a moment, I'm horrified to see that this figure is a woman in an old-fashioned dress, walking with some kind of terrible disability. Her legs seem almost bowed, as if she can't stand properly, and she's mumbling to herself as she gets to the top of the steps. Finally she looks through at us, and I can see the anguish in her eyes.

"She made me do it!" she sobs. "She whispered and whispered in my ear until I couldn't -"

Suddenly the basement door slams shut, cutting the woman off. I hear her scream on the other side.

"Move!" I hiss, starting to pull Toby through to the kitchen, only for him to slip out of my grip and hold back. "Ignore the ghosts! They're *just* ghosts, they can't -"

Before I can finish, he slumps down and I fail to catch him. Leaning against the wall, he lets out a pained groan.

"We have to keep going!" I yell.

"Leave me," he whispers, leaning forward and

almost slamming face-first into the floor before I manage to hold him up.

"Wait right here!" I continue, propping him against the wall before stepping back. "I'm going to check the back door, and then I'll come back for you."

I turn and hurry through to the darkened kitchen, but suddenly I hear panicked, stumbling footsteps nearby. Looking over my shoulder, I watch in horror as Toby hurries to the front door and starts trying to pull it open. It's as if sheer panic has suddenly forced him to act.

"Toby, get away from there!" I shout, filled with a slowly-growing sense of dread. "She's there, Toby! She's right next to you!"

"Why won't this goddamned door open!" he shouts, pulling harder and harder on the handle before stepping back and then trying to smash it open with his shoulder. "Let me out of this house!"

"Toby, stop panicking!" I yell. "Just keep your head and -"

"Help!" he screams, slamming his shoulder against the door again and again. "Somebody get us out of here! We're trapped! Help us!"

"Toby!"

"Help! We need -"

Suddenly he lets out a pained gasp and slumps against the door, panting heavily with his back turned to me. Something's clearly wrong, but I don't dare get too close, and after a moment I realize that he's starting to let out a low, anguished whimper.

"Toby, I need you to come over here," I continue, holding a trembling hand out toward him. "Toby, for the love of God, I need you to get over here right now!"

He tries to say something, but his voice sounds croaked and damaged.

"Toby!"

Letting out a sudden gasp, he starts turning toward me, and I see that there are now hundreds – maybe even thousands – of maggots wriggling through the flesh all over his face, as if they're all flooding out of his body at once. For a moment I can only stare in horror at the sight of them squirming in the moonlight, and I swear I can even hear the sound of their pale little bodies slipping out of his face and falling to the floor. Soon they're all squirming on the wooden boards, writhing next to Toby's feet.

"Toby," I whisper, stepping back as I feel a rush of panic in my chest, "what -"

Suddenly he gurgles and takes a stumbling step toward me, before dropping to his feet and reaching up to touch his face. He runs his fingers against the holes that cover his features, as if he can't quite believe what's happening to him.

"Toby!" I sob, edging toward him. "Come with me! We can still get out of here!"

I reach out to take his hand, but he lets out another pained gasp and I see that more maggots are starting to burrow out from inside his head. This second wave is fatter than the first, with maggots that are double the size of the ones that caused the initial damage, and I can barely make out Toby's features at all now as more and more maggots swarm out through the holes in his flesh. Finally, before I can think of any way to help him, he slumps down against the floor and I pull back in horror as I see that hundreds of maggots have eaten their way out through the back of his head and are now wriggling through his hair. There are flies, too.

Hundreds of fat flies come buzzing out from his head, filling the air.

"Toby!" I whimper, hoping against hope that somehow he might still be alive. "Toby, please -"

And then I see her.

The naked old woman is standing over him, grinning at me as flies buzz all around her.

"You didn't have to do that!" I shout, filled with anger but then pulling back as she steps over his body and comes closer. "He never did anything to you! Neither did I! If you're angry at someone, it can't be us! It you want something, it's not me that owes you! If anyone owes you anything, it's people who have been dead for years!"

She takes another step toward me.

"You're not Mary, are you?" I continue. "Everyone thought Mary was the ghost here, but you're someone else. I swear to you, you're not getting what you want. You can't have me!"

Panicked, I turn and run through to the kitchen. When I try to open the back door, however, I find that it's locked. I pull on the handle a few times, but I already know that I'm going to have to come up with a better plan. I look around, and finally I spot the gas cooker. My mind is racing, but deep down I know that there's no point getting away from this house and just leaving it standing. As long as the house is here, this *thing* will keep trying to get me back here. Even if I'm able to resist, if I have children myself I'll always know that they're in danger.

I can't get out of here.

But at least I can make sure that *here* doesn't exist anymore. Not after tonight.

Feeling an overwhelming sense of fear, I step back against the kitchen counter and slowly slither down onto the floor next to the cooker. I can't see the old woman right now, but I know she's close and I know she's coming. I'm too weak to fight back, and there's nothing I can do. She killed Toby, she killed so many people, and now she's coming for me. If they couldn't stop here, I can't stop her either. Not unless I take the only remaining way out.

"Please don't hurt me," I sob, trembling with fear as I wait for her to reappear. "Please, I'm begging you, don't make me do this..."

And then I see it.

An old Polaroid photo, resting on the kitchen floor. Reaching over, I pull it closer and see that it shows two smiling people standing outside the house. At first I don't recognize them, but after a moment I realize that I *have* seen them once before, in a photo I managed to track down a couple of years ago.

These are my parents.

Jonathan and Louisa Cruikshank.

My real parents, who died the day I was born. They died here, in this house.

"You killed them," I whisper, feeling a rippling sense of anger rising through my chest. A moment later I hear a creak on a nearby floorboard, and I turn to see the naked old woman standing in the doorway, watching me. I guess she thinks she has me cornered. "You killed them!" I sneer. "You killed them right here in this house!"

I stare at her face, and she smiles back at me.

"You're not going to get me," I tell her. "You're not going to get any of us ever again."

She starts stepping toward me.

"As far as I know," I continue, with tears in my eyes, "I'm the last in my family's line. It ends with me, so if I don't have children of my own, there'll be no-one else for you to go after. So really, you're not in a very good bargaining position, are you? 'Cause I'm guessing your curse is pretty specific about these things."

I watch as she takes another step closer, and then I reach up, turning the knobs on the front of the cooker. I immediately hear the hiss of gas, and once all the knobs have been turned I reach toward the button that'll cause a spark. I know I have to wait a little longer, and I know this is going to hurt for just a moment, but at least then it'll all be over. If I'm going out, then at least I'm going to be the one who ends this misery forever. With my finger still poised to hit the igniter, I wait as the old bitch comes closer and closer.

"You don't even know what I'm doing, do you?" I ask, as I start to smell gas filling the room. Not much longer now. "I guess they didn't have gas cookers in your day, huh? Well, you're in for a surprise. And when it's over, there'll be no house and no body for you to take. And no more children."

I wait, hoping for some kind of reaction, but she's simply grinning as she stops and towers above me.

"I don't know the story of my family," I sob. "I don't know the details of what you did to them all. But I'm damn well not going to let you do it to anyone else. This is for them."

I look down at the photo of my parents. I can barely seem them properly through the tears, but for a moment I stare at their smiling faces.

"This if for you, Mum and Dad," I whimper. "This is to make sure it ends. Right now. No more curse."

With that, I push the button on the cooker, and I close my eyes as I hear a rush of fire.

ROSIE

Six months later

"SO HOW DID YOU get out?"

Sitting on the chair next to the bay window, in Doctor Sutcliffe's office, I think back to that moment when the gas ignited. I can still feel the roar of flames, and I can still feel the immense heat, but after that...

After that, nothing.

"Rosie?" he continues. "The house was ripped apart. The whole story you've told me so far was clearly a figment of your imagination, but the one part that even you can't explain is how you got out of the house with barely a scratch or a mark on you."

"I don't know," I whisper, before turning to him and watching as he makes a note on my chart.

"You were found on the side of the road when

the firefighters arrived."

"I know."

"A group of men from the local town, led by a Daniel Langton, saw the fire and rushed to help."

"I know that too."

"But you don't know how you got out of the house?"

"No."

"And you're sure there was no-one else inside with you? I mean, no-one who could have carried you out?"

"Toby was dead," I reply, "and the only other person..."

My voice trails off as I see that awful woman's face in my mind's eye. The same face that I see in my nightmares. The face that makes me wake screaming and sobbing every single night in my room, bringing the hospital orderlies rushing to check that I'm okay. I don't think there's been one night when I haven't seen those dead eyes staring at me.

"The police are still looking into the circumstances," Doctor Sutcliffe mutters, making another note, "but obviously there was someone else in the house. It's just not possible for you to have been alone."

"I wasn't alone," I tell him.

"I mean flesh-and-blood people, Rosie."

"But the house was destroyed, wasn't it?" I ask.

He nods.

"*Completely* destroyed?"

"Torn down and bulldozed. Mr. Langton and some of his friends bought the ruins and dealt with it. Apart from some little girls who've been seen playing nearby, I hear the place has been left well alone."

Feeling a flash of relief, I pause for a moment.

"What about the wood?" I ask.

"Rosie..."

"What about the wood from the house? That was all destroyed, wasn't it? Nothing can be allowed to survive!"

Sighing, he takes a moment to clean his glasses.

"We need to focus on your health," he continues finally. "You remember why you're here, don't you? The court decided that you needed serious help, and in three months' time I'm going to have to make a recommendation about whether or not to keep you here at the hospital for another period, or whether some other option needs to be considered. Now, so far, I'm leaning heavily toward keeping you here. I would, however, like to see some more signs of progress. For example, if you could try to think about what really happened after you and Toby reached the house, I'd -"

"I told you."

"Well, I'm still not -"

"And you looked into the names I gave you, didn't you?" I ask. "The family names. The history. The witch. They were all real historical people, weren't they?"

"The details check out so far," he says cautiously, "but that doesn't prove anything."

"It proves I'm not making it up."

"You could have read about them before you went to the house."

"I didn't!"

"This is becoming a rather circular conversation," he continues with yet another sigh.

"I don't know how I got out of that house," I tell him, as I grip the arms of the chair in sheer desperation. "Believe me, if I knew, I'd tell you. But ever since that night, I've felt like... I can't explain it, but I've felt like something's protecting me. I know how that sounds, but it's the truth. Even right now, sitting here with you, I feel as if there's someone else in the room with us. Even when I have the nightmares about the old woman, about that witch-like creature from the house, I can tell that something's holding her back. It was holding her back in the house, and it's holding her back in my dreams. I can't explain it, but I know it's real. And I feel safe."

"Hmm."

He makes another note. Probably something about how I'm delusional, and about how I need my dosages upped.

"We'll talk some more tomorrow, Rosie," he says finally.

"We're done for today?"

"We're done for today. It's a nice afternoon, though. You should try spending some time outside with the other patients for once."

"Maybe later," I tell him, as an orderly comes into the room and I get to my feet, ready to be led away.

"I want to sleep for a while first."

"I thought you had nightmares when you slept?"

"I always know they're nightmares when they're happening," I reply, heading over to the orderly. "I'm more scared in the daytime, when I can't see her. Because that means she might appear at any moment."

"But you just told me you feel safe."

I open my mouth to reply, but the words catch in my throat.

"I do," I say finally. "I can't explain it, but I do."

I turn to leave.

"Oh, Rosie? You received another letter from Mr. Langton. Perhaps you feel ready to speak to him now?"

Glancing over my shoulder, I see that he's holding an envelope with my name written on the front.

"No," I reply, shaking my head. "Not ever. Burn it. Burn all of them."

A few minutes later, I'm back in my room. There's not much in here, since I'm not allowed anything I could use to hurt myself. I have some books, and some paper, and some pencils that I have to give back every night. I don't mind the sparse decoration, though, and to be honest I feel pretty calm when I'm in my room. I can't explain that feeling, but I was telling the truth to Doctor Sutcliffe earlier. Ever since I woke up after the night at Wetherley House, I've felt like I'm protected, like something's watching over me. Although I like to tell myself that the old witch was probably burned up with the house, I'm not entirely sure that it works like that. If she could reach out before, she can probably reach out now, but something feels different this time. Something I can't explain.

I know one thing, though.

Mary wasn't the monster in that house.

The monster was someone else, someone who must have hated my family for some reason. Maybe I'll never find out what really happened, but I'm certain the woman was some kind of witch.

Settling on the bed, I turn and face the wall. I can hear the other patients talking outside in the garden, but I don't feel like joining them right now. Instead I stare at the beigeness and wait for sleep to crawl over me. At the same time, I still feel as if someone is here in the room with me, and after a moment I turn to double-check that I'm alone. Once I'm sure, I turn back to the wall. I start to close my eyes, but at the last second I spot a faint scratch on the wall, poking up from behind the crumpled bed-sheets. Reaching out, I pull the sheets aside, and finally I spot some crude, barely legible letters carved into the surface.

They were there yesterday, and the day before too. But each day, four more words appear is from nowhere, and I can just about make them out. Even now, as I reach over and run my fingertips against the scratches, I feel certain that something is watching over me. And I read those four words again, words that must have been her way of making sure she finally remembered herself after she died.

"My name is Mary."

EPILOGUE

Four hundred miles away

"MR. PATTERSON? IS THIS okay?"

Glancing up from my marking, I see that Mikey Spode has brought his latest creation from the workshop. He's an eager kid, always trying to please, but he's never really shown any great talent in my class. This time, however, I can't help noticing that he's actually done a pretty good job.

"Let me see."

I reach out and take the carved wooden tiger from him, and I've got to admit that it's not bad. He's managed to get a lot of detail, and I reckon I'd be pretty chuffed if I made something like this myself.

"I like it," I tell him, and when I turn to him I see that he's grinning. He's proud of himself. "It's a real improvement, Mikey. This must have taken you a long time."

"Will I get a good grade for this unit now?" he asks. "I'm averaging A's in everything except woodwork."

"Well, no promises, but I predict great things if you keep this up." I continue to turn the tiger around in my hands for a moment. It feels light yet sturdy, and the grain of the wood has a very appealing quality. "What did you make this out of ?" I ask after a moment. "It's not material from the wood-box, is it?"

"I took some wood from that new pile that came in this morning."

"There's a new pile?"

"Mr. Garlinge said it had arrived and that we could use it. I'm not in trouble, am I?"

"You're not in trouble," I reply, setting the tiger on my desk as I get to my feet. "I'm very impressed, Mikey. You've obviously put a lot of effort into this, and I can see a real improvement in your skills." I lead him out of my office and into the main workshop, where the rest of the Year 11 students are hard at work on their own carvings. "Now prove to me that it wasn't a fluke and see what else you can come up with."

As Mikey heads back to his bench, I wander over to the wood-box. Sure enough, next to the usual supply of cheap balsa and off-cuts, there's a large stack of new wood. Eric Garlinge is always buying cheap consignments of wood from local merchants, usually just stuff that would've been tossed if the school hadn't taken it. As I pick a piece out from the box, I can't help thinking that this time he's struck lucky. The wood looks like old house timber, and this particular piece has a couple of dark patches, as if maybe it was lightly burned at some point. Frankly, I don't want to know exactly where it came from, but it's good quality wood and when I look across at the kids, I see that they're almost all using it. I guess I taught them well, and they recognize decent wood when they find it.

"Ten minutes to the end of class," I remind them as I head back to my office. Reaching the door, I turn and look at them again, and I can't help noticing that they seem very quiet and absorbed in their work. In fact, there's no chat at all.

I wait, but they're all just getting on with their work.

This is a miracle.

"Ten minutes," I mutter again, before heading back into my office.

Taking a seat, I'm just about to get on with the marking when I glance at the tiger again. It really *is* a great piece of work, although something about it is starting to feel just a little odd. I stare at the piece for a moment longer, before realizing that I really should finish up what I'm doing. Looking back down at the essay I'm currently checking, I spend a couple of minutes reading through the pages, and then suddenly I spot something moving at the edge of my vision.

A maggot.

"What the hell?" I mutter, before seeing another,

and then another.

Half a dozen maggots have crawled out of the wooden tiger. I use a piece of paper to squash them, and then I toss them into the bin before peering closer at the tiger. Sure enough, yet another maggot is starting to wriggle out. For a moment, I consider going into the workshop and telling the kids to down tools and toss their pieces away, but then I figure that there can't be maggots in all the chunks. I'm sure it'll be fine, even if the wood's clearly from some reclaimed dump.

I'll let the kids take their work home. After all, what harm can it possibly do?

The Murder at Skellin Cottage

Skellin Cottage is an oasis of peace and tranquillity. Miles from the nearest town, nestled far out in the English countryside, it's the perfect place for visitors who want to get away from the world for a while. And then the cottage's latest tenant, Deborah Dean, is found brutally murdered.

After several months of police inactivity, the cottage's owner Lord Martin Chesleford decides to take matters into his own hands. Hiring former police officer Joanna Mason, who now works alone as a private investigator, he demands that Deborah's murderer is brought to justice.

But while Deborah had tried to isolate herself at Skellin Cottage, she'd already begun to attract attention. And as the ongoing investigation uncovers old secrets and new rivalries, another murder is right around the corner.

Also by Amy Cross

The Ghosts of Hexley Airport

Ten years ago, more than two hundred people died in a
horrific plane crash at Hexley Airport.

Today, some say their ghosts still haunt the terminal
building.

When she starts her new job at the airport, working a
night shift as part of the security team, Casey assumes
the stories about the place can't be true. Even when she
has a strange encounter in a deserted part of the
departure hall, she's certain that ghosts aren't real.

Soon, however, she's forced to face the truth. Not only is
there something haunting the airport's buildings and
tarmac, but a sinister force is working behind the scenes
to replicate the circumstances of the original accident.
And as a snowstorm moves in, Hexley Airport looks set
to witness yet another disaster.

Also by Amy Cross

B&B

A girl on the run, hiding from a terrible crime.

An old B&B in a snowy city.

A hidden figure lurking in the streets, waiting for his next victim.

When Bobbie takes a room at the rundown Castle Crown B&B, all she wants is to get some sleep and make a tough decision about her future. Unfortunately, the B&B's other guests won't give her any peace, and Bobbie soon realizes that she's stumbled into a world with its own rules. Who is the mysterious bandaged woman? Why is there a dead man in the bathtub? And is something deadly lurking in the basement?

Before she can leave, however, Bobbie learns that the city of Canterbury is being terrorized by a mysterious figure. Every time snow comes, the Snowman claims another victim, leaving their blood sinking into the ice. If Bobbie leaves the B&B and ventures out into the empty streets, she risks becoming his next target. But if she stays, her soul might be claimed by something even more deadly.

Made in the USA
Middletown, DE
29 April 2017